SKYSHIP
ACADEMY

SKYSHIP ACADEMY
Crimson Rising

NICK JAMES

flux
™
Woodbury, Minnesota

First Edition
First Printing, 2012

Book design by Steffani Sawyer
Cover design by Kevin R. Brown
Cover illustration: Steven McAfee
Cover images © Boy: iStockphoto.com/luminis and stone desert: iStockphoto.com/peter zelei
Editing by Rhiannon Nelson

Flux, an imprint of Llewellyn Worldwide Ltd.

Library of Congress Cataloging-in-Publication Data
James, Nick
    Skyship Academy : crimson rising / Nick James.—1st ed.
        p. cm.—(Skyship series ; #2)
    Summary: When fifteen-year-old Jesse manages to smuggle onboard the Academy a mysterious red Pearl, a fragment of space debris that is a dying Earth's most important energy source, he sets forth a destructive chain of events.
    ISBN 978-0-7387-2342-6
    [1. Science fiction.] I. Title. II. Title: Crimson rising.
    PZ7.J154195Si 2012
    [Fic]—dc23

                                    2012002989

Flux
Llewellyn Worldwide Ltd.
2143 Wooddale Drive
Woodbury, MN 55125-2989
www.fluxnow.com

Printed in the United States of America

1

A sideways hailstorm of bullets sliced through the air. Cassius Stevenson had only a split second to jump from the rooftop before being hit.

No time for hesitation.

Bounding onto the outside ledge, he pushed forward and leapt.

Midair, one of the bullets ripped through the shoulder of his jacket, nicking his skin and forcing his left side forward at an awkward diagonal. A sharp pain tensed his arm. It wasn't enough to fracture his concentration.

The second rooftop approached quickly, nine yards below the first. He tucked his legs and prepared for impact.

The moment he hit the ground, the entire surface caved in.

Planks of rotten, damp wood cracked and exploded, sending a cascade of splinters into the air. Slum rooftops. Some were reinforced, some were as thin as cardboard. He should have known.

The building's top floor was sturdier. His thigh smashed into the ground first, followed by the rest of him. A jolt of unfettered pain spread through his body, meeting the sharp throb of his shoulder. It was all he could do to keep from shouting.

There was no telling how many of them were outside. Even if they hadn't seen him jump, they'd notice the massive skylight he'd carved out.

He shouldn't have upset the Locusts. Slum Lords were nasty individuals at the best of times. Tick one off and you're as good as dead. Cassius wasn't here to tussle with the locals. But the tussle seemed to find him, regardless of his intent.

Fight to stay conscious. That was the trick now. Black out and it was all over. He couldn't defend himself if he couldn't move.

He clenched a fist, mostly to see if he could still do it, and allowed his legs to spread onto the ground as he rolled onto his back.

A hoarse cough soon became a heave. Chunks of wood and insulation rained from the decimated ceiling, lowering the visibility to a thin haze.

Beating his chest to knock the breath in, he pushed himself back against the floor.

Too late.

The rest of the rooftop came down. Large slats of wood cut the floor like guillotines, crashing around him. Random intervals. Random landing spots.

Cassius flipped over, making himself as small as he could, keeping his head low and covered as the clatter of wood became a deafening wall of noise. Small pieces hit his back. Nothing big.

Please, he thought. Nothing big. Broken skin was fine. Bruises were better. Punctures? A full-on plank through the body? There was no recovering from that.

He felt his fist warm, skin sweating. He had fire inside him. He could burn the entire building down if he wanted, but what would that accomplish? He'd come up to Canada's Polar Cities to escape, to blend in. After what he'd done back in America—destroying a government building, betraying his commander—he knew the Unified Party wouldn't let him get away unscathed. Setting a city block ablaze would likely result in the kind of news item that could make him findable.

He forced himself to dismiss the past and focus on the present. He didn't know exactly where the Unified Party was looking for him—hopefully south of the border, far away—but the Slum Lords? They were here, and they were just as serious.

Shadows descended on the walls of the room, followed by heavy thumps as feet hit the floorboards. Then came the clicks of artillery. When Cassius pulled himself to a sitting position, he was greeted by a firing squad.

They stood in a semicircle around him, faces obscured by the dust in the air. They'd landed on their feet, decreasing pain and recovery time. Cassius cursed under his breath. How must he look, cowered on the floor, presenting himself willingly to these men? The thought of it sickened him. It couldn't end like this. It wouldn't.

The Slum Lands, even this far north, were a dangerous place—the Slum Lords even more so. They lived for this kind of thing, employing plenty of paid assassins, happy to carry out the dirty work.

All it had taken was a wrong turn that morning. Fate could have steered him toward any alley in the city, but Cassius had to stumble right into a local gang skirmish. Locusts versus Hoods, brawling over a deal gone bad. There were children caught in the middle, forced to the ground. Bargaining tools. Cassius had no choice but to get involved. It was none of his business, but he could hardly stand by and watch innocent kids be murdered.

His results? Two unconscious Locusts and a horde of new enemies. Fast, resourceful ones. Cassius had trained with the best Unified Party soldiers back home, yet here he was. On the floor. Disarmed.

The semicircle of slum assassins advanced as one unit. Cassius swallowed. His fingers scratched at the dirty floor. A trickle of blood dripped from the wound on his shoulder. The room was abandoned. That was at least some consolation. No one to get hurt. No one to watch.

"Anything to say for yourself?" The nearest man spoke.

Cassius coughed. "If your crappy roof would've held—"

A gunshot interrupted him. He flinched, only to realize that the bullet had slammed into the wall several feet from his right shoulder. The assassins laughed, enjoying the show.

"We don't actually want to hear your voice." The man sneered.

Cassius grit his teeth. This was it. He didn't have a choice.

It was fire. Fire or die.

He closed his eyes, just for a second. He'd have to fight through the pain to summon it. The flames were buried inside him, constantly held at bay ever since his power had been triggered four months ago. It had been nothing but trouble so far. It was time to project that trouble onto someone else.

The assassin moved forward, close enough for Cassius to see his pleased expression. Long, scraggly hair framed a pockmarked, sweat-dampened face. A pair of beady black eyes appraised him like he was a hunk of meat. An animal waiting to be put out of its misery. A trophy.

"You don't stick your nose in Locust business and live to brag about it."

"The kids," Cassius started, fire generating inside him. "They were going to be killed."

"That's slum life for you. No reason for an outsider such as yourself to get involved. You don't belong here."

He grit his teeth. "Hell no."

The barrel of the gun rose, aimed directly at his forehead. "Then I'm doing you a favor."

With a grunt of pain, Cassius pushed his fist out in front of his face and unclenched his fingers. Sparks danced along his skin, igniting into small flames. The assassin's eyes widened.

He hadn't seen anything yet.

The flames snaked into the air, twisting and winding until they formed an impressive torrent. Cassius winced. It took energy to control it like this, and he had precious little.

The rest of the guns cocked. Cassius's fingers spread.

A flurry of gunfire erupted. The flame extinguished as Cassius was forced to pull back, shielding his face.

The deafening ring of gunshots blocked out any other senses. For the first few seconds, he was convinced he was a goner. He'd taken shots before, but never more than one at a time. Was this what it felt like to be the victim of a firing squad? So thoroughly gutted that he couldn't feel a thing?

Bodies fell in front of him, hitting the floor with a dull thud. Cassius watched in horror as the men lay still. They'd never had a chance to fire. The gunshots had come from outside, somewhere on the roof. Somebody else had attacked them.

Another Slum Lord? A local police squad? It didn't matter. It gave him a chance. He could still escape this.

He tried to stand, and fell. A second pained effort brought him to his feet. He staggered back, hitting the wall. He needed to rest.

Everything was silent. The air began to clear.

Maybe he'd take one of the assassin's guns. He wasn't confident that he could conjure any more fire.

Before he could move, something caught his eye. He watched as a metal sphere, small enough to hold in his hand, dropped from the hole in the ceiling and hit the ground. It rolled toward him a few feet before stopping.

His stomach lurched. Panic flooded his heart. He recognized the weapon instantly. He'd used them dozens of times in training. Every Pearlhound knew what a Unified Party–issue gas bomb looked like.

Unified Party. This couldn't be a coincidence.

"Not now," he muttered to himself. "This isn't happening."

A tiny red light began to blink on the surface of the bomb. It would only pulse faster until the thing exploded and knocked him out for good. Seconds. Less than.

Pushing against the wall, he moved sideways until he found the closest door. He pulled on the handle in a blind panic, moments before the bomb exploded.

Expecting to enter another room, Cassius was surprised by the sudden drop. The planks beyond the door had been removed, leaving nothing to support his body. He fell to the next lowest level of the building, a narrow landing attached to a rotting staircase.

Half running, half rolling, he tumbled down the stairs. Gas seeped through the open doorway above him, slowing as it dissipated into the large open space.

When he finally reached the bottom, he dragged his bruised and battered body toward the nearest exit and slipped outside, desperate for fresh air. He took a deep breath and stumbled forward, all the while repeating the words in his head.

Unified Party.

There was no way a Slum Lord would've gained access to a gas bomb like that. Not this far north. It was government-issue, no doubt. Even in his weakened state, he couldn't forget something so obvious.

The skyline beckoned in the distance. It was his only chance. Laws were scarce in the slum lands. In the city, he'd have the protection of a more dignified crowd. Maybe.

He ducked into the nearest alleyway. He'd run until he passed out, if necessary. Anything to lengthen his distance from them. He'd let the city swallow him. It was his only hope.

2

They're going to find me. I have minutes, maybe. And when they do, I'll get the needle again.

Jesse Fisher. He doesn't look like much, but he's dangerous.

Jesse Fisher. We don't understand him anymore. He's not one of us. Not really. We'll pretend he is, but not really.

It's a foregone conclusion. Once the secondary lights cut off throughout the Academy, they'll know what happened. Kids who should be sleeping will look up from blank screens. Yank at silent headphones. The ship's control deck will flicker to emergency backup. This—right here in the reactor chamber—is the first place they'll look. And they'll find me. I won't have time to escape.

But if I can just do this one thing, maybe it'll be worth it.

The thought pins my fingers to the railing. It keeps me traveling up the ladder, rung by rung, each move another treacherous act. By the time I've pulled my body onto the warm metal of the platform, it's too late to talk myself out of it.

I stand in the center of Skyship's main reactor chamber,

the heart of our little operation. But instead of pumping blood, this heart runs on Pearl Power. Without it, the Academy shuts down. The Bridge'll trigger crisis mode and try to eke out as much power from our struggling solar panels as they can give.

It's okay. We'll survive. It's not like there's a danger of plummeting to the ground. We haven't been airborne in weeks.

I shield my eyes from the green glow that overtakes the room. A bulky turbine spins several yards from where I stand, stretching from floor to ceiling like an enormous hourglass—an ancient beast of a machine. Each revolution is a struggle. Loud thomp, thomp noises reverberate across the walls as the flaps scoop the air. Beyond that I see the source of the green light. Placed inside the bowels of the tube, sitting there like a treasure ripe for the picking, is a Pearl.

It pulses in my gut. It's so strong, it's internal. The energy crackles along the narrow walls of the spherical room. My heart flutters. The Pearl speaks to me. Maybe not the way normal people do, but it's calling me all the same. Telling me to break it.

I stand at the far end of the thin platform that surrounds the reactor chamber—metal scaffolding that's been in place long enough to be considered permanent. I step closer to the reactor and look over my shoulder in case I'm not alone. The room is empty, but full of spirit. This is a tomb. Hundreds have died here, sucked dry by the reactor. Thousands more have been killed these past decades.

Back when I was a simple Skyship trainee, we didn't know what was inside Pearls—that they carried living, sentient beings. It took a chance meeting with Cassius Stevenson, my brother, to trigger my power to break Pearls. And that changed everything. Now every flip of a light switch or click of a button is a kind of murder. Small things. They add up.

Pearl Power runs everything onboard, from the central thrusters to the tiny overhead light on the desk in my room. Every Skyship's like this. Every Chosen City too.

After discovering what was really inside Pearls, our technicians upped consumption of solar, biomass, and alternative fuels. We now burn twenty-eight percent less Pearl Power, extending each orb's lifespan from sixty-eight days to ninety-three. Captain Alkine's gone through the numbers, but it doesn't make any difference to me.

Pearls are people. My people. Cassius and I were sent to Earth to break Pearls, freeing allies who would help us fight the invasion that's to come. But instead of following my parents' wishes, I've been standing by, oblivious, while my own people are snuffed out.

Not anymore.

I wipe the sweat from my forehead and breathe in dank air. My balance wobbles on the platform. I make the mistake of looking down, right through the hexagonal holes between grids of metal underfoot. I'm not entirely sure this scaffolding is strong enough to support anyone for more than a few minutes, even a scrawny fifteen-year-old like me.

It was a long climb up here, which means an equally long drop if I were to fall. Below me are the docking bays, followed by the engine works, though the chute from the base of the reactor chamber would likely wind past everything until I landed unceremoniously at the very bottom of the Skyship. Pow. Splat. Dead.

I stumble forward, my fear a constant motivation to get this done quickly.

My hands tremble at my sides. I was able to bring a Pearl toward me back in Seattle last spring. I shouldn't have to reach far. All I've gotta do is focus.

I crouch and close my eyes, extending my hands in front of my chest like I'm ready to catch a baseball. I let the energy speak to me, connect to the whispers inside. Suddenly I feel heat, like I'm standing in the Fringes. Back in America. It's the Pearl.

The tips of my fingers twitch, shoved around by the force of the energy. Glass shatters in the distance. So much for the reactor's containment shield. I open my eyes and watch the Pearl fly at me—a stringless yo-yo heading straight for my waiting fingers.

The moment it connects with my hands, I feel complete again. There's no downplaying the sensation. It's as if a missing limb has reformed itself. Nobody in the world knows this feeling. Nobody in any world. There's only one Pearlbreaker.

Me.

I hug the swirling sphere of green closer to my tingling body. The hairs on my arms stand on end. My skin warms, coursing up from my hands and into my chest. I stare into the Pearl's seemingly endless abyss of energy and listen to the whispers. A language. One I can't even begin to comprehend, but mine all the same. The language of my ancestors. My history.

We huddle on the scaffolding for a moment like this, me and the Pearl. Connected.

The clicks and pops of broken transformers echo through the room as the ship's power begins to fail. I watch the reactor's turbines slow as lights shut down. Soon the glow of the Pearl is the only color I see.

I should break it as fast as I can. They may not be able to see me, but every waking soul onboard our ship knows what's happened. The night guards might assume it's an attack. Families will be alarmed. Blackout. No power. No light except for the stars and moon. There will be punishment. The only question is, how long do I have?

I stand, clutching the Pearl tight to my chest. This could be the one that holds my mother or father. Of all of the thousands of Pearls that have fallen on Earth since the Scarlet Bombings, this could be it. And there's only one way to find out.

The clatter of boots on metal breaks me from my thoughts. I spin around to watch a bulky figure pull itself onto the darkness of the scaffolding.

Too soon. No way they're this early.

I stagger back, forgetting the flimsiness of the ground. The metal shudders underfoot. I pull the Pearl tighter, like it's a child I'm trying to protect. Hell, it could be a child.

"Fisher." Captain Alkine spits my name. I recognize his gravelly voice from the shadows, even before his weathered face moves into the green light. He's taller than me by a foot, and still carries the frame of a soldier. Of course it would be him. "Put it down."

I take another step back. "No."

He scowls. "Listen to me. You're sabotaging us. You're hurting your friends ... your family."

This is where it gets tricky. He thinks this is going to sound rational. But there's no way it will, not when I've got two families and one is dependent on snuffing out the other.

I shake my head. Alkine knows his argument doesn't affect me. In another second, his words will give way to brute force. It's the only advantage he's got over me. He grits his teeth and stares me right in the eyes. His voice becomes a whisper. "You don't know what you're doing."

I extend my right arm to my side. With it the Pearl hovers in the air, held aloft by the force of the invisible energy coursing from my hands. Alkine watches its trajectory with slit eyes before focusing on me again. "Jesse, I understand how difficult this is for you, but you have to think."

I shake my head. I'd been thinking about this all night. I'd been thinking about it so much that I couldn't sleep. It's the one overriding struggle that's consumed my thoughts these past four months, ever since that day in Seattle when I found out who I really was.

I close my fist. The Pearl explodes.

Alkine's eyes widen and he falls to the ground in anticipation of the force. A shockwave of green energy shoots in every direction. It connects with the walls, warping them before flowing into the circuitry of the Skyship. Power surge. Lights will be flashing in the dorm rooms tonight.

I feel the energy flow through the chamber and turn my head to watch the body of a Drifter shoot out from the nexus of the explosion. Drifters, Alkine calls them, like he's hoping they'll just drift back out into the cosmos where they came from and leave us alone. But it's not as simple as that. I'm a Drifter. An alien. And aliens deserve to live too.

The figure soars into an open vent above the chamber before crashing down again and disappearing below us, flying in a blind panic. It'll likely find the chute to the nearest open docking bay and escape. It's not the best of scenarios. I don't have time to make out features or details or even tell if it's male or female, but the Drifter will live. And if it has any relation to me, I'll have done something good. We'll have a chance to find each other.

As the energy dissipates, I turn back to Alkine. Without a word, he jumps from the ground and rushes at me. I don't have time to react before he grabs me by my shoulders, spins me around, and pushes me into the wall. I collide hard with the metal, helpless against his superior strength.

His hands dig into my shoulders. I can barely look at his face.

"Now you've done it," he rasps.

I look to the side. "So what? Are you gonna kill me now?"

"Of course not."

"But it'd be easier for you, wouldn't it?"

His grip tightens. "You need to calm down."

I meet his eyes for the first time. "Calm down? That could've been my mother in that thing! It could be my dad!"

"That doesn't give you the excuse—"

"I don't wanna hear this again," I say. "Just pull out the gun and get it over with."

Alkine shakes my shoulders. "You're selfish, Fisher. That Pearl's the only thing that's keeping us operational. It's the only thing that's keeping us safe!"

"It's murder," I mutter.

"You're being irrational."

"Yeah, well, you're being a murderer." My lip shakes. "You promised and you ... you lied and—"

"I can't talk to you like this." He moves his hand to my chest, pushing hard. The other hand heads for his belt, retrieving the gun. I know this without even looking.

I keep my fists at the side, pushed against the wall. "Of course not. Never talk. God forbid we should talk—"

"You want to endanger the lives of my people? You deal with the consequences." He grits his teeth. I watch him bring the piercing gun to the side of my neck. I feel the cold metal of the muzzle against my skin. "You're not the only one on this ship, Jesse."

I swallow. "Last spring, after my first training mission, you said you wanted me to think of you like a father."

He moves closer. I feel his breath on my face. "I saved you in Seattle. I'll always save you."

I latch onto his eyes. I'm not scared, and he has to know that. "You're a hypocrite. You don't know what you're saving."

He sighs. I can't tell if it's out of frustration, sadness, or anger. Maybe it's a little bit of all three. "Go to sleep, Fisher. This isn't you. This isn't right."

A sharp pain strikes my neck as the needle's shot through my skin. The serum only takes seconds to work. Before I know it, I feel myself slump into Alkine's arms. My eyes shut. The energy in the room fades. Ghosts. That's all it is now.

3

I wake in a gray room. My face is pressed against the thin fabric of a too-tiny couch, its cushions sunken and hard. There's no table to go with it. Only one small, dirt-stained window on the unadorned, scratched walls.

This is how it is these days. I've woken in this room before—punishment for stealing a Pearl from Dr. Hemming's science lab, punishment for my last midnight adventure to the ship's core reactor two months ago. I've had time to study this room, from the crack in the corner of the ceiling to the one floor tile that sticks up a little more than the rest. This is where they put troubled people to cool off. Half holding cell, half observation chamber. They could never hurt me, but that doesn't mean they have to listen to me.

It all happened so fast, four months ago. After my chance meeting with Cassius in the Fringes, the Unified Party came after me. But it was Madame, head of the party's Chronic Energy Crisis Commission, who knew the truth all along. Cassius and I were more than brothers. We were the first Drifters to land on Earth, and the means of unlocking every one that came after us. Her cover-up cost more lives than I can imagine, and it continues to this day.

Cassius is out of the picture now, laying low in Canada. And I'm stuck here in Eastern Siberia. Chukotka. That's what they call this bare eyesore of a peninsula. I personally never imagined a life where I'd know a word like Chukotka, but that kind of stuff happens now that the Academy's on the run from not only Madame but the entire fraggin' Skyship Community as well. After Alkine illegally crossed the International Skyline into Unified Party territory to rescue me, we were forced to leave our perch above Northern California and head across the Pacific Ocean. There's too much uncertainty. Too many reasons for the Skyship Tribunal to find us guilty of sedition. That's the word Alkine uses. Basically, we screwed up big time. Skyshippers and the Unified Party are already on the brink of war, fighting for elusive Pearls, oblivious to the truth. The Tribunal doesn't know about my power. If they found out what really happened in Seattle, who knows what they'd do? Pearls are too precious. The fact that I can break them makes me dangerous too. A liability, or a weapon. Either way, I'm a trigger for full-blown war. So we wait in tundra and mountain. It seemed the smart idea at the time.

But it's not a war on Earth that I'm most concerned about. While we fight amongst each other, something's approaching from the stars. The Authority. I don't know much about it beyond what Cassius and I heard from my mother's voice recording last spring. I hope the Drifters can tell me more, but Alkine won't let me speak to them. And with every Pearl that's snuffed out, another potential ally disappears.

There are six Drifters on Earth. Well, seven after last night. Not much of an army. And no sign of my parents, if they're alive at all.

I close my eyes and try to remember their faces. I've only seen one picture, revealed to us on an electronic disc just before we heard our mother's recording. It fizzled out quickly until it was worthless. I can hardly remember what they look like.

The Drifters I've freed might be able to tell me more, but Alkine hides them away. He holds them underground, somewhere not far from the Academy. Or so he tells me. It might as well be on the other side of the Earth.

I straighten up as I notice the handle of the far door twist. It opens and in walks Mrs. Dembo, Head of Year Ten. *My* training year, as of two weeks ago when the new semester started.

She's a short woman, dark-skinned with bright clothing. Her graying hair's cut close to her scalp. She holds a drinking glass at her side as she quietly shuts the door and turns to acknowledge me.

I stare up at her. "I expected Alkine."

She approaches cautiously. "After what happened last night, Jeremiah thought it would be best if somebody else came and talked to you." Her tone is calm and reasoned. Somehow this makes me angrier.

I rest my elbows on my knees and look at the floor. "He's scared then?"

"I don't know what would give you that idea." She stops. "I brought water. Would you like some?"

"Depends. What's in it?"

She moves to the couch and takes a seat beside me. I inch away. "It's just water, Jesse. Straight from the reprocessor. Would you like me to take a sip first?"

"No." I reach for the glass and hug it with my fingers. "That's okay."

She sighs. "You have to learn to trust us."

I nearly laugh. After all the lies they told me, the fact that they think they deserve my trust is the real kicker. It wasn't too long ago that I was up in the ship's air vents, spying on their secret faculty meeting. The entire staff knew I was different. They knew there was something wrong with me. They'd known ever since they brought me onboard, plucking me from the ruins of a destroyed Seattle when I was only three years old.

Mrs. Dembo crosses her hands. "I wanted to give you the opportunity to talk. Tell me what you're thinking."

I take a sip of water. I didn't realize how thirsty I was. Then I point to the ceiling, to the pair of illuminated panels in the center. "The lights are on."

"Of course," she says. "You know the lighting runs on an automated system."

"It's sunny outside. Your system's ridiculous."

She frowns. "It's not my decision to make, but I can certainly bring it up at the next meeting."

I take another sip. It helps to calm me down. Even so, my hands shake. "They've got another Pearl going, then?"

"I don't think this is something we should discuss right now."

"If I knew where you were keeping them—"

She holds up a hand to stop me. "They're secure. Shielded"—her eyes pierce mine—"from those who would steal them."

I ignore her. "What happened to the one last night? Did anybody find who was inside?"

"No," she says. "It… er… the Drifter likely escaped through one of the air hatches below the engine works. Nobody saw, Jesse. We don't know age, gender. No details." She pauses. "You know, when I was an adolescent—"

I hold the glass in front of me and release it. It plunges to the ground, crashing in a mess of glass and water. I watch the shards dance along the tiles before turning to gauge her reaction.

Her fingers unclasp. Then she smiles. A small, fake one. "Hmm."

We sit in silence for a moment, watching the water pool along the indentations between tiles. Mrs. Dembo doesn't make a move to clean it up. Instead, she pulls her arm around my back and squeezes. I resist the urge to fight back. I let her think that she's comforting me.

Her voice is low and soft this time, like she's afraid

others will hear. "I never liked it. I know that's easy to say now, but I always felt rotten having to lie to you. We comforted ourselves in the knowledge that it was for your safety, but I've always believed that truth is more important than logic."

These are the types of things they say now. Sweeping, vague slogans that are supposed to make me feel better. All they're doing is trying to make themselves feel better. They know they're screwing up, but they've dug a hole so deep that the only way to get out is to keep lying to themselves. They think they have the luxury of doing that.

"I remember when you first came to us," she continues. "You were a confused little boy, always staring off into the distance like you needed to be somewhere else. Our nurturing staff took good care of socializing you, but you were terrified of loud noises. I guess every child is, to some degree. We didn't know what trauma you'd been through before we found you. We didn't want to make things worse, so we invented a story. We explained your parents away in the most respectful, honorable manner we could think up. It was only ever meant to keep you safe. Everything we do is meant to keep you safe." She extends her hand toward my knee. I pull away.

"You lied."

She brings her hand back to her lap, sighing. "It...wasn't my decision."

"Yeah, it was Alkine's."

"Jeremiah Alkine is a good man."

"I don't care how—"

"And more importantly," she continues, "he's your commander. Don't tell me that all the training we've given you thus far has amounted to nothing." She pauses. "Look, you and I both know that things would be different if we could make it so. In a perfect world, Pearl Power wouldn't be an issue. We could focus on what's happening to you without consequence. But the climate out there, especially after our rescue operation in Seattle ... we broke laws to help you. Important ones, to the Tribunal at least. I know it isn't easy to hear, Jesse, but we can't help the Drifters until we know that we're safe ourselves. It's a horrible choice to make, I understand that. We all do. But it's the logical approach."

I keep my eyes pinned to the broken glass, unwilling to look at her. "I thought you said truth is more important than logic."

"I *am* telling the truth," she responds almost immediately. "And that's why it's so difficult."

I close my eyes, wishing I could rewind time about six months. To think I used to be worried about scoring well on exams or passing skill courses. "Aren't you scared of being my teacher?"

"Why? Should I be?"

I open my eyes. "My last head teacher died, you know."

She scoots closer. "Mr. Wilson died protecting you. It's not something he would have been ashamed of and it's not something you should feel guilty about. So, no. I'm not scared." She stands, narrowly missing the broken glass, and crouches next to me. She tries to catch a glimpse of my face. I make it hard for her. "Jeremiah wants confirmation that you understand the repercussions of what you did last night. He runs a tight ship, Jesse. You know that. Nobody's interested in holding you prisoner. We don't want to confine you or restrict access to your friends. We want you to continue your training. We want you to be a vital part of this team. You're important. We have a great deal of respect and … fondness for you. And we haven't forgotten. We know what you're going through. We have to make it right. It's just going to take some time."

Somehow this sounds even worse coming from her. I've always liked Mrs. Dembo. I always thought she had my back, even when Alkine was less than cheery about my training progress. Suddenly, I feel sick to my stomach. Or maybe it's hunger. I haven't eaten since dinner last night.

So this is the choice I have. It's always the same. Play by their rules and wait, or become their enemy—work against the only family I've ever known, even if they're not the real one. Skyship Academy used to mean safety. Now I'm not sure.

Mrs. Dembo stands. "The Sophomore Tour is tomorrow afternoon. I'd like you to be able to participate. These types of activities are helpful to take your mind off of things you're unable to control." She paces to the center of the room. "Of course, we can't let you out of here consequence-free, but we're giving you another chance. I know I can't speak for the others, but you've always been very special to us. We hate to see you like this."

I glance up at her. I know she expects a response, a declaration of loyalty or something, but I can't stomach the thought of it. It's all about them, like always. But the bottom line is, I've gotta get out of this room. I can't do anything in here. So I make the only move I can. I nod.

Mrs. Dembo returns the gesture. "I'm going to give you just a little more time to think about it. Should I grab you some more water?"

"No," I whisper. "Sorry about the mess."

She smiles. "Don't you worry." She turns to leave, but stops before grabbing the handle. "Things are going to be alright, Jesse. I hope you know that. Days might seem dark now, but I'm confident that your turning point isn't as far away as you expect it might be."

I don't know what she means by that. It sounds like a mild threat, even coming from her. But maybe that's just me being paranoid.

I watch her leave in silence and kick the heels of my feet against the couch. When she's gone, I bend forward and pick up the largest shard of glass I can find. I run it across my finger, not strong enough to cut, but firm enough to feel. Then I chuck it at the door, hoping that maybe it'll stick. It doesn't. I watch it fall to the ground. Everything's silent.

4

Cassius pulled his head from the water and took a gasp of breath. He ran his fingers through his wet hair and used the splash to cleanse his shoulder. The bullet had only grazed his skin, leaving a shallow wound. Still, he couldn't afford an infection. The worst of it had closed throughout the evening. Even so, the cool saltwater stung.

He sat with his bare, calloused feet dipped into the Arctic. He'd found a sheltered area, a secluded grassy outstretch from one of the city's lesser-known waterfront parks. Trees surrounded him on all sides, save for a narrow walkway behind him that offered a brief snapshot of the city skyline.

The sunrise beamed a shocking orange, lifting from the edge of the skyline so close that it seemed like its fire could reach out and touch him. Back home, the chemicals in the Fringes obscured much of the sky's color, dulling sunsets and sunrises. The Polar Cities were lucky that way. By the time the chemicals from the Scarlet Bombings made their way up north, they were so dilute that they had little impact. A ten-degree climate increase, fifteen at the most.

He stared at his reflection in the ocean, trying to understand the face before him. Beyond the scratches and bruises, he'd lost close to fifteen pounds since running from New York. He looked more like Fisher now. Skinny. Or skinnier, at least.

It was just after three in the morning. The sun had been down for exactly one hour and twenty-seven minutes. He'd been keeping track. This time of year it was light almost all day and night in the Polar Cities. He'd tried getting some rest, but every time he closed his eyes, the thought of that Unified Party gas bomb shocked him awake. It killed him not to know who threw it. They'd done him a favor, finishing off those slum assassins. They could have easily killed him too. Instead, they sent gas. They wanted him unconscious, but not dead.

And they hadn't followed him into the city. He wasn't sure if he should be pleased or petrified.

He snapped his fingers and ignited a tiny flame that hovered above his hand and evaporated what beads of water were left. He played with it for a minute, quivering it sideways, expanding it, adding heat. Then he clenched his fist and extinguished it altogether.

There was a time, not too long ago, when the fire controlled him—built inside until it tore through his skin, triggering an explosion capable of destroying a room, a train car, a building. Now he could snuff it out with his bare hands, not that it had done much for him back in the slum building.

Madame had called it a sickness, tried to convince him

that there was something wrong, that he needed to shoot and kill to fix it. And in the end, that's exactly what he'd done. Maybe it hadn't been with a gun. Maybe it hadn't been by his hands directly, but he'd left her in Seattle, buried under the rubble. His mother, or the closest thing to it for twelve years, dead because he hadn't come back to save her. He couldn't face the thought of the murder he'd aided, even if it had been to save his own brother, so he remained up north. But even that had its dangers.

Providence was one of twenty-five Polar Cities the U.N. had nestled along the Arctic Circle decades ago in preparation for intense global warming. They all had fancy, quasi-religious names like Arcadia and Assumption. Most were in Canada and Northern Europe and functioned as normal cities had before the bombings. No Bio-Nets constantly stabilizing the environment. Rent was expensive and real estate even more so. The North Coast was incredibly desirable, and with a Unified Party ID socket carved into his wrist, finding legitimate work had been impossible. He'd managed to find shelter in the basement of a condemned building on the outskirts of town, dead in the middle of slum territory. Hardly beach-front property, but it had been hard-won regardless. Of course, the problems far outweighed the perks. Cassius didn't search out trouble, but it was difficult to walk through the slum lands without finding it. Narrow escapes, arguments that intensified to fistfights—they had all become part of the norm these past few months.

He didn't spend much time indoors. Most days he

roamed the city, familiarizing himself with every nook and cranny. Boredom compelled him, as well as the need to erase the past. And then there was his brother. Fisher.

Cassius carried his communicator with him everywhere he went. It was an older model, the last before the new line of com-pads made long-range contact more convenient. But it was untraceable. He and Fisher could talk candidly, and Fisher certainly had a lot to talk about.

He took things harder than Cassius, or perhaps he was just less afraid of discussing them. While Cassius spent most of his energy worrying about Madame and the Unified Party, Fisher had only one thing on his mind each time they talked. Pearls.

He'd become obsessed, but it was understandable. While Cassius could only store and manipulate the broken Pearl energy into fire, Fisher had the power to break the things open—liberate those from their home planet. Restore life, in a way.

It was suitable. Fisher could give life. All Cassius could do was take it. It had always been this way, from the murder of the Year Nine teacher back onboard the Academy to the massacre on the chute from Seattle to Spokane. Death followed him around like an old friend.

His stomach grumbled. Food was an issue. Without credit, he'd been forced to steal—especially at first. At the height of the summer he'd found a reasonably steady job loading and unloading smuggler's boats at the east-side dockyards. Pay had been under-the-table, and he hadn't needed to identify himself. He'd had steady payment for five weeks until the local authorities had raided and shut down the organization.

He lifted his feet from the water and breathed in the fresh morning air. The city lay quiet and still. He pivoted to stare at the bright, looming metropolis behind him. All Polar Cities had humble beginnings, but after the climate changed in America, they'd grown exponentially. A skyline of silver towers laying before him, nearly uniform in height and sprawled over the land in a vast sculpture of boulevards, catacombs, and wide sidewalks—the complete opposite of the smashed-together Chosen Cities he'd grown up in.

He ran his fingers over the scar on his wrist, just below his identification socket. Before breaking through the U.S. border on his trek to Canada, he'd been forced to carve out the microchip Madame had embedded inside his arm. A tracker, tossed to the ground somewhere in the Fringes, left to throw the Unified Party off track. Yet someone had still found him.

Around the opposite wrist wrapped a seamless black band, a gift from his home world fused to his arm after he and Fisher had learned of their past in Seattle. It felt like stone but with a heft no greater than a ring of paper. Alien in nature, he was sure. It'd been completely useless so far, but impossible to remove. Another reminder of things he'd rather forget.

Shaking the water from his feet, he stood and started into the city. His government suit—minus the seal and anything else that could identify him—had seen better days. It had served as his main set of clothing since he'd arrived, and it wasfraying at the edges. A thumb-sized hole slowly unwound near the waist where it'd gotten stuck on a splintered beam a couple weeks ago. And now the shoulder, blasted straight through.

The trees rustled to the left of him. A bristle ran up the back of his neck. Carefully, with as little sound as he could make, he rubbed his feet dry against the grass and slipped on his boots.

There was no wind this morning. No reason for the trees to shift like that.

Someone was here, watching him.

Panic flooded his body. He stood, fists balled at his sides. He could run if he wanted to, but then he'd never know what was happening.

"Who's there?" His voice came out a hoarse whisper.

Trees surrounded him on two sides—a hundred perfect hiding places for anyone wishing to spy.

He could hear breathing. Most people wouldn't even notice, but his senses had been heightened through years of training at the Lodge. A good quality in a soldier. Even better for a runaway.

Still, he couldn't help but doubt himself. Was this paranoia? Too much time spent alone, running things over in his head—it could make a person go crazy.

"Stop hiding," he continued. "I know you're there."

A branch snapped. Cassius spun to face it.

Nothing.

He felt his right fist ignite. He hadn't meant for it to happen, but now that the flames had erupted, his body followed suit. He felt his skin heat up. The invisible, organic generator inside of him produced more fire, drying any saltwater left on his face.

"Leave me alone!"

Before he knew it, fire spilled from his fingertips, bursting forth in a torrent as bright as the rising sun. Trees cracked and bowed as they caught ablaze. The fire spread fast, surrounding him within moments. Plumes of smoke rose into the air.

There were no screams. No footsteps or gunshots. Only fire.

Taking a choked breath, Cassius watched in horror as the blaze continued to spread. He'd done it again, let his fear and anger drive him to destruction. Whether or not there had been someone watching him, he'd lost his cool. And there wasn't time to fix it.

Keeping his head low, he bolted from the fire. Trees fell behind him. He forced himself to ignore the sound. He couldn't be linked to this.

He needed to disappear. Grab his communicator and leave the Polar Cities for good. But as he sprinted across the grass, he knew he couldn't run forever. They'd find him. They were the best, and the best don't give up, no matter how many of them he set on fire.

5

I sit at the edge of the bed in my dorm room, staring at the wall, scared to go outside for fear of what everyone else will say. Their eyes are scarier now, the way they dissect me. The corridors of the Academy seem endless. It's not just the faculty. It's the students. The families. Everyone.

There are two things they can't take away from me, and they're both in this room now. One winds around my wrist and the other sits securely in a safe below my desk, accessible only by my identification card.

The first is a black bracelet, weightless but solid as stone. It's fused so perfectly against my arm that it feels like a part of my body now. It was a sort of gift from my parents, meant for when I'd first landed on Earth more than twelve years ago. But Madame managed to hold that little party back until last spring. I still don't know exactly what it's supposed to do, but if nothing else, it's proof that my homeworld exists. Cassius shares this proof. He also shares what's in the safe—a direct line of communication between the two of us. The second of my untouchable objects.

If Alkine had his way, he'd take them both. Luckily,

the bracelet won't come off. And the communicator? Well, there's a reason I've got it locked up. Everybody gets to keep a secret or two. I have so few left.

I itch to head back to the core reactor and break the new Pearl they've got spinning in there now. My knee shakes. It's hard to keep still.

Avery would know what to do. If I could wish anything and have it be true, it would be for her to be here now, safe beside me on this bed. She'd know what to say. She's the one person I know who's worked for both the Academy and the Unified Party. It took me a while to trust her again after learning that, but I believe her now. She's on my side. She would've died for me in Seattle.

Maybe she has.

The Unified Party took her back. To reenlist her or to kill her—I have no way of knowing. Either way, the only person who really cared about me is gone.

I'm supposed to meet Eva and Skandar for lunch, but I honestly don't know if I'm up for it. Sure, they've been two of the only friends to stick by my side these past few months, but after spending the morning in the gray room I'm not exactly thrilled to face them. It's embarrassing, the way I am now. The way I feel.

A knock at the door jerks my shoulders back in surprise. My stomach sinks. My breath quickens. This is my home, my room. It shouldn't be like this.

I don't move. I wish I had a camera that could show me

who's standing on the other side of the door. Caller ID for people too lazy to stand up.

Another series of knocks. Maybe it's Skandar. That would be alright, I guess. Then at least I'd have someone to walk with up to the canteen.

I take a deep breath and work up the courage to stand and open the door. But before I can, it swings open and a man steps into the room. He stops just past the frame, arms crossed. I've probably seen him before—one of the hundreds of young agents onboard—but I have no idea who he is. Twenty-something, I'd guess, with a broad eager-to-please smile on his chiseled face. Cropped brown hair, button-up shirt and tie, the whole agent look. In short, a vision of exactly what I have no hope of becoming.

His eyes are bright and focused. I must look like an absolute mess in comparison. He leans on the open door, feigning a casual, at-ease persona. At the very least, he's not all that threatening. "Hey, buddy." His tone is overeager. "How's it going?"

My shoulders slump. I turn to look at him. "Who're you?"

His smile widens. "I remember when I was a Year Ten." He glances around the room like he's appraising a castle. "Level Two dorm rooms. Good times. Of course, that was back before they installed the content shields on the e-feed network, if you know what I mean." He moves from the doorway and sits beside me on the bed, almost shoulder to shoulder. After a moment, he holds out his hand in expectation that I'll do the same. "Agent Morse." I get the sense that if I grabbed it, he could throw me over his shoulder and chuck me all the way down the hallway.

I stare at him with an expression that can't help but come across more than a little insulting. "Um...this is my bed."

"Oh." He jumps to his feet. "Yeah. Sorry, man. I didn't mean to intrude or anything."

"Then you shouldn't barge into someone's room."

He laughs. He thinks I'm being funny.

I keep my eyes pinned to his face. "Did Alkine send you?"

He walks to the far window, dodging piles of clothing on the way. An agent like him probably has a mass clean room, probably folds his sheets with a straight edge. "It's a beautiful afternoon up at Lookout Park, Fisher. You shouldn't be cooped up in here."

I glare at him. Does this guy realize where I just spent my morning? I'd point it out, but I don't think the irony would phase him.

After another moment at the window, he turns back to me, his crisp suit at odds with the clutter around him. "Let me walk you to lunch."

"That's okay. I'm already meeting—"

"No," he says. "I insist."

"You know, there are privacy laws. Breaking into someone's room and—"

"Privacy laws?" He chuckles. "On Skyship Academy? Good one. They told me you were a joker."

"I'm already meeting friends."

He shakes his head. "I insist."

I scoot away from him, fingers forming fists. "What are you gonna do?"

Agent Morse holds his hands above his shoulders in innocence, that perma-smile still affixed to his face. "Whoa, calm down little man. I'm not here to hurt you."

Little man? Any chance of me listening to this guy is blown as soon as I hear these words. Tells me all I need to know. He's like all the others. Patronizing. He thinks I'm a kid. Maybe I should break a Pearl in his face and see if he still thinks I'm little.

He crosses his arms. "The Captain told me you'd have this reaction."

"Wonderful."

His posture eases. "He asked me if I would kind of, well, check up on you. You know, like a mentor program. He knows the way it's been between the two of you recently."

I stand and grip the door handle, seconds away from slamming it shut in his face. "You've got to be kidding me."

"It's not a punishment." He eases closer. "And it doesn't mean you're a ... loser or anything."

"Gee, thanks."

"It's just that you've got a different situation going on. And sometimes it helps to have someone to talk to. Someone who's a little older. Someone who's been through things."

My grip tightens. "You've got no idea."

"So fill me in. Over lunch."

"I already told you. I'm meeting people."

His brows raise. "I'd like to meet them too."

I shake my head. "No way. The moment we step out that door and people see me walking around with someone like you, they'll think something's up. Like, that you're walking me to the brig or something."

He sighs. "You really think people don't know already? Do you think the other students in Dr. Hemming's lab this morning didn't realize you were gone? Attendance hasn't exactly been first rate this term, has it? People know something's up."

My shoulders tense. "They don't know all of it."

"No. You're right. Hell, *I* don't know all of it. But I know you're different. I know that something happened back there on the Surface that changed the way we think about Pearls, and the way the Captain thinks about you. And, if I can be frank, from the rumors I've heard floating around the ship, you're lucky that Alkine's letting you stay onboard like this, protected."

I scoff. "Lucky."

"Yeah," he replies. "If I'm being honest. But I'd like you to prove me wrong. I'd like to discover that the file I read about a funny, good-hearted kid wasn't just a lie. He's in there. I can see him." He sighs. "Just give it a chance. It's like a big-brother thing. You've always wanted a brother, right?"

My heart sinks. "What did you just say?"

He shrugs. "A brother. Like, big bro ... toss the antigrav ball around and hang out."

That's it. Screw the people outside. I don't care how they look at me, or what they say. Nothing can be worse than this. Without responding, I head into the hallway and slam the door before Morse can follow. Then I run, and I don't stop until I reach the stairwell.

———

"You look terrible, mate. What did they do to you?"

That's Skandar Harris. Always tactful, always there to pick you up. Eva would say that he's too dim to be deceitful or manipulative, but I don't believe that. He sits across from me at the canteen table. His uncombed brown hair is tangled on top of his head, like usual.

Next to him is Eva Rodriguez, a firm, steady voice even when I don't need one. We've had our moments—we still do—but I think I trust her. I trust her enough, anyways. And compared to me, with her cropped, battle-ready hair and buff arms, she's mass good at this Skyship Agent stuff. She's the kind of student Alkine likes, and she's saved my butt on more than one occasion.

Agent "Big Brother" Morse didn't follow me up, thankfully, though it's only a matter of time before he corners me again. Especially if Alkine told him to.

Lunch is some sort of potato mush, halfway between a soup and a paste, with bread. It's bland, even with a fistful of salt mixed in, but I'm not paying much attention to it. Food's been a problem ever since we crossed the Pacific. It's mostly the same stuff every day, cans from deep within our rations storeroom, the odd crate our agents bring back from the States.

We sit at our old table, the one we always stole in Year Nine. It's lopsided, but pushed far into the corner of the room, shielded by rows and rows of students and faculty. Hopefully it's isolated enough to keep Morse from finding me. The din of the crowd is sort of comforting. I feel like I can blend in and disappear for once.

Eva sighs as she drags a spoon through her bowl. "At least they're letting you move around the ship. Class this afternoon?"

"I don't think so." I take a sip of water.

"That's a shame."

Skandar leans forward, whispering. "So did you really break it? Like, yank it from the reactor and give it the big explosion?"

I nod. "Right in Alkine's face."

Eva chokes down a spoonful of the paste. "Probably not the best way to endear yourself." She winces. "My god this is revolting."

"It was satisfying." I shrug. "Kind of."

She sets down her spoon and rests her elbows on the table, leaning closer. "Listen, Jesse. You know I have your back, whatever you do. But we really need to sit down and brainstorm some better ideas. There's got to be an effective way to look out for the other Drifters that doesn't cause this kind of chaos."

"Lights flickering off for a couple of hours is hardly

chaos." Skandar rolls his eyes. "I was asleep. I didn't even notice."

I nod. "If Alkine would stop using Pearl Power, every-thing would—"

"You know that's not an option," Eva interrupts. "He's doing what he can."

"You didn't meet with him after Seattle. You didn't hear the way he was talking, like we were gonna bust past the Skyline and take on the Unified Party until all the Pearls were broken. Project Pearlbreaker. That's what he called it. What a joke."

She grabs her spoon and attempts another go at the mush. "Military operations are always dependent on—"

Something flashes red. My vision blurs and I feel heat in my chest, like I'm back in the reactor chamber with the spinning Pearl. I close my eyes and the image of a coastline spreads across my consciousness. It's as clear as if I'm stand-ing there, right in front of the water. I hear the waves crash against the rocks, smell the gritty saltiness in the air. But I've never seen this place before. It's barren—no people or grass for miles—and flat.

Another flash and my eyes fly open again.

Eva gapes at me. "Are you okay, Jesse?"

I nod. "Fine." But even as I respond, the coastline lin-gers in my mind.

Skandar frowns. "You look like you just fell asleep for a second."

I give a slight nod, mostly ignoring him. "Yeah. Maybe."

Eva's eyes narrow. "It's not like last spring, is it? In Dembo's room on Visitation Day?"

"I'm fine."

I wish I could believe it. Every time I blink I see it again. And visions like this—weird, random flashes—are never good in my case. The last one led me to Seattle, but that was months ago. I thought it was a one-time thing, a symptom of my Pearlbreaker powers being triggered. Why would some empty coastline pop into my head now?

"Anyways," Eva starts up again. "I think if we run through this logically…get it all down in a…a chart or diagram, we can organize your thoughts into a coherent argument and present it to—"

"Cassius." I stop myself. I didn't mean to say his name out loud.

Her face drops. "What?"

"Sorry." I flash a fake smile while I think it through.

Cassius is on the coast. Back in Canada, a continent away. Was this some kind of warning? He's the type to get himself in trouble, even more than me, and I still don't fully understand our bond after Seattle. Maybe I was seeing something through his eyes. A connection.

Eva groans. "Are you even listening to me?"

Skandar pokes her shoulder with the end of his fork. "Jesse's not about to give Alkine some lame chart. That's like something you'd do."

"I'm just trying to help," she mutters.

I pull myself up from my seat, abandoning the rest of lunch.

Skandar leans back, fork pointing at me now. "Where are you going?"

"Don't worry. I just have to check on something."

Eva frowns. "What could be so important? You just got here!"

"Cover for me in Tech, okay?"

"I can only cover for you so many times."

"Thanks." I walk away before she can respond.

I don't look at anybody as I dart through the canteen on my way to the stairwell. I've gotten good at this lately, blocking out the curious glances and pretending that I'm the only one in the room.

I make it down four flights of stairs to my room in record time and slip inside. Door locked and double-checked, I head directly to my desk, pull my identification card from underneath piles of junk, and open the safe in the bottom drawer. Grabbing Cassius's secret communicator, I lie stomach-down on my bed and set the device against the deflated pillow. It's probably too late to hope that he'll pick up, but it's worth a shot. Our time difference is killer, but as far as I can tell Cassius doesn't sleep. Guy's a total insomniac.

I make sure that the dial hasn't been turned off our channel before speaking. Then, scooting forward so that I can keep my voice low, I whisper, "Cassius?"

I'm answered with static as the signal strengthens. This is old technology, even by the Academy's standards.

Cassius's voice spills from the speaker after a few moments, tinny and small. It's the only version of my brother I've gotten to know these past few months. "This isn't a good time." There's a hardness to his tone. Imposing, even now that we're allies.

I bring myself closer to the speaker, scared that Morse or someone could be out in the hallway listening. "Is something wrong?" I wait for a response that doesn't come. "You're still on the coast?"

"Yeah," he says. "Why?"

"I just had the weirdest flash. Like, suddenly my eyes shut and I saw this place, right on the water. I haven't had a vision that strong since last spring, when I saw Seattle clogged up with all that green mist."

He's silent. I'm not sure if he's thinking it through or if he's decided not to respond again, so I continue.

"I thought maybe, since it was a coastline, it might have something to do with you."

"What kind of coastline?"

I close my eyes and recall the image. "Dirt, mostly. Bare."

"That's not the Polar Cities," he responds. "There are buildings everywhere. Docks and … small forests."

"Oh." I move to a sitting position, resting on my knees. Suddenly the mad rush back to my room seems a little over-dramatic, something a crazy person would do. Or someone with a massive anxiety problem.

I stare into the speaker, wishing that we were sitting face to face. These short bursts of communicator conversation are never enough. And it makes it impossible to tell if he's being honest with me. "Where are you now?"

"Home."

"Where's home?" I know he won't tell me. He never does. He sighs. "Just *home*. Okay?"

"Okay."

His voice calms. "The Academy...how are they treating you?"

"The same," I start. "I broke a Pearl last night but they—"

"You've got to do something," he interrupts. "I don't have your power. I can't do what you can. They're still hiding the other Drifters?"

"They're in Siberia somewhere. That's all I know. We've had conference calls, but—"

"You've got to find them," he says. We've been through this before, countless times. And the conversation always follows the same path. I can nearly predict it word for word. "Talk to them. We're being kept in the dark. We can't do anything if we don't know what's going on."

"It would be a lot easier if you were here."

He scoffs. "Yeah? I'm sure Alkine'd be happy to have me after all I've done."

"But you've changed."

No reply.

I wince. "I don't know how."

"Next time they hook you up to the video feed, look for clues."

I think back to the last conference Alkine let me sit in

on. He schedules them every few weeks, heavily scripted sit-downs with Ryel, one of the first, and most English-fluent, of the Drifters I've freed. Their prison can't be far away. Otherwise Alkine wouldn't have been able to install a video link.

"It's only a room." I close my eyes and visualize Ryel's worried face filling the video screen. I picture the feed breaking in and out like it always does. I think the faculty manipulates the frames. I'm not even sure that the conference is live. The grammar Ryel uses, the words and phrases he chooses to put together... it never seems right. "There's nothing behind him. No markings or maps or anything. Just a gray wall and a pair of Academy guards flanking him."

"Maybe it's on the coast," Cassius says. "Maybe that's what you were seeing. The Academy has to have the coordinates stored somewhere. You have to look around."

"Yeah," I mutter. I know that finding Ryel is more important than freeing random Drifters from captured Pearls. He was the one who was able to relay the message from our mother on the rooftop last spring. He knows things that we need to know. But finding him—hell, getting to him—seems impossible.

There's a long pause. For a second I think Cassius has switched off his communicator. "Cassius?"

"I've gotta go, alright?"

"Is there anything I can do to help you?"

"From Siberia?" He laughs. "Doubt it. You focus on your end. Call me when you've got answers."

I nod, not that he can see it.

He grunts. Or maybe it's a cough. It's hard to tell over the communicator. "I'll talk to you when I know things are safe."

"Alright." That's about all I can expect from my brother right now. But things are never safe. Not with him.

The static fades and the line goes dead. I turn off the communicator and flip over on my back, staring at the ceiling. I close my eyes and try to visualize that coastline again. It appears in front of me, one little piece at a time until I recall the entire horizon. Problem is, there's not much to see. It could be any stretch of land. The whole of this country's crammed with coastline. If I'm gonna risk my butt hijacking a shuttle to go exploring, I've got to be absolutely sure that I know where I'm going. There can't be mistakes. I can't give Alkine time to find me and bring me back.

I try to wind around inside my little vision, see if the image will let me zoom out and reveal a path to our Skyship. No luck.

Water. Rocks. That's it.

I open my eyes and notice a ball of red light blotched on the ceiling—a flash like the ghost image left behind after looking at a lightbulb for too long. Another second and it's gone. I continue to stare, squinting to see if I can make the red appear again. It doesn't.

Water. Rocks. Red. My mind's playing tricks on me. Maybe it's an aftereffect of the meds Alkine pumped into my system last night. Or maybe I'm just going crazy.

I sigh, trying to forget the entire thing. That's when my bracelet starts to hum.

6

Cassius deactivated the communicator and clicked it to his belt, letting his tattered jacket conceal as much as possible. It was his only important possession, and now that he had it, he could leave.

He crouched behind a row of overflowing trash cans perched diagonally across from the half-collapsed building he'd called a home for the last several weeks. He needed to take a moment to catch his breath and prepare for the long journey out of the city, but more than that, he'd had an idea.

Being the victim of subterfuge had taught him a trick or two, and once he'd recovered from the panic on the coast, he remembered his training. Fleeing without gaining information on his pursuers would be a wasted opportunity. The more he learned, the better he'd be able to defend himself. And if someone from the Unified Party knew that he was in Providence, they'd likely know which building he lived in as well.

So far the morning had proven fruitless. People littered the street before him, crawling out of their dank, miserable little hovels for another day in hell. The entire place stunk of garbage and feces, both animal and human. Cassius had just about gotten used to it, much as he hated to admit it. It was a far cry from the sterile grounds of the Lodge—the private chefs and hot showers and endless credit. But it was how it should be now, after Seattle. He didn't deserve those things, not after everything he'd done.

He brushed thoughts of Fisher from his mind. He could never tell if his brother was being serious or not, especially about coming aboard Skyship Academy and playing happy family. It rang suspiciously of a trap, but maybe that was Cassius's default mode. Everything was a trap. He watched a crowd of children kick a brown, dirt-covered soccer ball through the streets, blissfully unaware of a Serenity deal going down in the far alley. Then a dark figure entered the street.

Its combat suit was black from head to toe, its face obscured by a mask seamlessly connecting with the rest of the outfit. With all of its protective padding, Cassius couldn't discern gender, though he assumed it was a man.

Cassius watched the reactions of the residents who stared at the figure with a mix of curiosity and fear as they moved about. He'd never seen a Unified Party soldier dressed like this, not even covert ops. Maybe the Slum Lords had sent him. Either way, something was definitely wrong.

The figure moved confidently to the entrance of Cassius's building, pushed on the wobbly door with his foot, and peered inside. The guy was thin and lacked the bulk of a foot soldier. Cassius could probably take him in a fight.

Something shifted behind him. A footstep. A splash of puddle water. Cassius spun around to see a second figure, dressed as the first but dangerously closer.

"Cassius Stevenson," the figure said, voice low. This one was definitely a man.

Cassius didn't give him time to respond. He darted out from behind the trash cans with instinctive speed. The first figure noticed this immediately, releasing his grip on the door and joining the pursuit.

So much for gaining intel.

Cassius pushed through crowds of startled onlookers as more and more of the black-clad figures shot from alleyways and side streets like a flurry of blow darts. Sneak attack. They'd all been waiting for him to move.

He cursed himself for staying back. He should have left the city when he'd had the chance.

The thickness of the crowd kept the soldiers at bay, giving Cassius the few seconds he needed to change direction.

He barreled down a twisting corridor. Shacks and hovels were arranged like a mixed-up jigsaw puzzle around him. At times the path required stepping through someone's house, but in this area it was hard to distinguish shelter from trash heap. His pursuers didn't know the slums like he did. It was the only advantage he had.

Arriving on another crowded street, he paused for a

moment and surveyed the surroundings, searching for hiding places. The breath caught in his throat.

A tattered flag hung high above him on a crooked pole, a sign that he had entered the southeastern corner. Locust Territory. That was all he needed.

He paused to decide on a course of action. Mistake.

The crowd scattered in front of him. He turned to see the entire fleet of dark soldiers move into the street, spilling from the city block with impossible speed and coordination. Ten of them, he thought. They were moving too fast to get an accurate count.

Slum dwellers retreated into buildings and alleys until Cassius stood alone in the center of the street, surrounded by a half-circle of silent Government Agents. They approached as one unit. He didn't have time. Running wasn't going to cut it. He needed to act.

He sunk to the ground and laid his right hand on the dirt, closing his eyes. He'd have one good chance, one opportunity to blow them away in a single motion.

He felt his insides boil. This had to be big. Even bigger than back in the park.

The heat spread to his shoulders, then down his arms until it reached his fingers. Focus, he told himself. Focus on the pathway, the arc. It's got to be just right.

Fire exploded where his hand met the ground and arced around him in a half-circle before spreading outward like a deadly scythe, tearing through the figures on its way to the wall of shacks beyond. He prayed it would cut off before catching on any of the buildings, but once it had left his body, there was no controlling it. The old wood went up instantly. The fire spread through the city block with dangerous speed.

Worse yet, the figures remained standing, completely immune to the flames. Cassius stumbled to his feet and stepped back, realizing with horror the true nature of their black bodysuits. Fireproof. Of course. If they had been sent to capture him, why wouldn't they take the necessary precautions?

Now he'd started a blaze in the most dangerous part of the city for nothing. People would lose their homes. There would be fatalities. It was the Washington Chute all over again. He'd killed. He'd been stupid and he'd killed.

The figures approached with ferocity now, surging at him like one multilimbed monster. Two grabbed his arms and pulled him to the ground. Others restrained his legs. He struggled, but they were too strong. There were too many. Fire didn't hurt them. Fire was all he had.

One remained standing. Cassius watched as the soldier removed a tube from somewhere at his hip. As the object neared, he recognized it as a syringe filled with a pale-blue liquid. Cassius's eyes widened as the figure crouched low, straddled his legs, and brought the point of the needle to his neck.

Then, with his free hand, the figure ripped off his mask.

Cassius's mouth dropped. For a moment the horror and futility of the situation melted as he stared at the face of

Avery Wicksen. Fisher's girl. The same one who had disappeared in Seattle, who had been captured and brought to Unified Party quarters. She'd helped Fisher run away from Madame. She was one of Alkine's good guys. Or at least, she was supposed to be.

"What are you doing—" He managed to speak, then coughed as a knee rammed his diaphragm.

She didn't smile or frown or show that she recognized him at all. Instead, she pushed down on the end of the syringe, sending sharp metal through his skin.

Immediately, he felt a surge of cool liquid in his blood stream. His legs and arms went limp, then numb. Avery stared down at him, her soft brown hair glowing in the sunlight, a hint of fading freckles on either side of her nose. Cassius could tell why Fisher had been so infatuated with her. She was beautiful, even now.

His eyelids became heavy and he found it harder and harder to stay conscious. Soon it wasn't even worth fighting anymore. The figures released their hold on him. He wasn't going anywhere.

7

Red. Water. Rocks.

Something's wrong, I'm sure of that, but it's too vague a feeling to act on.

My bracelet hummed for about twenty minutes yesterday afternoon, then again last night. It's trying to tell me something, just like it did four months ago after it first fused to my wrist. Back then, it was a message from my mother about the Authority. Now it's far less clear.

Today's the Sophomore Tour—an unnecessary distraction from the mysteries I really need to be solving. Maybe that's why Mrs. Dembo was so keen on me participating. It's a bizarre shift, coming from the gray room yesterday morning to the training room now. Agent Morse escorted me to breakfast this morning, and then to the locker room to get suited up. He's probably waiting at Lookout Park to watch me finish the Tour. I wouldn't be surprised if they had monitors tracking my every move. That way, if I step out of line, they can charge in here and restrain me.

The Sophomore Tour. They say it's a tradition for us

Year Tens. I hear public beheading used to be a tradition hundreds of years ago. It doesn't mean that it's okay.

It's the first Friday of the training year, a soul-draining obstacle course from the bottom of the Skyship to Lookout Park on the top level. The rules are simple: start at the entrance to the docking bay and "survive" until you reach Lookout. No elevators or stairs. That'd be too easy. The Tour's a mass big deal here, even for the adults. Even in these trying times, there are hoards of them up at the park now, sitting on the sidelines waiting to cheer on their favorite students like it's some sick parade.

Maybe it would be better if it was just an endurance thing, but it's not. Hiding within the Academy's nooks and crannies are agents waiting to get you. They've got these guns—not loaded, though in my case who knows—that shoot sticker tags. Each tag's a penalty, and the more you have on your body by the time you get to Lookout, the crappier you get to feel about yourself. We're ranked by time and number of penalties. My back is covered with the stupid stickers, so I guess I gotta count on speed. Too bad, because I've already seen half my class pass by, including Eva and Skandar.

I shift my grip and wrap my blistered fingers around the width of a sweat-dampened rope until I'm stable again. I hang in the center of one of the Academy's gym-sized training rooms, halfway between the battlefield and the balcony. No, not even halfway.

They usually use this place for games like Bunker Ball,

outfitted with projected battlefields and skills courses. Today it's empty, except for the ropes.

I glance above me. With every second I hesitate, the thought of pulling myself up to the balcony seems more impossible. After that, I've got to navigate the catacombs above the training room on my way to the secret underground exit leading to the park.

One hand in front of the other. One hand in front of the other.

I repeat the mantra in my head, willing my body to follow through. The alternative is letting go and hitting the mats below, but then I'd have to start all over. Not only that, but I bet an agent would pop around the corner and tag me with another sticker. They're heartless like that.

I grit my teeth and pull, wrapping my feet around the swaying rope. My muscles strain and heat up like I'm about to break a Pearl. I'll be feeling this for days.

I manage to move a foot closer to the ledge. Seems like nothing, but I'd kill to do it again. Across the length of the balcony hang a dozen other ropes, each separated by a narrow gap. Most are empty. Manjeet Rajah, another Year Ten, struggles four ropes over. I can tell he's hating this as much as I am. He's a science guy, not a soldier. But seeing him fight with his rope strengthens my motivation. This whole thing's meant to be a race anyway. At least I have someone to race against.

With that in mind, I yank up, ignoring my trembling, about-to-burst arms. Three more pulls and my muscles give out. I press my toes inward and weave my fingers together. I grip on for dear life as the rope wobbles, sending me in rapid, nauseous circles.

I close my eyes and try to recharge myself. I pretend I'm holding a Pearl, that it's covering me in its healing green glow. As the rope becomes still again, I take a deep breath and prepare for the final assault. One more strong pull ought to do it. The ledge is only a foot above me now. I can practically reach out and grab it.

Distracted by my own little struggle, I don't hear the footsteps above me until a dark-skinned hand reaches over the lip of the balcony.

I glance up and meet Manjeet's eyes. An exhausted smile spreads along his sweat-dampened face. "C'mon, man," he wheezes.

I cautiously release my right hand and grab onto his wrist, letting him supply the extra strength to get me up over the ledge and onto the balcony. I take a look down at the empty gym before sinking to my knees, panting. "How'd you get up here so fast?"

"Fast?" He laughs. "I think we're the last two."

"No." I run my hand through my wet hair. "I swear I saw Allison and Bernice down there."

He frowns. "The last two guys, then."

I fall on my back and stare at the maze of dark catacombs above us.

Manjeet sits beside me, breathing hard. "Hey, wanna help each other out?"

"Isn't that against the rules?"

"Not technically."

I rub my biceps, hoping they'll stop going all psycho on me. "I've been up there before, in the catacombs. Just once, with—" I catch myself before her name escapes my lips.

Avery.

I can't say it out loud.

"If we hug the left side, there's rungs fastened into the walls," I continue. "We can make it halfway using those before we have to do some jumping."

"Jumping?" Manjeet's expression wavers. After the Rope of Hell, I understand where he's coming from.

"There're these big panels up top. The gap's only a couple of feet at most. They'll hold us."

Manjeet sighs. "This is not how I wanted to spend my afternoon. Can't you just, y'know, fly us up there or something?"

I pull myself to my feet and take a deep breath while stretching. "What do you mean?"

"You know … some of the guys told me they saw you floating through the Level Three corridor a couple of nights ago. Like a ghost."

This is the worst thing. Captain Alkine's been vague with the student body about what's really going on. Rumors are bouncing around everywhere. Maybe it would be better to get it all out in the open. But I don't even know everything yet, and I'm not sure I could explain it to someone like Manjeet anyway. Part of me wouldn't want to see his reaction when he learned how different I am.

"They're making it up," I say. "If I could fly, don't you think I would've zipped up here instead of doing all this climbing?"

He's about to reply when a voice rings out from the entrance to the catacombs. "Fisher!"

I watch August Bergmann emerge from the darkness, flanked on either side by a pair of Year Eleven boys, each blockier and less-friendly looking than the other. August himself is the blockiest of all the blocky. His broad, smarmy face is impossible to stomach.

For a few weeks after Seattle he left me alone. I'm not sure if he was afraid of what I could do, or if he just needed time to reload. Whatever the case, he's back to throw dirt in my face.

I struggle to my feet. "What are you doing here? Aren't you supposed to be up at Lookout, cheering us on?"

He crosses his arms, blocking our path. "I *was* at Lookout, but you're taking so long that I figured I'd have time to come down here, run a few laps, and make my way back before you were done."

Manjeet freezes beside me. He stares at the floor. I'm sure he's had his fair share of run-ins with people like August.

"That's a lot of stickers, Fisher." August points his finger at me like a gun, cocks it, and shoots. "Blam blam blam blam blam blam blam."

"You're gonna be in trouble when they find out you're on the course."

An eyebrow raises. "Not as much as you. That was you two nights ago, yeah? With the Pearl?"

I shrug.

He grabs the shoulder of the guy to his right. "Jensen here was in the showers after a late-night training run."

Jensen frowns. "The lights went out." His voice is an almost incomprehensible, deep mumble. "Water turned cold."

I nearly laugh, but if I do it'll send August's fist flying right into my face. "I don't know what you're talking about."

August steps forward. "I'm not stupid. I didn't suit up and head to Seattle last spring just so I could rescue a traitor."

The fact that he thinks that he rescued me is beyond hilarious. Yeah, he was one of dozens of soldiers sent down to fight the Unified Party, but as far as I'm concerned, he was lucky not to get himself killed in all of the commotion.

"Me and the Year Elevens," he continues, as if he speaks for *all* Year Elevens, "we're not happy with what you're doing. Destroying Pearls—whatever's going on—that's Unified Party stuff. That's Pearlhound work. And the fact that the teachers let you carry on like normal makes me sick. Just admit it. You're a traitor. Everything since Seattle has been planned. You've been working with the Unified Party behind our backs. Some of the guys are even saying you're related to one of them."

I bite my lip. "People say a lot of things."

"It's sabotage," he continues. "Alkine's keeping you onboard, but he's gotta know."

Manjeet's hands quiver. "Maybe you shouldn't rush to judgment until you've got all of the facts. Dr. Hemming would want you to—"

"Did I ask you a question?" August fumes.

His head goes down. "No."

August continues to approach until he's within striking distance. He could do anything. He could trip me and push me off the platform altogether if he wanted to. "You know," he whispers, "if I were to knock you out and drag you outside the ship ... leave you in the middle of nowhere so that you couldn't find your way back, there are plenty of people onboard who would call me a hero, including some of the adults."

My back tenses. I inch away from him, but I can't go far. A few more steps and I'll be falling back to the mats. If I had a Pearl right now, I'd show him what I can really do. I'd wipe the smug look from his face.

My lip quivers. I try not to let it, but I can't help it. My voice is small, retreated somewhere inside of me. "So what are you gonna do?"

His eyes narrow. "I'm not sure yet. I've been thinking about it, you know ... the consequences. Weighing the good and the bad. I always knew there was something different about you, Fisher, but I never gave you enough credit. That's my mistake. It all fits together now."

"You're an idiot." I refuse to meet his eyes.

"What did you say?"

"An idiot," I repeat, louder. "A moron. You know ... *stupid*."

He shakes his head, visibly distressed.

"You're jealous," I continue. "Aren't you? That's what it really is. You're just upset that all of Alkine's attention is on me. You're ... you're not the important one for once."

Manjeet grabs my shoulder. "Jesse ... "

August stands still for a moment, shoulders tense. Then, before I can react, his fist connects with my stomach. I bend forward, then stagger to the side. The heel of my shoe hangs off the edge of the platform for a split second before I stumble back to safety. I can't talk. Can barely breathe.

He's about to punch me again when a voice rings across the ceiling, emanating from speakers all around us. It's Mrs. Dembo. "Year Elevens!" she bellows. "Get off my course!"

August's friends scatter. August sneers at me for a moment longer, unwilling to move. But I barely see him.

Something else happens.

My vision goes red. I don't know if it was triggered by the force of his punch or not. I topple onto my side.

Manjeet panics. "You've killed him!"

August prods my leg with his foot before stepping away. "No, I haven't. He's just a freak, doing what freaks do."

I barely hear him. The heavy red begins to fade. Then, clear as a photograph, the coastline pulls into view again.

Only this time it's different. I can manipulate it now, like I'm a bird staring down at the land. I pull away and steal a wider view. I twist in the air and see the pathway to the Academy—every last inch of it, all at once. Coordinates flash in my mind, exact crosshairs targeting the destination.

I see everything, and in such detail that it's almost too much. I imagine the Drifters sending the information to me. They've got to be doing it. They're reaching out. They're helping me.

My eyes snap open. The ceiling tiles of the training room blur into view, but the memory of the coastline remains. It's burned into me.

"Jesse." Manjeet crouches by my side. "Are you okay?"

I nod. Never been better.

I've got it. I know where to find them.

8

Cassius woke with a start. His head jerked back and banged against a wall, sending a jolt of shock through his skull. His hands were pulled unnaturally to his sides, his legs bundled together and secured to the metal behind him.

He smelled it instantly, like coming home. Even after the fire he had conjured had destroyed much of the main floor last spring, the sterile, scrubbed-down smell lingered—the hint of lavender that she insisted must always hang around. Memories flooded his barely conscious brain. Training courses, conversations, faces. He had no doubt. He was in the Lodge.

He took note of his surroundings, trying to discern what wing he was in. He knew the building inside and out, yet this room was unfamiliar. It was no bigger than the infirmary he'd woken in after his first explosion, and empty. A wall of cabinets hung to his right, each door shut and locked. Temperature-controlled air seeped in through the ceiling, pristine and cool.

He struggled against the restraints. No use. He was trapped.

His mind rocketed back to the slum lands of Providence—Avery Wicksen's cold, emotionless face staring back at him as she injected the fluid into his neck. If he was truly in the Lodge now, they'd have traveled thousands of miles past the border and into New York State. He'd been unconscious the entire time, unable to remember any of it. Helpless for hours. They could have done anything to him.

He nearly lost it for a moment. It was the smell, mostly. He knew all of the officials at the Lodge on a first-name basis. He'd had friends here. Not real ones, but acquaintances nonetheless. Had they watched him being carried in? The murderer who had double-crossed their leader and left her for dead? If Cassius had been in their position five months ago, he would've wanted revenge. They'd be right to hate him.

His breathing quickened. He forced himself to calm down. Panicking would cloud his mind.

The door handle turned.

He tensed as he watched the single door crack open. A shadow fell across the wall.

Then Madame entered.

His heart sunk. He blinked twice to make sure he wasn't seeing things. His expression lost all composure. She'd be happy to see that, he knew.

Madame. Alive. Walking.

"No," he started. "No, I saw you … " He trailed off. Words couldn't express it.

She stepped into the room with the same authoritative ease she'd possessed when he'd last lived at the Lodge, when he'd still considered himself her son. Her dark hair was tied back, not a single strand out of place. She wore a custom-fitted business suit. The sleeves of her white blouse spilled over her wrists. The familiar pair of delicate spectacles rested over her cold eyes. Below that, a scar ran down her left cheek until it met with the folds of her smile. But she wasn't smiling.

"Cassius." She shut the door behind her. He bristled at the sound of her voice. "Welcome home."

"No." It was the only sound he could make.

He watched her approach. He didn't dare speak for fear of what she would do. He'd seen her handle enemies before. Mercilessly. He'd watched her lock away Skyshippers without food until they were skin and bones, until she had drained everything she needed from them.

She shifted toward the cabinets, leaning her shoulder against the wood. "You'd have never seen this wing. Experimental. One needs the proper clearance to gain access. You were nearly there. Another three weeks, maybe, and I'd have let you take a peek."

She crossed her arms. Cassius scanned her hands for weapons. They were empty.

"Tell me about your vacation." She gave a cold smile. "I've heard the Polar Cities are particularly nice this time of year."

"You're supposed to be dead." He choked out the words.

"Am I?"

He glared at her, unable to speak. It was like talking to a ghost. How could she have been so strong? And that scar...

She followed his gaze. "Admiring my little souvenir?" She ran her finger against her cheek. "The doctors offered to sew me up completely, but I asked them to leave a little something. I've grown too vain, anyway. It's a sort of gift. Your gift to me, Cassius."

She took a deep breath and approached him, her eyes latching onto his. "Oh, don't be so serious." She leaned her hand against the wall, inches from Cassius's face. "It's good you escaped for a little while. A boy your age... what kind of a mother would I be if I didn't let you go off and find yourself?"

"You're not my—" The words hurt as they came out. He couldn't finish the statement.

"Shh." She held a finger to his mouth. "Don't strain yourself. You've had a very long day." She turned on her heel and strode back, pacing through the small room. "Things have been different since you left. I'd imagine you would have guessed, but you don't know the extent of it. Skyship has been all over us, infiltrating every sector of our organization. The President caught wind of it too late, as is usual for him." Her delicate fingers balled into fists at her side. "Things are even more combustible than before." She paused, smiling. "Combustion. You'd know all about that, wouldn't you?"

"I don't—"

"That's right," she interrupted, as if reading his mind.

"You don't care about affairs of the Unified Party anymore. You're a little maverick now. Good for you." She moved back to his side, grabbing his right sleeve and pulling it up to reveal his wrist. "I see I'm not the only one with a scar. I'm impressed, Cassius. You had the force of will to remove your microchip and manage to get across the border undetected." She pressed hard on the scar with her thumb, sending a jolt of searing pain up his arm. "Pretty clever." She released his throbbing arm. "Don't think about summoning any fireworks today. I've got you on strong medication. You're not going anywhere until I want you to."

He winced in pain as she slid to his shoulder, whispering in his ear, "Why did you have to do it, Cassius? You showed such promise. I was prepared to give you everything, but you threw it away."

She spun forward and grabbed his chin, pushing the side of his face into the cold metal. Her polished nails pricked his skin. "You don't leave your mother like that, buried under rocks in the middle of a wasteland. It's inhuman. I taught you better than that. You were weak, Cassius. It was a coward's move."

He sputtered, stealing a breath as she let go of him. His head hung low. He glared up at her through exhaustion. "I didn't—"

"Don't talk back to me." She straightened her blouse. "You're in no position to talk back to me."

He analyzed her cold, distant eyes. They were emptier, somehow, like she'd lost more than her flawless face these past few months. For a moment he felt sorry for her, but it was a fleeting emotion replaced quickly with anger.

"You sent Avery Wicksen after me," he muttered. It came out part declaration, part question.

"So I did," she replied. "People have their uses long after you'd suspect. Even you, Cassius, still hold some value to me."

He scoffed. "Is that why you've got me chained up in here?"

Her brows raised. "After all you've done, you'd expect me to let you roam free?"

"I want out," he said. "That's all. I don't want anything to do with you."

Her eyes slit. "I'm afraid that's a choice that you don't get to make. We have a history, Cassius. It's not so easily erased."

He swallowed and found his voice. "I ... I saw you there, buried under the rocks. There's no way—"

"I know you did." She paused. "Did that make you upset? How long did it take before you forgot about me?"

He rattled his restraints. "Let me go!"

She laughed, which only made him angrier. "You're so aggressive now. You'd have never spoken to me like that before. Maybe Canada was good for you." She removed her spectacles and pulled a cloth from her pocket to polish the lenses. "But you're not equipped to be on your own, Cassius. You belong here, with me."

He met her eyes and knew instantly that it was a mistake. This was what she wanted. A connection. And once she found it, she knew exactly how to exploit it.

"You're getting older," she started. "I've noticed it these past years, but things have grown out of hand. There's normal teenage rebellion and then there's you." Her eyes latched onto his. He felt helpless, unable to break free from the bonds and do something. "Harnessing, I call it. This entire wing's devoted to the study of it. A personal interest of mine, I suppose you could say."

He coughed. His arm jerked uncomfortably to the side. "I don't understand."

"You harness a weapon, correct? Why not a person?" She stepped forward until she was near enough to touch. "Our first attempts were sloppy. Scientific waste. But with Avery, I've got my first living, breathing weapon. She brought me you. She's proven my success."

Cassius grit his teeth. "Mind control? You're telling her what to do?"

"Harnessing." She grabbed his chin and pulled his head up, forcing him to look at her. "The vocabulary is very important to me. She can still process ideas on her own, but it's within a framework of my design. As long as the apparatus remains under her skin, I own her instincts."

"You and your microchips," he muttered.

She pulled away from him. His head slumped to his chest before he could get control of his muscles again. "It's a simple process—a slim device inserted at the back of the neck, connected to a similar device of my own ... "

"You've already gotten to me, haven't you?"

"The cocktail Avery injected into your system enabled installation of the device. You can't feel it, but it's there. Your synapses are ready for reassignment. You're mine again." She crossed her arms and appraised him. "I'm sorry it had to come to this."

"You won't get Fisher, you know. No matter what you do."

"Oh, Cassius. You never see the big picture." A smile crept over her face. He didn't understand how he could have mistaken it for love all those years. There was no warmth left in her.

Madame grabbed his arm, gently shaking his wrist in excitement. "I've already got your brother," she said. "He just doesn't know it yet."

9

It's late. These are the hours that Alkine knows to watch for me. Every time I've tried to pull something, it's been at night. They've taken to stationing guards throughout the hallways. Alkine says it's in case the Unified Party comes knocking on our door, but he can't fool me. Some of the guards are here for me. I know this because there was one stationed outside my door tonight.

Eva and I sit in the cockpit of a shuttle in the smallest and darkest of the Academy's docking bays, waiting to take off.

"Do you think he's coming?" Eva whispers. "Three more minutes. I say that's all we give him."

"He'll be here," I reply.

I have Skandar to thank for getting rid of the guard outside my door. Just after midnight, he came strolling by my dorm room and told the guy he'd seen me sneaking around the Level Five rec room. I pushed my ear against the door and listened as the guard questioned him. In the end, the guy insisted that Skandar lead him to the spot he'd seen me.

That's the slight wrinkle in our plan. Now we're waiting for Skandar to come back. Who knows what kind of questions the guard could have asked him.

Eva shivers. "We could leave without him—"

"No."

I need my friends here. If we're really going to see Ryel and the other Drifters, I want witnesses. Otherwise, anything I say to Alkine afterward will be twisted into the ramblings of a crazy teenager.

I stare out at the stars beyond the opening of the bay. I was up there once, shuttling between planets. It seems so impossible.

Eva squirms in her seat. "I think I see him."

I turn to watch a thin shadow creep through the empty bay. The shuttle shudders as Skandar steps onboard and seals the entrance behind him. "Whew." He takes a seat behind us. "I thought he'd never let me go. It's okay, Jesse. I think we've bought ourselves some time."

Instead of answering, I begin to power up the shuttle.

"Are you sure you don't want me to do the piloting?" Eva grips her seat belt.

"I've got to learn. Just tell me if I'm about to do anything stupid."

Her teeth clench. "Can I preemptively tell you now?"

I flip on the radar. "Very funny."

———

The stark Siberian landscape rushes beneath our shuttle. Fields of endless tundra stretch miles in every direction. If I stare long enough, it's like we're not moving at all.

Identical, that's it. All of this Siberia crap is mass identical.

And yet somehow I know exactly where I'm going.

Eva's grip tightens as the cockpit bumps. "You know, chances are Captain Alkine's going to find out we're missing. Or that a shuttle's missing, at the very least. Are you sure this is worth it?"

"You're not seeing what I am," I reply. "Trust me. It's as strong as Seattle. And look what I found when I went *there.*"

"Yeah. A trap."

I shoot her a glare, but she's kind of right. I might know the pathway. I might even have a reasonable idea of what's at the end. But things like this—strange, cryptic visions—rarely go off the way I expect them to.

I glance over my shoulder at Skandar. He's slumped in the passenger seats, barely awake. A tangle of brown hair pokes over the armrest. He's still in his pajamas.

"For god's sake, pull up!" Eva bolts back in her seat, eyes wide.

My attention darts to the front window. Land fills nearly three quarters now. The shuttle tilts, losing altitude. I yank on the console. We whip into the air, wobbling sideways.

Eva cups her mouth, looking sick. "I'm going to die. You're going to kill me."

Skandar shudders awake and whoops like he's on a rollercoaster. "Keep it up, Jesse! Gun it!" If he had his way, we'd be doing loops in the sky. Of course, with me behind the wheel, it'd be more like one shaky corkscrew right into the ground.

I fight the steering, struggling to bring the shuttle level again. We dip sideways. The seat belt cuts into my torso. Eva's arm weaves under my elbows and moves to a switch beside the console. We slow to a crawl. I straighten us out.

"Velocity dampener." She recoils. "Keep you under control, Fisher."

I lay on the accelerator. Nothing. "So we're gonna drive like grannies now?"

Her brows raise. "Grannies come home alive."

Skandar joins us in the cockpit, kneeling beside Eva.

I glance at him briefly until a tug forces my attention back to the windshield. "I feel it."

Eva stares at me.

"Something's yanking me forward," I continue. "Can we speed back up?"

She sighs. "Flip the dampener, but be careful of rocks. You're awfully low."

Even with our front beams on full tilt, anything not spotlighted by our shuttle disappears into the same black hole. I ignore Eva's warning and dip the shuttle until we're less than a few meters from the dirt.

Skandar grabs onto my seat as we accelerate. "What exactly are we looking for?"

"Red. Water. Rocks." I wince. If they hadn't been with me from the start, they'd think I'm crazy, but they know I wouldn't make this stuff up. "I don't know what it is, but it's right on the coast."

Eva grips the console. "A bad dream, maybe?"

"I wish."

We pass over a patchy area of grass before the scenery gives way to dark tundra once more. It looks different from my vision now that the sun's down. For a moment I start to doubt myself. Then I see it, out of nowhere, like a mirage.

Snow.

It's not a large plot—maybe football field–size at best—but it's here. The clouds put it here, not some weather program or Bio-Net. Growing up in the Skyship Community, none of us has ever seen honest-to-goodness real snow. It's as alien as I am.

"Wow." Skandar stands and stares beyond the windshield. The moonlight casts a soft blue glow over the thin layer of white. "Should'a brought my sled, huh?"

I crane my neck to catch more of it. "This shouldn't be here. I didn't see this."

I trace the line of our headlights until I notice water, twinkling in the distance. The coast. We're here, but it's all wrong. There was never snow.

The pull intensifies. This is definitely the spot.

I slow the shuttle and extend the landing gear. Eva grabs onto the armrest as the cockpit rumbles. We arch around the blanket of snow as I prepare to bring the ship down.

I point at a lever to the right of the steering console. "This one?"

She nods. "But not—"

Too late. I yank it and we sink fast and slam into ground with a reverberating thud. Skandar flies an inch in the air before landing back on his feet.

"—all at once," Eva finishes.

"Oh." I flip off the power. The shuttle sputters as it settles down. Skandar rubs the back of his neck, mumbling expletives under his breath. As the headlights dim, a pinprick of red light pokes through the snow beyond our windshield. It's muted, not at all like in my vision, but it calls me forward all the same.

Eva rubs her elbow. "Well, we didn't die. That's a start."

I unbuckle my seat belt as the side door slides open.

"Yeah." Skandar winces in pain. "Way to go, man. Best landing ever."

"Sorry." I step around him and jump out the door. I nearly slip on the snow as I land. It crunches beneath my sneakers.

I reach down and grab a handful of white powder, balling it in my fist until it's hard and compact. This shouldn't be here, not with the planet warming the way it is. The air is refreshingly crisp and cool—cooler even than the temperature-controlled stuff inside the shuttle. I'm used to stepping into triple-digit heat back in the Fringes. This has got some bite to it. It's a freak snow globe in the middle of a wasteland.

Skandar leaps into the snow from behind me, kicking it into the air and flipping over to lie on his back. Eva lowers herself carefully until she stands beside me, shaking her head in disapproval.

My skin buzzes. The hair on my arms stands on end. My chest warms. I know this sensation.

"Jesse." Eva grabs my tense shoulder.

I step away. "It feels like a Pearl."

She bristles at the word. "But the Academy's radars would've picked up any energy trails. We're not that far out." She grabs my arm again, stopping me. "When's the last time you heard of a Pearl landing in Eastern Siberia anyway?"

I shrug. "If a tree falls and there's nobody around to hear it…"

"That is such a load of…" She sighs, loosening her grip. "Seriously, we're standing in the middle of snow. This isn't natural."

"Neither was Seattle." I pull my wrist up in front of her face to reveal the band of black. "Neither is this bracelet."

As if on cue, it begins to hum, vibrating wildly until it forces my arm back to my side.

Eva stares in disbelief. "This isn't good, Jesse."

I steady my wrist with my opposite hand and trudge through the powder.

Eva freezes. "Jesse!"

I ignore her and continue on toward the water.

She turns to Skandar. "Are you gonna come with us or play around like a child?"

He pulls his snow-covered body from the ground and follows without a response.

I speed to a sprint. The arctic air pushes against my face—icy brambles rubbing my skin raw. I do my best to ignore the weather. Waves crash gently along the coastline in the distance. The sound is familiar. The smell too.

Almost there.

My arms buzz with electricity, eager to reach the energy. My strides lengthen until it feels like I'm floating. The glow comes from inside a snow drift a few yards away, deep and red. Strong, like a traffic light, visible even under a layer of powder.

It is a Pearl. I can see it clearly now.

But Pearls are green. That's the problem. Every one I've come across, all the hundreds I've seen since I was a kid, have been the same.

I kneel to analyze the strange object, transfixed. I could hold it in my palm, easy. But something about that color—it's like a warning.

Eva and Skandar pull in behind me, wheezing. Skandar wipes snow from his pajama sleeve. "Whoa."

Eva leans down next to me. "This was the red from your vision?"

"I guess." I stretch out my arm. My hand shakes, pushed around by invisible layers of energy. I struggle through the force field and extend my fingers to touch the Pearl.

First I feel the cold numb of the snow. But when my fingers press against the red surface of the orb, I yelp in pain.

I recoil immediately, skin on fire. My hand burns like

I've dunked it in a pan of boiling water. I whip my body away and clutch my throbbing fingers in a fist of snow.

Skandar chuckles, like I'm putting on a show for his amusement. "Did it bite you?"

I shake my head, cursing under my breath. Energy waves ripple around me. I'm attracted to it, like a normal Pearl. Why would it burn me?

"It's all covered in snow." Eva stretches out her fingers to touch it.

I thrust my arm in front of her. "No!"

She brushes me away and proceeds to dust the rest of the powder from the beaming red surface. Then she hoists the Pearl from the ground. I wince, fully expecting her to drop it and stagger away in pain.

Instead she cradles the Pearl in her arms with ease. Red light illuminates her skeptical expression. "I don't see what got you so riled up, Jesse."

"It burned me." I stand and survey the ball of red light from a safe distance. "Hurt like hell too."

She frowns. "Then I must have magical hands or something because it feels like a regular Pearl to me. Weird color, though."

Skandar steps to her side. "Looks like blood."

She shifts the Pearl to her right hand and holds it in the air. "It's thicker, isn't it? I mean, usually you get the sense that you're staring into something. This is too murky to see."

"It *burned* me," I repeat, frustrated that neither of them seem to care. "Why aren't you screaming in pain?"

Skandar cautiously lays a finger on the side of the Pearl. "It's a little warm, but nothing weird. It didn't even melt the snow."

I scan my palm for marks. It's clean and pale. Normal. I briefly consider touching the Pearl again, but decide against it. It'll hurt me. I know it.

Skandar backs away. "Break it, Jesse."

Eva nearly drops the Pearl. "What? That's the worst idea—"

"I wanna see what's inside." He leans his hands on his knees, staring intently.

The truth is, I do too. I thought the vision was leading me to Ryel. Could this be some sort of message from the Drifters?

Ignoring Eva, I hold my hands in front of my chest and clench my fingers. "Get behind me," I warn them. Whatever force flies out of this thing won't hurt them if I'm in front to deflect it.

I can tell Eva wants to argue, but she's afraid I'll trigger something before she can get out of the way. After a moment of thought, she drops the Pearl into the snow and darts behind me. I watch it roll through the powder without melting a thing.

I raise my fingers in the air and try to pull the Pearl off the ground. It doesn't budge.

I close my eyes and concentrate on the heat pooling in my chest. I imagine the Pearl right in front of me, floating there. I ball my hand into a fist and feel for the explosion.

Nothing. I try again.

This time, I try so hard that I fall forward onto my knees. Snow begins to creep into the lining of my pants. I open my eyes in exhaustion.

"I can't do it."

Skandar leans out from behind me. "What do you mean?"

"I can't break it. I can't even *move* it."

Eva steps forward and crouches beside the orb. "Maybe it's not a Pearl at all."

I pant. The exertion took more out of me than I'd expected. "I'm not leaving it out here."

Eva scoops the Pearl from the snow. "Let's get it in the shuttle. We can worry about it on the way back."

I nod, still staring into the red light. "I can't break it," I repeat to myself. "Why the hell can't I break it?"

10

We race back to the Academy at double-speed. Skandar sits with the Pearl on his lap, blissfully unaware of how badly I want to be able to hold it. This means nothing to him. It's just another Pearl. New color, yeah, but that's a novelty.

My mind clouds with possibilities. The thing's hot, like the fire that comes from Cassius. Maybe that means it's related to us somehow. It won't break. Maybe that means there's no Drifter inside. It could be something else. Information. A map. A weapon.

I lean forward as we pull into the docking bay. "Something's wrong."

When we left, the lights in the bay had all been shut off. Now a row at the far end is illuminated. It's enough to cast shadows along the wall. And there's a big shadow there, shaped like an X with arms at the hips. As we pull closer, I realize who it is.

Agent Morse.

Skandar and Eva met him briefly this morning during breakfast, but they'd seen him at his best. Heck, I think *I've* only seen him at his best. By the way he's standing now, I can tell that this is going to be anything but.

I slap Skandar on his shoulder. "Quick. Lock the Pearl in the floor panel before he sees." There's no way I'm getting this thing up to my room tonight, whether I can touch it or not. And the last thing I want is for Morse to tell Alkine about it. He'd want to analyze it, hold meetings about it—do anything he could to keep me from having it.

"Go, go!" I push Skandar back to the passenger seating before we're close enough for Morse to see inside.

Eva mutters something in Spanish. She turns to me, whispering, "You better be working on a good excuse."

I grit my teeth and hope for a perfect landing. Adding a scuff to the underbelly of our shuttle would only make things worse.

"You do have a good excuse, right?"

I bring the shuttle down—a little wobbly, but we make it without any scratches. "That's your thing, Eva. You're Excuse Girl."

I turn to see Skandar secure the floor panel and flash a thumbs-up. I scan the seating for any hint of a red glow. There's nothing. As long as nobody looks, we're good.

Agent Morse doesn't move. He's like a chess piece, all still and intimidating but ready to end the game. A knight. Alkine's knight.

Our eyes meet through the windshield. His expression reveals nothing.

Knowing I'll look more suspicious the longer I stay in the shuttle, I push the button to open the side door, remove my belt, and step outside. I can't say I'm nervous exactly, not in front of someone like Morse. I've gotten in trouble too many times these past four months to be nervous about it anymore. Now it's disappointment. Annoyance that I'll have to wait to see what's inside the Pearl.

I stand in front of him, separated by about a dozen floor tiles, for what seems like minutes before either of us talks.

Morse lets out a dramatic sigh. "Evening, buddy." He clasps his hands in front of his waist and shakes his head like he's staring at a two-year-old. "It's a shame, isn't it? And you had such a good day too."

I swallow. "I don't suppose we can just forget about this."

"Afraid not," he replies. "Captain Alkine's already waiting. You're coming with me, kid."

———

It's our first training mission all over again. We sit in the middle of a plain meeting room, not unlike the one Mr. Wilson had picked to give us the better-start-working-as-a-team lecture last spring. We're lit by a series of bright ceiling panels, making it difficult to gauge time. But I know that it's still dark outside. Most everyone's asleep.

It's the first time I've seen Alkine since the incident in the reactor three nights ago. He barely looks at me.

Morse sits across from us at the table. Alkine stands, unable to keep still. Like last night, he's wearing his official Academy suit, which makes me question whether he sleeps at all.

Eva cracks her knuckles, nervous. If I had to pick between

her and Skandar, she's the one who could betray me here. After all, she's spied on me before—reported back to the teachers in secret. She swears she'd never do it again, but I'm not sure what Alkine's going to throw at us yet. She might be easy to persuade.

Alkine stops pacing and leans his hands on the table. "I've got no other choice," he says finally. "I give you a chance to obey and you do the opposite. You're constantly putting yourself in danger, you and the Academy as a whole. I can't have that." He pauses, staring directly at me for the first time. "You'll be spending your nights in the brig from now on."

My mouth drops. "What?"

"I can't trust you." He shakes his head. "During the day, you'll be in classes. The teachers can vouch for your whereabouts. Agent Morse can escort you through the hallways. But at night? You've found our weakness, Fisher. It just isn't safe."

Eva clears her throat. "We were only getting some air, sir."

"Quiet." He frowns. The creases in his face become more visible. "Be thankful I'm not confining the two of you as well. You should be ashamed of yourselves, encouraging this kind of reckless behavior."

I slap the edge of the table. "It's done, then."

Alkine sighs. "Excuse me?"

"I'm a prisoner now. You've been building up to it for weeks and now it's done."

"*You've* been building," he responds. "Do you think I want this for you?" He turns his back and paces to the wall, muttering to himself. When he faces us again, his expression has calmed. "There are ways to go about this. Procedure. Anything less will get you hurt."

Eva frowns. "You can't tell me you have a procedure for how to deal with aliens ... "

"Exactly," he replies. "That's why we have to be careful. And hijacking a shuttle, even to get some air, is not careful." He glances at Morse, then back to us. "You're a minor, Fisher. All of you are. You're under my protection. My responsibility." He pauses. "We could have thrown you out. After what happened in Seattle, after we knew what you were capable of ... I could have left you there. Instead, I'm taking care of you. Don't throw it in my face."

Skandar leans forward. "But ever since we fled from the Tribunal ... " He stops himself. "You don't have to take care of us, sir."

Alkine sighs. "I wish that were true." His eyes meet mine directly and linger for a moment. I can't read him exactly, but for the first time I see something that could be fear. Fleeting, but it's there. Then he glances to the far wall, breaking our connection. "Maybe we're out of Skyship Territory at the moment, but that doesn't mean we're without rules. Things continue as normal, even in Siberia."

I try to meet his eyes, challenging him as I say the words he wants to hear. "You're the commander."

"Yes," he says. "And more than anything, it's my duty

to move us into a position to reconnect with the rest of the Skyship Community with as few consequences as possible. This was never meant to be permanent. We need allies."

I lean my elbows on the table and rest my forehead on my clasped hands. "They're burning Pearls. All of them. I don't want to reconnect just so we can kill Drifters."

He shakes his head. "Well, we have to do something. Do you think we can stay here forever? Even if they're not looking for us, we'll run out of resources eventually. My crew is working on a presentation to the Tribunal explaining why we crossed the Skyline. This is a delicate situation. Pearls mean so much to so many people. We can't expect them to believe anything we say. We need to prove our credibility first."

"We're wasting time."

"It was wrong," Alkine continues, "the way we went about rescuing you. No matter how noble it felt. You forced me into making a rash decision. Don't do it again. I won't be able to forgive you the second time."

I could argue this. I could argue that it was because of the lies Alkine and the others told me that I went running to the Surface in the first place. I could point out that it was Alkine's lack of security that let Cassius board our ship and drive me away. But anything I say will only be denied.

Alkine glances at Morse. "Escort Fisher to the brig." He motions to Skandar and Eva. "Harris. Rodriguez. You may leave. We'll talk about consequences in the morning. This was severely boneheaded of you both."

Eva stands. "Look, Jesse may not always know what's best, but don't you think it's a little—"

Alkine extends his hand, silencing her. "I'll make the decisions, Rodriguez. Thank you." His eyes fall squarely on me. "This is what happens when you back me into a corner, Fisher. Don't push me again."

———

Agent Morse actually tries to make this imprisonment deal sound like a good thing.

"It's so much quieter down there, buddy," he says with a smile. "You should hear the guy in the room next to me. The snoring seeps through the wall. Maybe I should spend a night in the brig too."

His humor fizzles like dud grenades. I'm sick of how everything sounds like a camping trip with this guy. It's like being escorted to the slammer by a Boy Scout.

Eva and Skandar stay with us until we reach the doorway to the brig, which is good because it takes me nearly that long to figure out what I'm going to do.

I smile and nod in Morse's direction, all the while taking miniscule sidesteps toward my friends.

Morse's eyes narrow as he notices. "Wait a minute." He yawns. "You heard what the Captain said." He gestures to Eva and Skandar. "Maybe you two should head to your rooms. I'll take it from here."

"Calm down." I continue toward them, keeping one eye on Morse the whole time. "I just want to say goodnight."

He stops. "Say it closer to me."

I ignore him and head toward the wall.

Morse shakes his head, visibly uncomfortable. "Thirty seconds, alright?" Then he mutters to himself. He thinks I can't hear. "They couldn't do anything in thirty seconds."

I nod and move to Eva and Skandar, not wasting a moment before whispering, "There's an old laundry bag in the corner of my room, stuffed between the dresser and the wall. It's black, so it should block most of the light. Grab the"—I look over my shoulder to see if Morse is listening—"the you-know-what and bring it to my cell."

Eva's face drops. "Jesse..."

"Okay," Skandar answers without hesitation.

"Good." I meet his eyes. "If Morse is still here when you come back, skip the cell and bring it to my room. Just get it out of that shuttle before they find it."

"Got it, mate." Skandar grabs Eva by the shoulder and starts nudging her away. His eyes widen and his voice becomes slightly too loud. "Have a good night, Jesse. Don't let the...er...don't...be positive, okay? Smile."

Eva pulls away from him. "Hands off, Skandar. I know how to walk."

I watch them head down the hall, hoping that she won't convince him to play it safe and forget about the Pearl. She's mass good with that persuasive stuff, and Skandar's good at falling for it.

I turn to Agent Morse. He waits by the entrance to the brig, arms crossed. For once he's not smiling. It's not a frown, either. He's concentrating on something. Hopefully it isn't me. I march through the entrance, totally ignoring

91

his presence. This breaks his concentration. He moves in behind me and leads me down a hallway to the left. "You should seriously consider some new friends," he says. "A guy like you should be hanging with guys like me. Agent material, you know? You want to graduate, right?"

I don't respond, which seems to throw him off. He bolts in front of me and leans on the nearest open door. "I don't mean they're bad people. I'm just thinking, wouldn't it be cool for you to find some friends who will challenge you? Without some of my buddies, I could've made some very different decisions. It's a slippery slope." He nods to himself. He doesn't realize that I stopped listening as soon as he opened his mouth. "Tomorrow I'm gonna introduce you to some guys I met back when I was your age."

I point to the empty cell. "I'd rather go in there."

He sighs. Then, after another moment of deep thought, he motions me forward. "Whatever you think is best, little man. You can't fault me for trying to help."

I walk into the cell and grab the handle behind me. Morse nearly jumps out of his shoes as I yank on the door and shut it myself. I watch his face appear on the other side of the barred window. He stares in disapprovingly. I stare back. It's silent warfare.

He blinks. A minute later, his face moves out of my sight.

Footsteps. He leaves.

I win.

Of course, I'm the one stuck in a cage, so maybe it's more of a tie.

11

It is quiet in here, like Morse said. Too quiet, really. The kind of quiet that's begging to be interrupted by something horrible. It will be hard to fall asleep like this, but I need to be awake anyways. Eva and Skandar will be here any minute. That is, if she hasn't convinced him otherwise.

I wait at the far end of the cell, back against the wall, sitting. A square of moonlight hangs on the door in front of me.

We don't use the brig often. Every once in a while, a minor offense onboard will result in an overnight stay, but we've never harbored any real criminals. The thing is, Alkine could've chosen to stick me in the gray room again tonight. At least there would be that ugly couch for comfort. The fact that he chose a prison cell speaks louder than the crap he was spewing upstairs. He really thinks I'm going rogue.

Am I going rogue? I know so little, and all of it muddy. I've never seen my parents. The voice on the rooftop last spring could've been a fake. The picture disc could've been altered. I don't know any specifics about this "Authority," and I haven't been able to ask the Drifters anything. I'm risking my life—and if Alkine's right, the entire Academy's life—on guesswork. Guesswork and hope.

And now, a red Pearl.

Alkine must know something. He wouldn't be on me like this without a good reason. Instead of antagonizing him, maybe I need to find a way to interrogate him. Pick his brain without him knowing it.

Or spy. That's what Avery would have suggested. She was always a snoop, even when I didn't see anything worth snooping for. But I've isolated myself too much to start sneaking around. They're on the lookout for me now.

Which leaves me with my third option.

Leave.

I can't do anything here, not the way they've got me cornered. The only other choice is the most dangerous of all. If I cross the Pacific, I'll have the Unified Party and the Tribunal after me. I'll be like Cassius—living by my wits, struggling to survive without capture. And I'm not Cassius.

I don't get much time to consider it before I see red.

Not a vision this time. It's the real thing. Faint light beams through the window of my cell, too muted to cause commotion in the main corridors. But in the darkness of the brig, everything shows up.

I jump to my feet and rush to the door, craning my neck to look between the bars. Eva and Skandar stand just beyond my cell carrying a dark bag between them. A circular lump hangs at the bottom, radiating through the cloth.

It's not as obvious as a green Pearl would be. People won't be looking for red.

"I pulled my jacket over it," Skandar whispers as he shows me the zipper of a coat he must have grabbed from his room. "It felt good." He smiles. "Warm."

My hands recoil at the thought of the heat I felt when I touched it. Boiling water. Lava.

"Leave it here." I keep my eyes on the bag the entire time.

Eva approaches the bars. "You're in a prison cell. We can't exactly get in."

"There's an electronic key system at the front desk. I didn't see anyone sitting there when Morse brought me in. The brig's empty."

She leans against the door, staring sideways. "It's not a good idea breaking you out. You heard what Alkine said. We're lucky we—"

"You won't be breaking me out," I interrupt. "Just open the door, toss the Pearl inside, and lock it again. He didn't mention anything about that."

Skandar grins. "Way to go. Loophole."

Eva grabs his arm before he can head down the hall-way. For a moment, she looks like she's going to give me a lecture, but then her expression falls flat. "This doesn't get traced back to us, okay?"

I nod. "Alkine won't even know."

She hoists the bag and releases Skandar. I watch him

disappear around the corner and wait until I hear the bolt on my door unlatch.

Eva grips the bars. "Please don't do anything stupid, Jesse."

"Like you said, I'm in a prison cell. What could I possibly do?"

She closes her eyes, shaking her head.

"Hey." I lean sideways against the door. "You don't know anything that you're not telling me, do you?"

I push on the door to open it a crack.

"Of course not," she grabs the handle and yanks forward, tossing the bag through the opening. "I'm on your side, Jesse."

I nod.

"Now promise." She shuts the door. "Nothing stupid."

I glance at the bag. Part of it has slipped below the Pearl, revealing a beam of red that hits the opposite wall.

"And don't get yourself hurt," she continues. "Remember how it felt when you touched it. There's no snow in here to cool your hands if you get burned."

"Got it," I say. "Thank Skandar for me on the way out."

She grits her teeth, clearly uncomfortable at the thought of leaving me alone. "Goodnight, Jesse."

"Yeah." I kneel next to the Pearl and get lost in the depths of crimson. "Goodnight."

———

I gaze into the Pearl so long, I lose track of time. Sometimes I close my eyes and try to sense it without looking. It's like other Pearls in some ways. The pull's there, a desire to scoop it into my arms and hold it close, but there's something else too.

I get close to touching it a few times, hover right over the top with my fingers. I feel the heat radiate off the surface. But before long, I have to retreat for fear of getting burned.

I clench my fist and try to break it. I stomp on the ground, point my finger like a gun, speak to it. I do everything I can think of to get it to do something. But it never responds. I can't pull it up or forward or sideways. I can't make the slightest movement at all. It just sits there, taunting me.

Eventually, I cover the red light with the blackness of the bag and lean against the opposite wall, prepared to admit defeat and go to sleep.

And I do, for a while.

I'm not sure how long I'm out, but when I wake I yelp, forcing my hands over my mouth even though there's nobody around to hear me. I'm covered in sweat. My hair clings to my forehead. My shirt's shellacked to my back. I roll up my sleeves and take shallow breaths. How did it get so hot in here?

And then I see it. A white dusting lines the floor. Snow, like on the coast.

My mind struggles to work it out. It feels like more

than one hundred degrees in here, yet the snow stays crisp and solid. I swipe a section off the floor beside me. The flakes melt the instant they touch my warm hands.

The bag slips away from the Pearl.

I watch it move, impossibly, from the ball of red, as if the cloth has come alive, wriggling along the floor in retreat. Free from the dark material, the red Pearl pulses with an intense glow. Waves of heat push into me—concentrated blasts like scorching currents of Fringe air. Snow continues to pour from the other side onto the ground, collecting in piles. I shield my eyes from the light. There's nothing I can do about the heat.

It's in control, I realize. This isn't like the rest of them, where I have the power. I can't touch it. I can't even get near.

My bracelet vibrates, forcing my wrist into my lap. I feel the tips of my fingers bake as the heat intensifies. The Pearl trembles, quivers back and forth. Then, without a sound, it rockets straight into the air.

I'm convinced it's going to slam into the ceiling, but it stops midway and hangs in the center of the room like a red star. Whatever's inside wants out.

The bracelet spins around my wrist, matching the heightened frequency in the room. I pull in my knees to make myself as small a target as possible. The Pearl energy fills the entire room now, radiating off walls, flipping on the overhead lights only to yank them off again. It's a physical presence—a spirit set on pushing me away.

The heat fizzles, replaced by an arctic blast that hits me in the face with gale force. Particles of ice settle in my hair and along the ground—a snowstorm in the middle of the jail cell.

The Pearl explodes.

I shout as energy collides with my skin and envelops me. It's not the bolstering feeling green Pearls give. This scratches all over my body like a thousand little insects biting me at once. My skin revolts. I'm convinced that I'm burning alive, though from heat or frost I can't tell.

The cell door flies from its hinges and shoots into the hallway, leaving a chasm behind. The corridor fills with red. The outside wall bulges with the added force before bursting open. A gaping hole spreads across the metal. I see insulation, pipes, wires—inner workings of the ship before the view of the dark mountains outside is unencumbered. The blast has blown a hole straight through the side of the Sky-ship.

Fragments of dust and shrapnel swirl about the room, kicked up by the force of the explosion. Everything's murky red. I can't tell what's happening around me.

Something tackles my side, so forceful it feels like a boulder after a mile-long build up. I'm helpless to react.

Before I know it, I'm thrown into the air. Something grabs me. Arms, maybe. I can't see anything but red energy, a blinding wall of light directly in front of my face. My skin screams.

We land on the ground. My ankle twists. I hardly notice

it past the other agonies. I'm pushed against the floor like a dummy, then lifted up again.

The prison cell disappears altogether.

It takes a moment to understand what I'm seeing. The air is cooler now, and cleaner.

I watch the side of the Academy pull away as we tumble through the sky. Whatever was inside that Pearl knocked me through the hole in the outside wall. There's nothing to grab onto, even as invisible arms hold me tight.

Mountains swallow me on all sides. The Academy walls grow distant. We're in free fall, half a mile straight to the ground.

I can't see anything but Pearl energy in front of me. I feel like I'm floating in fire. I know there are mountains. I know the ground's approaching fast. The air pushes on my back with so much force that I'm certain I'll snap in two.

All the while, something holds me tight.

I watch as the energy begins to fade, sucked into the swirling wind on both sides of me. I expect it to disappear altogether and leave me falling like this, alone—a tiny kid lost inside the sky.

But the red glow warps into something else. A figure appears from the light, a dark silhouette against the stars.

Features begin to carve themselves into the ether and I suddenly realize how close we are. Face-to-face.

Arms stretch up around mine, connecting with hands that interlock below me, holding tight in what could either be an embrace or a stranglehold. Body definition, beneath an unadorned black shirt, gives the figure shape. Brown hair flies wildly around the face, whipped around by the wind as we plummet.

The face.

A mouth appears, grim and silent and inexpressive. Not concerned or worried at all. A nose, then wrinkles. Lines on the forehead, under the eyes.

Eyes. Pearl energy forms around them, swirling and crackling until it disappears altogether. The irises turn red, like two Pearls right in front of me.

The man doesn't blink. He doesn't open his mouth or move his face at all. For a moment I wonder if he's dead, but he continues to stare at me, eyes locked onto mine as we tumble.

His grip tightens on my back. My own expression loses all composure. I must look more horrified and pathetic than ever, but if the man notices, he doesn't say anything. He doesn't scream or shout. His attention never strays.

In one fluid motion, he puts pressure on my right arm and flips me. We twist so that his back is to the ground. I watch the tundra grow closer and closer, a dark sheet of dirt and rock that will mark my last living moments.

We begin to slow. The wind calms as we defy gravity. The sky feels heavy. We crawl through it. I have a moment to tilt my head and watch the mountains. But I can't see the Skyship. We've drifted too far away.

We fall, slower, until it's like we're not moving at all.

The man stares at me the entire time, wide-eyed and mute. Never blinking.

I consider speaking—screaming, even—but before I can make any sound at all, his fingers unlatch and he brings up his knees to prod me in the stomach. I fly in an arc over his head, rolling through the air until I hit the dirt and land hard on my chest.

It takes a moment before I'm able to compose myself. The breath flows back into my lungs. I push myself onto my hands and knees and cough. I'm covered in dirt. Tiny shards of rocks dig themselves into my skin.

As soon as I'm able, I stand and spin to see if the man is still there.

He is. Closer than I remembered.

He stands several yards from me, arms at his sides. Black shirt, black pants. Only his face is visible in the moonlight. From this distance, all I can see clearly are the eyes.

They pierce the darkness like twin beacons, reflective in the night like a cat's.

And there's something else—a loop of black metal attached to a chain around his neck. I wouldn't notice it against the dark shirt, except that it shines with a glint of moonlight. It's the only adornment on his simple clothing, and matches the sheen of my bracelet.

I back away, fearful of what he might do. But the fact is, at the last possible moment, he saved me.

I cough again, trying to find my voice. The man stands in silence and stares. Then, with the only whisper I have left, I clear my throat and speak. It's probably a shot in the dark, but I have to try.

"D-dad?"

It comes out smaller than I mean it to. The wind snaps most of the sound away before it even reaches the guy. I try again.

"Dad?"

He blinks. Then, without a word, he turns and runs.

"Wait!" I follow the best I can, but he's too fast. "Don't run away!"

His legs pump like pistons along the barren terrain until he's running with more velocity than a shuttle. I keel over in exhaustion and watch him. His silhouette shrinks as he escapes into the distance. Then, just as he's about to disappear altogether, he crouches and jumps.

And flies.

I watch the man shoot into the sky like the blast of a cannon. A blink of an eye and he's gone.

I collapse to my knees and stare at the stars, waiting for him to loop around and come back.

He doesn't. Maybe he never will.

12

Cassius squirmed in the restraints. His left foot had itched for the last twenty minutes, right on the sole where he didn't have a chance of scratching. Worse than that, he desperately wanted to reach behind and pull Madame's device from his neck, but she was right. Even if he'd had control of his arms, he couldn't feel a thing back there. No tingle or rawness from a scar. But he knew it was inside. That was enough.

Various Unified Party officials had been in throughout the day, spoon-feeding him breakfast and lunch. The woman in the morning had been downright chatty, blabbering like he was her long-lost grandson. The lunch guy—younger and less smiley—hadn't said a word. Instead, he'd glared at Cassius through thick glasses as he ladled a stew into his mouth.

He looked at the clock on the far wall. It had been more than an hour since anyone had visited. The silence was becoming unbearable. His limbs stiffened. They'd started to cramp early in the morning. Now they were nearly numb. Numb would be better.

He longed to conjure the fire inside of him, to break free of the shackles and shake the stillness of the room. But, true to Madame's word, his body remained unresponsive.

He tried not to think about mind control. Harnessing. She'd told him his mind would function fully, but impulses would steer him in directions he didn't want to go. Madame's impulses, his body. It was a dangerous combination.

It couldn't happen. He wouldn't let it.

But Madame knew him too well. Without his power, he was as helpless as any other prisoner. The thick metal bands locked him in place. Strength didn't matter. All the agility and combat skills in the world were useless to him now. There had to be another way.

The door cracked open. He balled his fingers into fists, expecting Madame. Instead, a brown-haired kid—twelve or thirteen—crept into the room and shut the door carefully behind him. His messy hair stuck in a diagonal across his forehead, framing a youthful, dirt-specked face at odds with his intense, rattled eyes. Cassius had seen this kid before. Only once, but he remembered it clearly.

Last spring, a day before boarding Skyship Atlas in search of Fisher, Cassius had watched this boy leave Madame's office. The thought of someone else having a direct line to her had bugged him then. It didn't matter so much now, but seeing the kid evoked immediate anger. Bad memories.

As soon as the door was safely secured behind him, the boy's shoulders relaxed. A ratty undershirt hung over his gaunt body. Cassius caught the glint of metal hanging from the back of his belt.

The kid took a step forward. A devilish smile spread over his face. "So you're the legendary Cassius Stevenson? You don't look like much."

Cassius stared, unsure of what to say, or whether to say anything at all. The boy's immaturity showed in the way he carried himself, bobbing around the room like he had too much energy for his body to contain. He could be a mirage—a vision of his half-conscious mind.

Cassius closed his eyes. When he opened them the boy was still there. He swallowed and found his tired voice. "What are you, the court jester?"

"Nah." The boy continued to approach. "My name's Theo. Theo Rayne. I guess we're kinda brothers, in a way."

Cassius grunted. "Great. Another one."

Theo's smile straightened, though the corners of his lips still curled slightly. "She's always talking about you. I get sick of it sometimes. I mean, look at you, chained to the wall like a human sacrifice. What's so great about that?"

Cassius's eyelids drooped slightly as he fought to stay lucid. "You're one of Madame's kids, aren't you? I saw you coming out of her office last spring."

Theo's shoulder twitched. "My real mom was gunned down before I could speak. So yeah, Madame's the only mother I got."

He sighed. A part of him knew this kid, everything he had thought and felt while growing up in the Lodge—everything Madame had told him, every stupid line she'd used to manipulate his behavior. In a different situation, he might try to convince the boy to leave while he still had a chance, but he wasn't feeling particularly charitable at the moment. There were more important things on his mind. Chiefly: *How can I exploit this kid to my advantage?*

"She's using you," Cassius mumbled.

Theo smiled. "Sure is. Woman's got a use for everything, doesn't she? Definitely got a use for you. She's always got a use for the great Cassius Stevenson."

He chuckled. He hadn't felt so great when Madame had abandoned him in Washington to capture Fisher, or when she'd let him destroy a train full of innocent passengers without even trying to clean up the mess.

Theo moved closer until Cassius could feel the kid's breath on his neck. He paused for a moment, staring up at him with wild, dangerous eyes before turning abruptly and strolling to the far side of the room. Cassius noticed the glint of metal beside his back pocket again. A knife. How antiquated.

"Even after you go and get her killed," Theo mumbled, talking to himself. "Took a while to get her walking again, you know? The brick crushed her left tibialis." He turned. "Do you know what a tibialis is? I've memorized every muscle in the human body. It's good to know where to aim your bullets."

"Are you trying to impress me?"

"No," Theo said. "No one can impress the great Cassius Stevenson."

"Stop calling me that."

Theo grinned, clearly enjoying himself. "Even after you betray her, she's still obsessed with you. I can't figure it out."

Cassius grit his teeth. Like this kid knew anything about what it meant to be the object of Madame's obsession. "Is that why you strolled in here? You wanna find out why she's got me tied up?"

"I know why she's got you tied up, stupid." Theo reached up and patted the side of Cassius's head—the way a parent would, or an older brother. If he hadn't been restrained, Cassius would've punched the kid just for that. "Harnessing." Theo emphasized the word like it was some imaginary voodoo curse. "It's gonna be funny watching you toddle around the Lodge like an obedient little android."

"You've got quite the vocabulary."

Theo grinned, that same twisted, unnatural smile he'd worn when he'd first entered the room. He lowered his hand to the side, fingers playing with an empty belt loop. "I don't like you, Cassius Stevenson. I don't like you coming in here after all you've done and playing around with Madame's head."

Cassius sighed. "You wanna set me free, then? I'd be happy to leave."

"Not really." His eyes settled on Cassius's wrist. "What's this?" He ran his fingers along the surface of the black bracelet. "Did Madame give you this?"

Cassius remembered when the bracelet had been a simple black box, presented to him by Madame's hands. That was before it had transformed and clamped around his wrist like a shackle. "You could say that."

Theo's eyes locked onto the shiny darkness, analyzing it. "Does it come off?"

"What do you care?"

"I'll pry it off your dead arm when she decides to kill you." He reached behind him and pulled out the knife, thrusting it into the air and slamming it into the metal inches from Cassius's ear. "It's inevitable, you know, with the way you've behaved. But it probably won't be for a long time." The tip of the blade screeched along the wall as he dragged it downward in line with the contours of Cassius's face. "Wouldn't it be easier to get rid of you now?"

Cassius tried to control his expression, though the scream of metal on metal rattled his ears. "Madame wouldn't like that."

"No." Theo's expression froze. "She wouldn't." He lifted the knife from the wall, then ran his fingers along the blade, nonchalant. Cassius grit his teeth. Someone his age shouldn't be this comfortable with violence. Had he been the same before Seattle? Was this what Madame did to kids?

Theo shrugged. "But you know what? She'd get over it. She's still too close to you to see that you'll betray us again. Even harnessed, you can't be trusted. Not fully." He pricked the end of his index finger with the blade's tip. "She'd be proud of me after she realized."

Cassius pulled at the restraints. He should think of something. He always thought of something. But his mind wasn't strong. Fifteen hours hanging against the wall and he was starting to lose it.

Theo got closer. He pressed the blade into Cassius's chest. "You know, she always told me I was special. That I could do things that most people couldn't. Did she say the same things to you?"

Cassius shook his head. He felt a bead of blood drip down his stomach. The pain intensified.

"I saw what you did to the lab," Theo continued. "You're a real pyro, aren't you?" He blinked. "I think it's a little messy, myself. Leaves too much to clean up. You do things right and nobody even knows where to look."

Cassius winced as he felt the blade twist, peeling skin. "Wait! Before you do anything you'll regret, listen to me."

Theo's eyes widened. He steadied the blade.

"Theo!" Madame's voice echoed from everywhere at once. Her condemning tone was enough to send shivers through both boys. Theo pulled the knife back to his waist. His wild eyes darted around the room, eventually landing on a pair of circular speakers in the corner of the ceiling. He sighed.

"My office." Madame's voice continued, as if she was looking down on them from the heavens. "Now."

Cassius breathed a sigh of relief, even though Madame's interference meant the room was surveilled. She was probably watching them on video screens right now.

Theo sheathed the weapon behind him. He took two steps back and admired Cassius for a moment before grabbing the door handle. "Later." He saluted. Cassius watched him bound from the room like a schoolboy eager for recess.

Cassius let out a fractured sigh, cursing himself. He needed to get out. Now.

Madame's voice came from the speakers once more. "I'll see you soon, Cassius. Don't let Theo antagonize you. He's a troubled boy. I'm sure you understand."

He closed his eyes to shield tears. It wasn't the wound or the shackles that undid him. It was how it all looked, how he must look to her, tied up at the mercy of a child. It was pathetic.

But emotion didn't last long. It wasn't going to help him anyways. He fought past it and gave all his attention over to thought. Strategy. He wouldn't have long before his brain was useless against her. He needed to make the most of the time he had. Devise a plan, and get rid of her. And this time he'd make sure she was gone forever.

13

I can see a sliver of the Academy from where I stand. From here it blends in with the surrounding mountains. Dirt and rust covers the hull, eliminating any reflection. My eyes trace the pathway up to the opening I'd fallen from only minutes ago. It's tiny from my vantage point, but I remember what I saw before the guy tackled me. Heavy damage, inside the brig and throughout the corridor. To say I really screwed up doesn't even cut it.

I back away until the peak of a neighboring mountain blocks the Academy from sight. I can't return after what I've done. There's no proof of the red Pearl, and even if there was, it's my fault for bringing it onboard. The brig would seem like time-out compared to what Alkine would do now. August Bergmann was right. In their eyes, I look like a traitor. I've damaged my own home more than once. I'm dangerous.

Hand shaking, I dig into my pocket and retrieve my com-pad. I switch to Eva's code, hold it to my ear, and wait for her response.

It comes almost immediately. "Jesse? I heard the explosion. Are you okay?" Her voice is frantic. Anger will come later.

It takes a moment to compose myself and form words. "I did something stupid, Eva."

"What? Where are you?"

"Outside," I stammer. "I don't know the coordinates. Maybe a mile or two north of the ship."

"By yourself?"

I glance at the sky, still expecting the stranger to come back. "Yeah. I need a shuttle."

There's a long pause on the other end. I can tell she's fuming. "Jesse—"

"Look, we can't talk about this. Who knows if they're tracing my CP. Just get me a shuttle. Please."

She sighs so loud that it breaks up communication momentarily. "I'll see what I can do."

"Thanks, Eva."

The reception fractures again halfway through her name. I listen for a second more before bringing the compad back to my waist. Gripping it tight, I pivot and chuck it through the air. I watch the device land a dozen yards away and slip between rocks. If Alkine wanted, he'd be able to pull up the tracking system and trace me. I can't give him the chance.

I glance around one more time for the man from the red Pearl before sinking to the dirt.

I wait.

I'm not sure how much time passes. Without the screen

of my com-pad, I can barely see anything. I rest my fore-head against my knees. All the while I imagine the stranger, plunging downward, gripping me in his arms. Had he rec-ognized me? It was impossible to tell. His eyes seemed lost in the distance. He stared without any actual recognition.

If he's really a friend, he'll come back. Once he realizes what's going on, he'll turn around and find me. After all, the red Pearl found me. It weaved its way into my vision. It was meant to break in front of me.

But that's the scariest part. I didn't break it. It exploded.

I don't look up until I hear the sound of an engine in the distance. The atmosphere trembles. I try to trace where the sound is coming from. The horizon is still—triangle shadows against the night. A distant flash blinks in the sky. I watch a circular blotch, slightly darker than the moun-tains, cruise around a crest on its way toward me.

Spotlights. A pair of blazing beams ensnare me. I hold up my hand to shield my eyes.

A shuttle pulls in overhead. There's no telling who's inside. By the time it gets close enough, I won't be able to escape. If it's Alkine or another teacher, it'll be too late.

I stand and back up, squinting against the light. I have to take a chance. There's nothing I can do out here by myself without transportation. I wave my arms above my head.

Suddenly, I realize how tiny I am. If the Academy is an insect compared to these mountains, then I'm microscopic. I can flail about all I want. It doesn't guarantee that anything's going to happen. I try to imagine if I was in that shuttle, looking down. At this time of night, the landscape would be a black, lumpy carpet with far too many hidden places.

By some miracle, the shuttle continues forward in my direction.

I continue to jump around, loosening dust and dirt from my clothing. The spotlights fall directly on me again. The shuttle settles on the ground. Its thrusters kick up a cloud of dirt as the landing gear extends. The lights dim. I grit my teeth and wait to see who comes out.

The side door pulls open. Two figures bound onto the dirt. My heart floods with relief. Even without seeing their faces, I can tell it's not Alkine.

Eva rushes up to me, face filled with worry. "Jesse, what happened?"

Skandar stands beside her, brows creased.

I exhale deeply. "I'm so glad it's you."

"There's a hole in the side of the Academy," Skandar says.

"I know."

Eva grabs my arm. "You had something to do with it—"

"We can't go back," I say. "Get in the shuttle. I can explain."

She lets go. "This is a horrible—"

"Stop." My heart flutters. Everything warms. My head darts up to the sky and I lock onto it instantly.

Skandar moves to my side. "What is it?"

I don't answer him. It's as if I can't even hear him.

A Pearl. Green. Falling fast.

I'm exposed, I remind myself, standing directly in its path. It's going to come straight at me.

Eva backs toward the shuttle. Skandar stays closer, keeping a cautious eye on the sky.

I watch the Pearl hurtle forward. When it's close enough, I stretch my arm in front of my chest and point at the stars. I decide to free the Drifter inside before someone from the Academy sees it. And if it's farther away, the blast will dissipate before it hits our shuttle.

I clench my fist. The Pearl explodes in the middle of the sky, a hundred yards above us. It ripples through the air like a firework—a bursting star. Energy spreads in bright green waves, illuminating the scenery around us. The flashes continue for several seconds before the light scatters. Soon it's faded altogether, leaving behind a bright green figure that zips through the air like an oversized firefly. A Drifter.

I sidestep and run into Skandar's shoulder by accident. I push him toward the shuttle. "Get inside!" I steal another glance at the Drifter to make sure I haven't lost it. It does rapid curlicues in the sky. It seems agitated.

We shut the side door and rush to the cockpit. Eva moves to the pilot's chair, staring out the window.

I grab the seat beside her. "Follow it."

"What? Are you crazy?"

"I want to see where it goes."

Without time for a defense, she powers the engine and we lift into the air. I secure my belt and dip low, scanning the corners of the windshield for the green figure. It's easy to spot in the darkness.

"That way!" I point to the left. "Hurry, it's moving fast."

We move in a sharp loop, gaining altitude until we're at the same level as the Drifter. Skandar pulls himself up to the cockpit and finds his usual spot between us.

Eva continues to lay on the accelerator. "I've got him now."

Skandar grabs my shoulder. "Hey, are you alright, Jesse?"

"I'm fine," I mutter, keeping my gaze on the windshield.

If the Drifter notices us following, it doesn't show it. It doesn't speed up or change direction or anything. Whatever it's doing, its path isn't being dictated by us.

Eva shakes her head. "I can't believe I'm doing this."

Skandar pulls something from his side and hands it to me. I glance away from the sky and see my old communicator. Cassius's communicator.

He smiles. "I swiped it from your room before we grabbed the shuttle. Thought it would be important."

"Are you kidding?" I set the communicator on my lap. "You're a genius! Thanks." After all that's happened, Cassius has barely crossed my mind since I last contacted him. He'll want to know about what's happening.

The mountains give way to coastline, then water. The

Drifter continues to soar northward. I wonder if it'll keep on going until it runs out of energy. If that's the case, we won't be able to follow forever. Our shuttle's solar reserves will be on empty before dawn.

Then, right in the middle of the ocean, it dips toward the water. Eva follows. She cranes her neck to see over the console. "What is it doing? There's nothing there."

"Are you sure? Check the map."

Before she can, the Drifter makes a loop in the air, then makes a dramatic dive, like it's going to plunge right into the ocean. I expect a splash, but the Drifter corrects its trajectory at the last moment and skims inches from the surface. It travels in a straight line, quick as a dart.

"Bring us down," I order.

Eva grits her teeth. "Not too close. It's dangerous."

Skandar stands to peer over the console. "The little bugger sure is fast."

"I don't understand," Eva starts. "There's nothing here."

"Wait." I see it, suddenly—a dark shape in the distance, invisible except that it doesn't reflect moonlight like the ocean. "What's that?"

Eva squints, then consults the radar. "A small island, maybe. I don't know. The topography's pretty flat, but you're right. There's something there." She tilts the shuttle just enough so we can look down upon the expanse of land. The Drifter slows as it approaches the island. I watch its body pivot. Its feet point to the ground. I wonder if this is where the man from the Red Pearl went too. I hope so.

"We've gotta land. It's slowing down."

Eva hits a button. "Might as well. You've already dragged us out this far."

I watch the Drifter meet the island with gentle grace, like a feather falling to the earth. After a moment's hesitation, it walks forward.

"Set us down at the edge. We can follow it on foot."

Eva winces. "We don't know what's on this island."

"Calm down," Skandar replies. "It's probably deserted. Like every other lousy island out here."

———

We stay far enough behind the Drifter not to startle it. I want to run closer and ask questions, but Eva says we'll learn more by keeping our distance. She's probably right. After all, the Drifter hasn't been on Earth long, which makes its behavior even more curious.

Each step is deliberate, like it knows where it's going. But that's impossible.

Beyond squat outcroppings of rock, there aren't many hiding places for us. We move slow, sometimes on our hands and knees. It's not long before the ocean disappears behind us, replaced by thin patches of grass. After half a mile's walk, the Drifter stops and crouches.

It runs its hand over the ground. I poke my head up to see above my rocky hiding spot, but it's useless in the darkness. The three of us huddle close together.

The Drifter bounds from its perch and staggers back,

startled by something. Eva moves to grab my arm, but she's too late. I move to my feet just in time to see the ground in front of the Drifter open up.

"Jesse!" Eva yanks me back behind the rock.

A man lifts himself from the dirt, just a foot or two from the confused Drifter. Then another.

There must be a trapdoor of some sort—an entrance to an underground room. The men emerge on the grass, dressed in light body armor. They each carry what looks like a large pistol. The polished metal glints in the moonlight.

"Those are agents," Eva whispers. "See their uniforms? They're Academy."

I peek over the rock. "Do you think they know what happened back home, with the red Pearl?"

"Shh." She leans forward, keeping her eyes on the action. "They could have gotten radio, I suppose. Or maybe they were stationed here already."

I watch as the smaller of the two agents approaches the Drifter. He extends his hand in a calming gesture. His mouth opens. We're too far away to hear what he says.

The Drifter waves its arms, motioning wildly. The agents back away. One leans in and whispers to the other.

Then, a shot.

I watch the Drifter slump to the ground. The larger agent steps forward and catches the body before it hits the dirt. They drag it along the ground, hoisting the upper half and letting the feet lie still.

I stand again. I can't help it. I want to shout. I feel Eva grip my leg and pull, trying to get me back on the ground.

"You don't know what you're—"

I pull free and stumble two steps away to steal a better look.

It's a mistake.

As the agents force the Drifter through the trapdoor, the closer one turns and sees me. I don't know how—maybe they've got high-range specs or something—but the way he pauses and stares, I know I've been spotted.

"Oh no." I back up, nearly crushing Eva's hand in the process.

Skandar flattens against the rock. "Don't say it, man."

"They saw me." I risk another glance in the agent's direction, only to catch him tromping forward. "They're coming."

Skandar winces. "But we don't have any weapons."

"They're Academy," Eva whispers. "We shouldn't need weapons!"

I shake my head. "You're wrong."

And I know it in that instant. I know exactly what we have to do. Alkine and the others have been treating me this way for a reason. I am dangerous. I am treacherous. The way these guys are looking at me? They wouldn't do that unless they considered me a threat. And when Skyship Agents target a threat, they defend themselves.

I turn to the others, hands shaking. "Something's wrong here. We have to fight."

14

Eva crouches in front of me, eyes wide. "Hell no, Jesse. Sneaking out is bad enough. You're talking about turning against our friends!"

"That agent shot the Drifter." I shake my head. "He might've killed it."

"We're too far away. You could've seen anything. Calm down a second before you—"

"Uh, guys?" Skandar glances over his shoulder. "We don't really have a second."

I turn. The agent barrels toward us, closer than I expected. Instead of arguing with Eva, I break into a sprint and head in a wide arc, keeping my distance from the agent while heading toward the fallen Drifter.

The agent extends a gloved hand. "Stop!" He doesn't recognize me in the darkness, though I wouldn't be surprised if he'd attack knowing full well who I am.

I freeze. I'm in the center of flat land, totally exposed. Eva and Skandar duck beneath the rocks. I catch my breath and glance to the side. The bigger agent's got the Drifter half-way into the ground. There's no way to reach him in time.

Instinctively, I hold out my left arm. The closest agent reaches for his holster. I ignore him. I'm not sure what I'm going to do without a Pearl, but I have to do something.

I hone in on the energy surrounding the Drifter. It's not hard. It's the only light available on the island. But I'm not worried about seeing it. I need to feel it.

Something clicks. Connects.

The hairs on my arm bristle and pull toward the light. I close my eyes and forget everything else around me. If I can manipulate Pearls, I can do the same with Pearl energy. I'm sure of it.

When I open my eyes, I know that I've got it. The tips of my fingers pulse. I tense my hand, pull it inward, and watch as the green light streams from the Drifter's body into the air. A band of energy snakes through the sky, curving downward with the slight guidance of my fist. I bring it in a figure eight, gain momentum, and send it slamming against the nearest agent.

My index finger points forward. The energy follows suit, gaining speed as it shoots in a straight, bladelike path above the dirt and connects with the second agent. He topples onto his back, unconscious.

My concentration fractures. The energy splits into pieces, bursting in all directions. The field's a brilliant green flash until the last of it dissipates. Then, darkness.

Skandar and Eva run up beside me. My breathing's fast, exhausted.

"This is bad, Jesse," Eva says. "Imagine how this is going to look."

I ignore her. "I'm going under. I want to see what's down there."

Before she can argue, I take off toward the Drifter. He hangs halfway out of a wide manhole. I notice a metal cover lying in the sparse grass off to the side before turning my attention back to the body. He's unconscious, at the very least. Maybe dead. I can't look for long. I don't know how much time we have, and I need to see what's down there before Alkine sends reinforcements.

I grab the Drifter's hands and pull his legs from the opening. The hole is a well of darkness below.

I turn and let my foot fall until it makes contact with what must be a railing. Cautiously, I descend, grasping the rungs of a side ladder to steady myself. It's impossible to tell exactly how far I'm going.

The moonlight disappears overhead, replaced by a soft glow emanating from somewhere below me. Seven steps and I reach a dank ledge of dirt. I release my hold on the rungs and step backward. My shoes connect with concrete.

I spin and focus on the light. It's dull. The hallway before me is twisted, obscured by mazelike walls. The glow probably seems farther away than it is. I extend my arms and walk forward, right into a wall. Using the stone as a guide, I shift sideways and head deeper underground. I hear someone descend the ladder behind me. Hopefully Eva or Skandar.

Another twist, then another. All the while, the light

grows stronger. I push my back against the wall and quiet my breathing. The silence is more concerning than reassuring. I expect to feel something—the pull of a Pearl, the bristling of my skin. But all I really feel is cold.

I tiptoe around the corner of the wall and arrive in an open room. Three chairs are scattered unevenly around a table. Behind it, several yards deep, runs a dark, semitransparent wall. If I stood close, I might be able to see through it. Or maybe it's not transparent at all, but reflective. Either way, it's not natural. Not underground like this. A row of bulbs flicker softly overhead, casting the empty bunker in a dim spotlight.

I rush to the strange wall and lean my forehead against it, staring in. At first I can't see a thing, but as I focus, outlines appear. Soon, I'm looking at an entirely different room, twice the size of this one. But it's not the room itself that I notice.

A man sits right in the center, quiet and still.

His back is arched, his legs crossed under him. And his eyes are closed. Even with the shield of the dark wall blocking my vision, I recognize his face from conference calls. From the Kansas rooftop last spring.

Ryel.

This is where Alkine's been keeping the Drifters.

I bang on the wall with my fist in hopes of getting his attention. It must be soundproof, because his expression doesn't change. His eyes clamp shut as if in meditation. His hands clasp in his lap.

He wears all white, like when Cassius and I first met him. He doesn't look as though they've been mistreating him; not too thin or weak. No shackles or cuffs. But this is a cage all the same. I can feel it.

Ryel.

They don't have last names, these people. That's one of the few things I've been able to learn since spring. They have numbers. Rankings. But no last names. Ryel's the 7,085th to bear his name. I saw it once on Alkine's memopad. I think the numbers must be mass important to them. Something to do with their place in society.

The Academy's given him an age of forty-five, though I don't know if Drifter years are the same as ours. To me, he looks younger.

I lay my hands on the wall and take another look, praying for Ryel to open his eyes. I can't get over how human he looks, at least from the outside. They all look this way, at first. It takes a closer analysis to spot any differences. I overheard Dr. Hemming saying that their arms have a different ratio to them. Shorter at the bicep, longer forearms. Flatter nose. Slightly dilated pupils. A greater arch to their backs. None of it's enough to make them stand out in a crowd, but up close you can tell that they're foreign. Not quite right.

I guess I'm not quite right, either. I always wondered why Alkine had insisted on so many medical checks when I was a kid. Turns out that while I might seem like a normal teenager on the outside, inside's a different story. Again, not enough to ring alarms, but different. Like Hemming said, it's all in the proportions.

"Jesse." A hand pulls at my elbow, breaking my attention from the second room.

I jump and turn to see Eva standing before me. "What?"

"I think I heard something."

I glance around, searching for figures, shadows, anything. "Where's Skandar?"

Her eyes widen as she scans the room for him. "I thought he was right behind me. Maybe he—"

Footsteps interrupt her. Skandar rounds the corner, scratching the back of his neck.

Eva's whisper intensifies. "Where were you?"

"Rifling through the agent's side pack," he whispers. "You know, Alkine always says to use what you've got. Most of the guy's stuff was standard issue." He holds up a palm-sized, semicircle device. It looks like some kind of remote. "Except for this. It's got buttons." He shrugs. "It must do something, right?"

I grab the device from his hands. "I've never seen anything like this."

Skandar's eyes fall on the wall in front of us. "Wow. That's different, isn't it?"

I step back and analyze the remote. There are three buttons on top—hardly complex. Of course, there's no telling exactly what they'll do. Knowing my luck, I'll push one and end up setting off some kind of explosion. But I've got to try.

Before Eva can push her way in to have a look, I press each button in turn.

Nothing happens.

Eva shifts beside me. "You know, we shouldn't—"

"Wait."

I watch as a border of blue light appears from the darkness, illuminating the edges of the wall. The line spreads from the corners and stretches across the boundary of the floor and ceiling. Once the two pieces meet in the middle, the light changes course—moves vertically and splits the wall like someone's cutting it open with an invisible blowtorch. Without a sound, the pieces slide apart. The light fades and we're left with two slabs pulling across the ground, retracting into the walls. I haven't seen technology like this in the Academy. Unified Party, maybe, but not our dinky little ship.

Ryel doesn't notice the movement at first. His eyes remain closed until the walls are halfway retracted. When they open, he has a sort of glazed look on his face, like he doesn't know where he is or who we are.

Then, as if a switch has been triggered, his mouth falls open and he realizes.

I can tell by how quickly he moves that he knows it's me. Even though we've barely seen each other—only once in person—there's recognition in his wide eyes.

He bounds from his seat on the concrete, barefooted. "Please don't tell me I'm imagining this."

He speaks perfect English. It wasn't like that back on the rooftop, but Pearl transport energy allows for language recognition and processing. He doesn't have any discernable accent, more like he's studied every different way of speaking and crammed it into one voice.

"Ryel." I stare at him, unsure what to do. Shake hands? Hug him? Bow?

He stops several feet in front of me and takes a moment to survey what's left of the walls before refocusing on my face. "I'm going mad. I've had visions of shadows. Don't know if they're real or not. Are you real?" He clutches my shoulder. "Jesse Fisher?"

I glance behind me at Eva and Skandar. "We've gotta get him out of here."

"There are more of us"—he motions past the retracted wall—"in the holding chambers."

Eva cringes. "I told you this wasn't a good idea."

"You're here," Ryel continues. "You're standing right before me."

I step back. "Yes. It's me."

He presses his hands together as if in prayer, allowing himself a smile, though it looks more like a strange grimace. "The others! Our brothers and sisters."

I peer over his shoulder, expecting an agent to rush from the darkness and tackle us. "Yeah. Okay."

"Guards." Eva steps between us, expression tense. "Alkine's bound to have them."

"There's one room," Ryel says. "Halfway down the corridor, secured. They're sleeping now."

"Go back to the entrance," I tell Eva. "See if you can grab some weapons from the side pack. Then meet us down here."

"I am not pulling a weapon on one of our own people."

"They'd pull one on you."

Skandar retreats, pulling her with him. "Don't worry, Jesse." They disappear around the corner.

Ryel's head cocks to the side, his posture unusually rigid. "Do you hear it?"

I shake my head.

"The agents are coming. My plan … it won't work."

The corners of the room erupt in a flurry of activity. Six agents burst from the hallways beyond, each armed and decked in full battle gear. They come at us quick. Too quick.

I grab Ryel by the wrist and pull him forward. "Run!"

As we push forward, I fiddle with the remote in my hand in the hopes that it'll do something. It's too late to close the wall again, but maybe I can trip some emergency security system.

We sprint through the mazelike corridor on our way to the escape ladder. I grab the closest rung and climb. My arms still ring from the Sophomore Tour. The agents will have a harder time negotiating the ladder with all their gear. I saw the weapons they were holding. No stunners. That was lethal force. They wouldn't shoot me. They can't. Not if they know what I mean to Alkine.

I reach the surface and emerge on the dirt gasping for air. Ryel follows, struggling to his feet.

"Jesse!" Eva stands next to the fallen agent, brandishing a small pistol. Skandar crouches beside her, digging through the guy's weapons pack.

"They're coming." I stagger from the hole. "We've gotta get back to the shuttle."

Skandar stands. "All this guy's got is stunners."

"It doesn't matter. Which way's the shuttle?"

Eva consults the stars before pointing behind her. "There."

I take off in a sprint, followed by the others. Ryel runs beside me, easily matching my pace.

A shot fires into the sky behind us. It's meant to intimidate. All it does is tell me where the agents are. They've made it up the ladder.

We jump across rocks—over ridges and through plots of mud. All the while, the agents pursue us. I can't even see the outline of the shuttle yet. With each step, escape becomes more unlikely. Without a Pearl, I'm helpless.

Skandar bumps into Eva. "Give me the stunner."

She resists, but he grabs it from her hand and sidesteps away.

"What are you doing?"

"Get to the shuttle!" Skandar shouts. "I'll hold them off!"

As my lungs scream for air, our shuttle pulls into view. I look over my shoulder and watch the agents approach, closer and closer. A second shot breaks the silence. I cover my head, expecting to be hit.

Instead I see Skandar freeze and pivot in the grass, brandishing a stunner in each hand. It's tricky enough to accurately shoot one of those things in training modules. Trying to stun a guy through full body armor is near impossible.

"Skandar! No!" Eva slows, desperation on her face.

He doesn't listen. He stands his ground, waiting for the agents. "Go! Go!"

The shuttle grows closer. We're almost there.

Skandar fires—two darts laced with tranquilizer. One connects. I hear a body fall.

I slam into the side door of the shuttle and plug in the code to open it.

More shots. The agents' attention is diverted. Skandar's bought us the seconds we need. They better not hurt him.

The door opens. We scramble inside. Ryel follows us.

Eva cranks up the engine before she has a chance to sit. I watch the skirmish through the side window. A pair of agents tackle Skandar to the ground. His stunner flies from his hand. He's defenseless. We could shoot—harness what meager defense equipment this shuttle has—but then we'd risk hitting him. Shuttles don't fire stun darts. We could kill.

The landing gear retracts. We bolt into the air. I half expect the agents to open fire. Maybe it's because we're in an Academy vehicle. Maybe they did recognize me back there. Whatever the case, they keep their weapons still.

We gain speed and pull away from the island. It's only when we're a safe distance from land that Eva turns to me. "They've got Skandar, Jesse." She chokes on the words.

"I know." I pace uneasily. "What have we done?"

"They've got him," she repeats. Her eyes widen. "They—"

She can't finish the sentence. It finally happened. She can see what the Academy's become. Otherwise she would've chosen different words.

They've got him. They. Not we.

They.

15

Cassius relished the chance to leave his cell, to move freely without shackles pulling him back.

The Unified Party Cruiser had landed in the Fringes several minutes ago, opening its door to a world far different than the temperature-controlled room inside the Lodge. Madame had surprised him earlier in the morning, arriving in place of the usual breakfast lady. "We'll be going on an errand," she'd said, and left it at that. It was like old times. She never revealed more than she had to.

His wrists had welts on them from being restrained for so long. He walked with a slight limp. His leg cramped.

Keep moving.

Madame's voice echoed in his mind. She hadn't actually spoken, but the device on his neck relayed her commands.

They were at the edge of a Fringe Town. Syracuse, just a short distance from the Lodge. Cassius couldn't think of a more uncomfortable place. Every time he breathed, the air felt thick and sandy. Sweat dripped from his neck, staining the collar of his shirt. A dry wind ripped like sandpaper against his skin. And the sun ... it was unstoppable.

Syracuse, more than any other Fringe Town, had special significance. It was where everything had started, where he'd first met Fisher and triggered his power, where Pearls stopped being energy and became something else. He hadn't been back since.

The town could be dangerous. The lawlessness of the Fringes wasn't too far off from the slum lands back in Providence, though they were far emptier. Every time he'd ventured outside in the past, something had gone wrong. Fringers, like Slum Lords, were not to be trusted. Even though he'd denounced the ways of the Unified Party, he could still become a target. No Fringer would be happy to see someone like Madame walking through their town, not after the government all but banished them to a life in this hellish wasteland.

Madame wore a loose white blouse and tan pants. Casual for her. He assumed she wanted to blend in. Beside her was the boy, Theo Rayne, trotting along like an obedient puppy. Cassius didn't know why she'd insisted on bringing him. As usual, she'd offered no explanation.

Cassius surveyed the buildings on either side of them. Gutted, dusty storefronts bordered the vacant street. This was a ghost town—brown and lifeless. There were thousands like it scattered throughout the country, each as dead as the last. He hoped all the Fringers had scattered to different parts of the state.

Keep walking.

Madame wrapped her arm around his shoulder and pulled him closer. "Lovely morning, isn't it?"

He wanted to push away, summon fire, and fight, but the harnessing kept him at bay. It was an odd half-life, hazy and unfocused like a dream. He could move. He could talk. But he couldn't break through.

Madame released him and steered Theo to the right. She pointed to a building on the nearest corner. "That's a fine example of turn-of-the-century architecture." Cassius glanced up. The windows had been blown out on all three stories. "Things were quaint back then. I would love to crawl inside a time machine, take an excursion back before it all changed."

Theo tensed his shoulders. "Do I have to wear this jacket?"

"I know it's hot, dear, but you don't want to walk back into the Lodge with a Surface Tan. Besides, the material's designed to help regulate your body temperature. You'd be less comfortable without it."

Cassius dragged his feet beside them. "Isn't it dangerous for someone like you to be out here?"

"It's a dangerous world, Cassius." She led them down an alley. "The trick is not caring."

Theo's head poked around her back. He grinned. "The great Cassius Stevenson's not scared, is he?"

Cassius ignored him. The truth was, he didn't think he could be scared if he tried. He couldn't seem to summon any emotion at all.

"Now Theo," Madame chuckled. "Play nice. I don't want the incident in Cassius's cell to repeat itself. It's important to me that the two of you get along." She paused. "Come. We're nearly there."

She led them halfway down another street, identical to the last, and stopped before a wide, boarded-up building. Cassius thought he recognized it from his last venture out, but it was tough to be sure. Everything looked familiar.

Madame gripped the cracked door handle. "Cassius, you know I care about you. Everything, even what happened back in Seattle, I did for you. I dream of the day we can walk like this without the use of devices." She pulled open the door without waiting for a response. A cloud of dust dislodged from the opening.

Keep walking.

They stepped into the foyer. It was identical to the ones he'd explored as a boy when he found it necessary to escape the pristine cleanliness of the Lodge. They ascended a short flight of stairs and turned the corner, heading for a room on the second floor.

Theo stopped in his tracks and blocked the way forward as Madame disappeared into the room. He turned around, eyes slit. "I don't know why she brought you here, but I'm watching you."

Cassius pushed past him. "I'll keep that in mind."

He followed Madame into the small room. It was empty except for a disheveled bed in one corner and a table in another. She stood at the foot of the bed, hugging a girl.

Avery Wicksen.

Without the Unified Party suit she'd worn in Providence, she seemed much more like the girl Cassius remembered. Her straw-colored hair was tied back off her face, revealing soft features. A hint of freckles. She looked common, in loose jeans and a dirty T-shirt. Like a Fringer.

Avery's eyes met his own. Any glimmer of recognition was fleeting. Dulled. Madame released her embrace and Avery perched at the edge of the bed, oblivious to him.

"My dear girl." Madame backed up two steps to admire her. "Forgive me for these dreary surroundings. I hate to think of you out here in this heat."

Avery opened her mouth. For a moment, Cassius expected to hear anger—brash confidence like she'd possessed months ago. Instead, her voice was quiet. "I'm comfortable. I have water."

"Still." Madame smiled. "A place like this, a town filled with rousers and thugs, is hardly what I want for my daughter."

Cassius crossed his arms and leaned against the doorway. Avery was as much Madame's daughter as he was her son. It didn't count. It wasn't real.

Straighten up.

He arched his back, standing tall without even realizing it.

Madame strode to a wide window at the opposite end of the room. It had been covered with wood planks, but lines of sunlight poked through. "It won't be for much longer, I assure you. You'll have Jesse Fisher back in good time." She looked over her shoulder. "And when he sees you like this ... well, he'll be concerned. And rightfully so."

Cassius watched Avery tense up. Her fingers gripped the bedspread. Her heel tapped against the ground. "Do you know where he is now?"

"No," Madame responded. "That's why I've come here. I have a surprise for you."

She motioned Theo to her side. The boy pulled the pack from his shoulder and handed it to her, backing away without a sound. Madame unbuttoned the top flap and pulled a communicator from inside. Cassius recognized it instantly. Badly worn, unrealistically large. It had belonged to him only a few short days ago. Fisher's communicator.

She tossed it across the room to Avery's waiting hands. "Old Unified Party technology. Cassius was using it to speak with Jesse Fisher. We've switched it off until now. Go ahead and turn it back on."

Avery ran her fingers down the side of the device, searching for the switch. Cassius knew exactly what to press, but he remained silent.

Madame threw the pack back to Theo. "It's only a matter of time before Fisher tries to contact his brother. When he does, he'll find you instead. And that's when we'll construct our story. The two of you will be reunited." Her brows rose. "See? I do keep my promises."

Avery examined the communicator. Her hands shook. Her face remained blank.

Madame crouched on the ground beside the bed. "I

know about love. It may seem disingenuous, coming from me. The two of us have been strangers for some time now, but I remember it. At times it seems there's nothing more important."

Avery switched on the communicator.

"That's a good girl." Madame patted her knee. "You remember the plan. Everything hinges on timing and trust."

Cassius stepped forward. "What are you going to do to Fisher?"

Quiet.

Madame stood, a half smile on her face. "I'm not going to do anything to him, Cassius. Calm down."

"You're bringing him here," he continued. "And obviously it isn't so he can see *her*."

"What exactly are you accusing me of?"

Theo laughed from the window. "Maybe the great Cassius Stevenson needs another dosage."

Cassius glared at the kid. "I am so sick of you." He bolted toward the window and shoved Theo into the slats. His fingers tightened around the boy's neck, eager to snap it.

"Stop!" Madame shouted.

Cassius's grip loosened, half under his command, half from the sound of her voice.

A shot punctured the silence, coming from the street beyond the window. Theo ducked. So did Cassius. Madame froze before striding to the window. She bent to peer between the slats, then gave a great sigh. "Fringers," she said. "And their guns. Always bullets. So unrefined."

Avery stood, still clutching the communicator. "They don't know about me. I expected them to scavenge the building, even just for shelter, but it's been safe."

"They've probably seen the cruiser." Madame turned. "That ought to have set them off." She pulled Theo to his feet and dusted off the corner of his jacket. "Go outside and make yourself useful."

The boy swallowed. He hesitated a moment before nodding. As he went for the door, he made a point of bumping into Cassius's shoulder. Cassius eyed the kid in disbelief before turning back to Madame. "You're sending him out by himself? You don't even know how many Fringers are out there!"

"I saw three. There may be more." She held out a hand to stop the boy. "Names. I'd like names, if at all possible, Theo."

Theo nodded before sprinting out the door.

Cassius scoffed. "They're gonna kill him."

"They won't."

"Trust me. If they've got guns—"

"They won't kill him," she repeated. "You and Theo have a lot in common. Don't underestimate him."

Cassius stared at her, searching for the truth. Her face was impossible to read.

"Why do you want names?"

She clasped her hands at her waist. "There have been rumors of an uprising in these parts. It's the closest Fringe

Town to the Lodge. It would be fantastic news if any of the Fringe leaders were disposed of today."

"You mean—"

"You felt the blade of Theo's knife yesterday." She glanced at his chest before meeting his eyes once more. "It's his favorite. I gave it to him several years ago. You didn't know about it, of course. You didn't know about him." She paused. "But you soon will."

"What's that supposed to mean?"

"Shut the door," she said. "He'll knock when he's ready."

Cassius took a moment to peer into the hallway before closing the door. Theo had already disappeared.

Madame moved to Avery's side and placed one hand on her shoulder. "Let me show you how this communicator works." She coaxed Avery into a sitting position. "This is all we had back in my day. Primitive, yes, but it does the trick." She tapped the bed with her free hand. "Why don't you come join us, Cassius?"

He stood still, listening to the sounds outside. There were more shots. Two, then a third half a minute later. After that, nothing but silence.

To the bed, Cassius.

He moved to the side of the bed, positioning himself as far from Madame as possible. He wished he could do something. If he'd had his full senses, he could break free and warn Fisher.

He stole quick glances at Madame. The way she hovered over Avery, the hint of lavender coming from her skin . . . it was all too familiar. He recalled nights when he was a boy and she would come to his room to read to him. The classics—never anything trivial or childish. She'd been like a mother then. She looked like one now. No one had ever made him feel more important.

A knock came at the door. Three equal thuds.

Madame passed the communicator back to Avery. "That was quick." She smiled, then raised her voice. "Come in."

The door opened and Theo entered the room, jacket torn at the shoulder and hair stuck to his face. He raised his knife, wet with blood, and dropped it to the floor. "Randy, Paul, and Joseph," he panted.

Cassius stared at his face, then down at the weapon, the dark-red splotch against the wood.

Madame frowned. "Pity. Not an important name among the three of them." She stared at the tear in his jacket. "You can take it off now if you want, darling. No risk of Surface Tan in here."

16

There used to be more of Japan. That's what they say, at least. There are still underwater ruins, proof that civilization once existed here. But above the water it's just a string of small islands. Once mountains, now buried.

Some are wide enough to land a shuttle or two. Most look more like oversized stepping stones. It's a necessary pit stop for us—a chance to get our bearings. Away from the Academy, but not too far in case we have to turn back.

It won't be long before they start tracing us after what happened on the island. We have a limited window to talk—decide what to do—before we'll need to get airborne.

The shuttle sits behind us, empty and quiet. Waves lap upon the rocks at our feet. The Pacific stretches endlessly before us. This place is as silent as Russia, probably more. The grass that remains is eternally marshy. Sinkholes abound, but we've found a relatively stable piece of land.

Eva chucks a pebble into the water. She's got a handful of them ready to go. I think it makes her feel better to be doing something. "They'll take him back to the Academy," she says. "That's the first thing they'll do. And knowing Skandar, he won't talk."

My leg shakes with nervous energy. "Alkine wouldn't hurt him, right? I mean, it's Skandar."

"I don't know." She shakes her head. "At the very least, they'll get a story out of him. I'm going to have to see if I can disengage the trackers on our shuttle. That'll mean sacrificing our radar, but I don't see . . . " She trails off.

Ryel sits on the rock beside me, utterly still. His chin rests on his fingers. His eyes slit as he stares at the water.

"We found you," I whisper. "I did it. Finally."

He turns to look at me, his expression fragile. "I am . . . the only one?"

I open my mouth to speak, but end up swallowing my words before I settle on the right thing to say. "I've been trying . . . I mean, I've been doing what I can."

His brows furrow. "I thought your leader was rational. I thought, if we gave him what he wanted—"

"Captain Alkine doesn't know what he's doing," I reply. "He didn't hurt you, did he?"

"Does it matter? We weren't sent to this planet to worry about our own well-being. He confined me." His jaw hardens. "That was enough."

"I'm sorry."

"Don't be sorry for me," he says. "Or for any other Drifter. Be sorry for the time we've lost. Those hours . . . those pointless video conferences . . . I prayed that something was being accomplished. That I was an anomaly." He turns back to the water. "But you have nothing."

"That's not true." I push my wrist in front of his face.

The blackness of the bracelet reflects his worried features. "I have this."

He glances at it, frowning.

"It's been shaking," I continue. "It won't come off. Sometimes it's strong enough to pull my entire arm. What is it?"

He sighs. "That material is called Ridium. It's the most powerful element on Haven."

"Haven?" Eva scoots forward.

"The name of our home planet," he responds. "Or, rather, a rough translation."

Haven. The word slots into the framework of ideas in my mind. Right now that's all it is: a word.

"What's it doing around my wrist?"

"Ridium can be controlled, but only by a chosen few. Shifters, they're called. I am not a Shifter." He meets my eyes. "Neither are you."

He grabs my wrist and pulls the bracelet closer to his face, running a finger along the surface. "There are forces inside. I don't fully understand them, but they go beyond what exists here on Earth. All Ridium is controlled by the Authority. And the Authority, in turn, by Shifters.

"In the end, it formed the very infrastructure of our civilization. Buildings, technology, weapons ... they were all influenced by the endless powers of Ridium. It's a synthesizing element, which means those with the power to Shift can bend it to their will. In addition to changing its physical shape, it can be imbued with programmed instructions. Like a computer. It can send signals, relay messages, store video or holographic information … the possibilities are limited only by its Shifter's imagination." He releases his grip on my wrist. "The Resistance risked great peril to create this for you. It must be important." He sighs. "I was a simple pilot. I'm not qualified to be your guide."

I swallow. "You're all we have. For now."

He runs a hand over his face, exhausted. "Your parents wanted you to have that bracelet. That's all I can tell you."

"My parents … "

"Great leaders." He shakes his head. "Strong."

My lips tremble. I can't tell if he's taking a dig at me or not. "What … what were their names?

He pauses in thought before answering. "Savon. That was your father. And Adaylla, your mother. Numbers 3,038 and 5,017. Founders of Haven's Resistance."

Eva drops her pebbles. Somehow hearing the names changes things. They're real. People knew them.

Savon and Adaylla.

Even with the string of numbers behind them, the words sit comfortably in my consciousness—missing puzzle pieces.

The crashing of the waves takes over the silence. The ocean brightens with the rising sun.

I choke back emotion. "What were they like?"

"I never met them," Ryel says. "Not in person. I only know what I've been told."

I pound the rock with my fist. "You can't leave it at that."

"I can't?" He turns to me. "Don't let yourself be clouded by the thought of them. It won't serve any of us well."

"Then tell me what they were fighting for. They started the Resistance, right? What were they resisting?"

Ryel's eyes widen in disbelief. "You've been kept in the dark. It's worse than I thought. Your leader has told you nothing."

"Go on." I grit my teeth.

"I am not a school teacher." He closes his eyes, grunting in frustration. "Very well. A history lesson." He takes a deep breath. "Haven was approximately half the size of Earth."

My brows rise. "Was?"

"Let me finish."

I rest my chin on my knees, determined not to interrupt him again.

"Our climate was dry, but the resources bountiful. Ridium pits existed in the southern hemisphere, dark and endless before they were scavenged by the Authority. In the north, vast fields of gold-flecked grass. No oceans, but many lakes." He pauses, as if recalling the scenery upsets him. "Your scientists would have never spotted us. Not with their ... limited technology. The universe is constantly stretching. Mirroring itself. Haven existed more than fifty million of your light years away from Earth. But it's gone now."

"How?" Eva asks.

He glares at her. "Our home became unstable years ago—tremors that evolved into great fissures. Haven was eating itself alive. Self-destructing." He pauses. "Some blamed it on our actions. Others took a more philosophical stance.

Everything has an expiration date. Either way, an evacuation was called for."

My memory fills with historical videos the teachers made us watch about the founding of the Skyships, crowds of people taking off from the chemical-stained Surface in search for a better life. It helps me visualize Ryel's words. Otherwise it's too big to imagine.

"It was gradual," he continues, "especially at first. Day-to-day, it was easily ignored. The Authority looked to the stars for suitable replacements. They found Earth. Led by King Matigo, they sought to send a battalion to conquer. This planet was large and plentiful with resources. With a few adjustments, we could live well here. At your expense, of course."

"Tell me more about this guy," I say, forgetting that I'm not supposed to interrupt. "Matigo."

Ryel doesn't seem angry. "Number 207. A rare name."

"He's a Drifter, like you?"

"Like you. Like us, yes." His shoulders tense. "He's a Shifter as well, and a very powerful one. The ability to shift Ridium guaranteed him an important role in our society. With his power and ambition, it didn't take him long to become the figurehead of the Authority."

"He's the leader," I mutter. "He's the one."

"He is dangerous. And he's on his way." Ryel pauses. "When Haven's destruction became imminent, it wasn't difficult for him to convince our people that invasion was their safest option. Behind closed doors, he'd been planning to conquer other galaxies for years. It was a convenient excuse to … how do you say it … get the ball rolling." He turns back to me. "And that is what your parents were fighting."

"I don't understand," I reply. "They'd rather die than come to Earth?"

He shakes his head. "They believed there was an alternative. Riskier, and far less luxurious. Others had discovered another planet in a neighboring galaxy. It was closer than Earth and held the resources we would need for survival. Managed right, it could have been a fine home for us. And, most important, it was uninhabited. No need for an invasion. They called it Haven II.

"But Matigo was intent on populating Earth." He sighs. "The Resistance went behind the Authority's back. At first they planned to splinter and take Haven II for their own. Start a new society, free from the Authority's rule. But your parents were too honorable for that. They knew they couldn't live their lives at peace while Matigo destroyed another planet. They waged war. Gaining supporters wasn't difficult, especially among those in the outer regions, far from the central cities."

"Are they alive?" The words pour from my mouth without me realizing it.

"I told you. I've never met them." He leaves it at that and continues his story.

"Outnumbered at every turn, your parents devised the Pearl Transport System to get off-planet and warn the people of Earth. Though he had been born into a life of farming, your father showed a great interest in many of the sciences and eventually became one of the planet's leading physicists. He found a way to reverse the body's growth process and shield the resulting material in what has now become known as Pearl Energy. In a way, Pearls are like a portable womb, carrying and protecting bundles of genetic information. Atoms. Molecules." He pauses. "Utilizing a wormhole at the edge of our galaxy, Pearls were sent to Earth.

"Your parents hoped that if they could get here first, they'd be able to fight back. With the help of humans, of course. When the Authority learned of this, your family was targeted. You and your brother were targeted. You would have been killed, too, if your parents hadn't managed to get you off-planet before the Authority showed up."

My whole body shakes. I didn't notice it before, but my heart's pounding like a drum. My mind hurtles back to the dream—*memory*—I had in the security center last spring with Avery. The syringe filled with liquid. The pops and hisses from the small laboratory. The cloudy green energy. There were soldiers there, when my parents put me inside the Pearl and set me loose. The door busted down. There were gun shots.

Ryel bows his head slightly. "That was the night the Authority discovered Pearl technology. They've been augmenting it ever since, playing around with the formula. Strengthening it. When they land, they'll be more powerful than us." He grits his teeth. "But you have no army. You haven't done your job. Your parents would be—"

"Don't say it." My fingers clench.

"Your leader is incompetent. He fears that we are the invaders, that every Drifter is the same. You people have yourselves to blame for your destruction."

I wince.

"Where's your brother? Please tell me he's still alive."

"Cassius is . . ." I look down at the rocks. "It's complicated."

"Can you contact him?"

"I can try."

"Good." Ryel stands. "We've much to do. Pearls aren't meant to stay locked."

I pull myself to my feet. "Don't you think I know that?"

Eva slinks away. "I'm going to go see about disabling our radar. The longer we stay here, the more likely the Academy will—"

"No." I hold out a hand to stop her. "I'll call Cassius inside the shuttle. I want to be alone for a minute."

Ryel crosses his arms. "You're the Pearlbreaker, Jesse. Don't forget it, even for a second."

"Yeah." I don't meet his eyes. Instead, I turn and trudge to the shuttle. I can't do this without Cassius. Not anymore.

My arms tremble. It's real now. These past weeks, it's been all I can do to stay sane, but now that I know the truth, I'm not sure I can handle it. There are too many things coming at me at once, each stealing a piece of my attention.

Water surrounds me on both sides. My feet sink into the ground. Below me are cities, subway cars, and skyscrapers, all buried by time. A look at our future, perhaps.

There used to be more of Japan. Hell, there used to be more of *me*.

17

Cassius sat cross-legged on the stripped floor boards, back against the wall. It had been several hours and Madame hadn't shown any sign that they'd be leaving the abandoned Fringe building. He wondered if she'd told anyone at the Lodge what was happening. Or maybe she didn't care. Maybe this had become too personal.

She was off in a different room of the old hotel now. Theo acted as her watchdog, standing just beyond the closed door, guarding. Madame's voice remained ever-present in Cassius's head. It was only a precaution.

Sit. You're not needed now. Not yet.

Avery sat on the side of the bed, kicking her heels back and forth, silent. Cassius hadn't gotten to know her very well last spring. She'd been raised at the Lodge until Madame planted her as a spy in Skyship Academy, but Cassius never remembered seeing her. Of course, back then he'd only been a child. The more he learned, the more he began to doubt his entire opinion of the Lodge. How many kids did Madame have running around, harnessed as weapons?

Avery cleared her throat. "I remember when we were scared of you."

"You were never scared of me." He glanced up.

"That's true. But Jesse was."

His eyes shifted to the communicator beside her. "What are you gonna say to him if he calls?"

"What Madame told me to. The words she's forcing into my brain."

"I can try to dig it out," he replied. "I ripped the old microchip from my wrist. If you're not afraid of a little blood—"

"No, you can't," she said. "You'd like to think you can, but you're harnessed. The moment you laid a hand on me, she'd know. Trust me. I've tried."

Cassius's shoulders deflated. "So what's her plan? Bring Fisher here so she can collect the pair of us?"

"I'll bring him here," Avery replied. "After that, I don't know."

"Do you still love him?"

Her heels fall still. "What do you mean?"

"You did love him, didn't you? He talks about you like you did."

She sighed. "I'd do anything for him. I don't know what you want to call that. Guilt, maybe. For spying on him."

"You're gonna feel much guiltier after this."

She reclined on the bed. The room fell silent for a moment before she spoke again. "Do you ever think about what your life would be like if Madame hadn't found you?"

"I try not to."

"The way I see it, I've lived two lives, one with her and one at the Academy. And neither one was really mine." She paused. "When Jesse and I were running through the Fringes, away from you, it was scary. But even though we didn't know what was going to happen to us, at least we were making our own decisions."

Cassius's gaze fell to the floor. "Madame's the only mother I've ever known."

"Pretty screwed up."

"We're all screwed up. And that kid, Theo? She's done it to him too. But he's still young. Maybe someone can knock some sense into him. If he's lucky."

The door swung open. Theo strode into the room, cutting a line between the two of them. His eyes blinked rapidly. His steps were uneven.

Cassius backed up. "Were you listening to us?"

"I don't know why she hasn't separated you two," Theo replied, twirling the handle of his knife around his finger. "It's asking for trouble." He turned on his heel and paced to the opposite wall, feet kicking the ground as he went.

"Stop that." Cassius crossed his arms.

The kid's dirt-specked face hardened. "Or what? You gonna do something about it?"

Cassius's fist tightened. For a moment, he thought he'd be able to break through Madame's control and strike the boy.

The moment passed.

Theo chuckled. "Didn't think so."

Avery yawned. "Just ignore him."

"No." Cassius took a step forward. "We don't know each other very well, do we kid? Where did Madame pick you up? Some trash heap behind her office?"

"I told you." Theo paused, wiping the sweat from his brow. "My real mom was a—"

"I don't care who your real mom was. That wasn't what I asked you."

His knife stopped spinning. "How's that harnessing treating you? We could get you on the floor if you want." He grinned. "Make you cluck like a chicken."

"You didn't answer my question." Cassius smiled. Maybe he couldn't lay a finger on this kid, but that didn't mean there weren't other forms of abuse.

Theo's eyes narrowed. He retreated to the foot of the bed, leaning on the frame. "I don't know. Where'd she find you?"

"In the middle of a war zone," he replied without hesitation. "Wading through a haze of chemicals, fresh from outer space."

Theo laughed. "Hmm. Funny."

"It's true."

"You can actually remember that?"

He shrugged. "Only bits and pieces."

"Then how do you know that it's true?"

He crouched low, eyes at the same level as the boy. "She told me."

Theo looked away.

Cassius smiled, content in the thought that he was getting to the boy. "She hasn't told you anything, has she? You don't even know where you come from. And yet you follow her around like she owns you. It's pathetic."

He frowned, eyes fixed on the wall. For a moment, he looked like the child he was.

"How old are you, anyways?" Cassius continued. "Eleven? Twelve?" He laughed. "Not past puberty. That's for sure."

"There was an accident." Theo grit his teeth, glaring at him. "I don't remember anything past that."

Cassius's brows rose. "An accident can mean so many things with Madame."

Theo pounced to his feet and resumed his irritating pace. Back and forth. "Yeah, well, at least I didn't run away like a coward." He paused. "There were Fringe Towns. I remember the heat. I hated it. I'd look at the Chosen Cities in the distance and think that I was imagining them. Then one day I collapsed, face-first into the dirt. I would've died, but the Unified Party picked me up. Saved me."

Cassius watched him move, more loose and agitated than before. "Where'd you learn how to do that, with the knife?"

Theo froze. His fist gripped the handle of the weapon. "This thing?"

"Those Fringers out there didn't stand a chance against you. That's what Madame said."

He shrugged. "I've been good with a knife since before the accident. Madame said I didn't even need training. Said I was a natural."

"Sure."

"But that's none of your business, is it? I see what you're trying to do. It's not gonna work. She loves me. And I love her. Like a son."

Cassius laughed. "Right. Like a son."

The town rumbled behind the window.

Cassius cocked his head. "What was that?"

Theo smiled.

Avery rose to a seated position. "This town's been quiet for days."

The rumbling strengthened. Cassius stood and turned, crouching to stare through the open slits of the window. He could just make out the obstructed horizon, clogged with rows of buildings. Patches of spotless blue sky.

Then shadows.

Something descended on the town. Several somethings.

Ratty flags whipped in the air on the tops of buildings as a fierce wind kicked up. Sharp, black shapes fell to the earth. They reminded him of detached shark fins. Impenetrable.

Unified Party Cruisers.

Cassius had piloted several as part of his training at the Lodge. They were sleek and menacing, designed for aerial fights. They were also excellent transports for troops.

He turned. "Madame's blanketing the town."

Theo's smile widened.

Cassius moved back to the window and watched the cruisers set down in the streets. Most disappeared behind buildings, but he could imagine the troops pouring out of each one, hiding in derelict structures, waiting to strike.

"An army," he whispered. "She's brought an army."

"They'll shoot Fringers on sight," Theo said. "Clear the town before getting in position. Then reload."

The outside door swung open and Madame marched into the room. She moved immediately to the window and gripped the boards. "Marvelous, isn't it?"

Cassius backed away from her. "You never said anything about—"

"This is the best sort of town for hiding," she continued. "A hundred men can disappear."

"Why bring me here?" Cassius glared at her. "Why didn't you let me stay at the Lodge?"

"I want you to see this," she said, still gawking through the cracks. "You've forgotten. All those weeks in Canada and you've forgotten where you truly belong."

"I don't want—"

"I've always had big plans for you," she interrupted. "You're capable of such great things."

"Like killing."

"Look at the cruisers." She ignored him. "Like beautiful black birds seeking prey. He'll be here soon. Our little Pearlbreaker."

A succession of beeps sounded from the side of the bed.

Cassius turned, instantly recognizing the call. It was his communicator. Fisher was on the other line.

Madame bristled at the sound, then turned with a smug smile on her face. She nodded at Avery. "Go ahead."

Cassius took a step forward, prepared to leap to the bed and grab the communicator away.

Stop. Madame's voice echoed in his mind. *Watch.*

"No," he forced the word out.

"Quiet, Cassius." She turned back to Avery. "Please answer his call. I will be listening."

Avery's hand shook. For a moment Cassius thought she was going to drop the communicator. But she'd been harnessed by Madame far longer than he had—possibly months. She had her orders.

She pulled the communicator closer and stared at it. Madame nodded, egging her on. Lips trembling, Avery raised the device to her ear.

She hit the button. It was done.

18

I sit in the passenger seating of our shuttle, head bowed, communicator pressed firmly against my right ear. My shaking finger presses the contact button. It beeps several times before Cassius picks up.

Silence.

"Cassius?" I whisper at first. Then louder. "Cassius?"

No answer.

He's usually reliable, but there have been times he hasn't picked up. He'd seemed worried the last time we spoke.

"Cassius? Are you okay?"

I set the communicator on the seat beside me and give in to panic. Static comes over the upside-down device, muffled by the cushion. Then a voice. "Jesse?"

It's not Cassius.

But I recognize it immediately at a gut level, though it takes my brain a moment to catch up with my heart.

No way.

I reach for the communicator and flip it over. The voice pours from the speaker again, more clearly this time. *Her* voice. "Jesse?"

I dip low and hover over the speaker, refusing to believe it's true. "A-Avery?" My voice trembles as I say her name. I haven't said it out loud in weeks. "Is that you?"

Silence.

"Avery?"

"Thank god, Jesse," she replies, and I can almost see her smile like she was in the room with me now. Her face begins to etch itself into my mind, every last piece. I see her standing outside my dorm at the Academy. I see her la\ying beside me in the Fringes of Washington State, in the old playground outside of Lenbrg.

"Avery." I repeat her name like it's the only word that exists. My brain can't process it. It's really her voice on the other line. "How are you...? How do you—"

"Shh. Don't worry. I'm okay. I was hoping you'd call. Cassius said that you had the other communicator."

"Cassius. Is he alright?"

"He's on the run, Jesse. In the Fringes."

"Wait... where are you?"

"I'm okay," she repeats. "I'm in New York."

"The city?"

"No." She pauses. "Syracuse."

She knows what this word means to me. It was the town where I first met Cassius. It was the place where we triggered our powers. The rooftop. The first time I felt Pearl energy.

"Are you—" I stop myself and try to slow my words. "I

thought they had you, Avery. I thought the Unified Party captured you and took you away."

"They did." Her voice sounds tired. "But I escaped several weeks ago. I thought I'd make my way back to the Academy, but I didn't know where you'd gone."

"You won't believe this." I pause. "I hardly believe it myself."

"Where are you?"

"Siberia," I say.

"On the other side of the world?"

I swallow. "Afraid so. Look, you could—"

"I was working on getting a shuttle or a cruiser or something," she interrupts, "but it's dangerous. I didn't want to go back into Unified Party territory again, so I've been hiding in the Fringes."

I try to picture her in Syracuse somewhere, eking out a horrible existence in the wretched heat. "I should've come—"

"No," she says. "No, it was too dangerous. You were smart for running away. Remember what I said last spring in Portland? I'd do anything for you, Jesse. Don't worry about me."

"I want you here."

She pauses. For a moment I think I've lost her. "There are other things to worry about."

"What do you mean?"

"Cassius needs your help," she replies. "He's in trouble. He doesn't want to ask you, I can tell. He doesn't even really want you involved. That's why he passed the communicator on to me when we ran into each other."

I shake my head. "You and Cassius ... ?"

"He found an old shuttle outside of Providence," she says. "I think he came to Syracuse to investigate. You know, after what happened between the two of you. He was scared, Jesse. He tried to hide it, but I could tell. He says they've been after him for weeks. He doesn't know where to go. He's heading south, hoping that he can lose himself down there. I told him that it was a mistake. The Fringes are more dangerous than ever." She pauses. "He gave me the communicator, told me to get in touch with you—"

"Why would he—"

"He said that we needed to talk. But I was worried. I decided not to call you. It's just too dangerous. But when I heard the beep, I ... " She pauses. "I'm so stupid, Jesse. I should have never picked up."

"You're not stupid."

"Now I've started something."

"No. I'm glad to hear your voice. You don't know how much I've wanted to—"

"Come," she says. "Oh god, forget about it. Ignore me. I should hang up."

"Avery, I need to see you."

"I know. But it's not safe."

"I don't care if it's safe. It's been almost four months. I'm not just gonna leave you there!"

"It's dangerous, Jesse, even worse than it was when you left. The Unified Party is everywhere and—"

"Doesn't matter. You have no idea what I've been through." I pause. "Anyway . . . I've got someone I want you to meet."

"Oh?"

"And I've been working on it, the Pearl thing. I'm stronger now, I think. Ryel says we need to build an army. I can't do that without you."

"Who's—"

My mouth keeps spewing out words. "Once we pick you up we can find Cassius and then it'll be good again. We won't all be split up around the world. We can do it if we're together."

"Slow down." Her voice is low, almost a whisper. "You're not making sense."

"I've got so much to tell you. We've got a shuttle."

Silence.

Avery's voice is quieter now. "You need to be careful."

"Of course."

"No, Jesse. Really."

"Don't worry about me," I say. "You're safe in Syracuse, right? No Fringers?"

"They're taken care of."

"Good." I look out the window to see Eva and Ryel approaching. "Stay there, okay? It'll take a while for us to get to Syracuse. I'll call you every hour to make sure you're still alright."

"That's probably not necessary."

"Are you kidding? It's totally necessary. You know how bad I felt about leaving you in Seattle? I'm not letting that happen again."

"It wasn't your fault. I—" Static cuts through her last words. When she comes back, her voice is garbled. "I've gotta go."

"Stay there," I repeat.

"Of course."

"And Avery?"

"Yes?"

My fingers drum along the bottom of the seat. "I missed you."

"I missed you, too, Jesse. Remember—"

Static. The connection fractures.

Still, I can't help but smile. I haven't felt this way in weeks. Just hearing her voice was better than a hundred Pearls. A few short hours and I'll actually see her—alive and well! My brain can hardly process the thought.

I'd forced myself to imagine a life without Avery. Now everything's changed. She's something to fight for.

19

I barely get the chance to tell Eva and Ryel about Avery before the Academy tries to break through the shuttle's communication blocks.

We're in the air when it happens, minutes after taking off from the island.

"They're tracking us through the radar." Eva crouches below the front console, gripping a fistful of wire in her hands. An unscrewed panel covering lies in the corner of the cockpit. "I'm really no mechanic, Jesse."

"Just keep going."

The sun's fully risen as we speed over the Pacific Ocean. I try not to look out the window. I don't like the sameness of it. If we were to crash, or our solar power was to fail, there'd be no one around to help us. If we didn't drown, we'd starve.

Eva curses. "They'll know we're going back to America. They're probably watching as we speak."

I glance at the spotless sky. "As long as we have a head start."

Eva wipes her forehead and returns to her work. "You didn't even talk to Cassius?"

"We can pick him up," I say. "Trust me."

I hear her sigh under the console. "I know you miss Avery. It's great that she's alright, but—"

"It's a distraction," Ryel interrupts. It's the first time I've heard him speak for a while. He sits in the pilot's chair, eyes locked on the path in front of him. "We need your brother."

I sink into my chair. "We'll get him. She knows where he is."

"I hope you're right."

I'm about to respond when I feel my bracelet start to hum. Before I know it, the Ridium tugs on my wrist, pulling my arm forward where it connects with the top of the navigation console. I jerk forward.

Eva bolts from her work at the sound of the bracelet clanking on the metal. "What was that?"

I stare at Ryel while trying to pry my wrist from the console. "See? I told you. Sometimes it does this."

His eyes slit, then widen as something shoots past our shuttle. A red flash of light hurtles by my window over the ocean. I turn my head to catch a glimpse of it, but before I can make out any details, it's gone.

Maybe I imagined it.

The bracelet falls still. I pull back, rubbing my arm.

Ryel grips the steering. "Crimson."

"You saw it too?" I swallow. I'm hesitant to tell him

what I'm thinking because I don't really want to know the answer. But as far as I'm concerned, the flash could only be one thing. "Ryel," I start. "Have you ever heard of a red Pearl?"

His thin brows furrow. His fingers tighten. "No."

"I…I found one last night. It broke. But I didn't do anything. It broke by itself. And it made my bracelet go crazy, like right now."

"There was a Drifter inside?"

I nod. "A man. I thought maybe he was…"

Eva crouches beside me. "Maybe he was what?"

I shrug. "Never mind. I don't think he recognized me. I'm not sure he even knew what was going on. But the way he stared at me…He didn't fly away like all of the other Drifters."

Ryel's shoulders tense. "Do you know why Pearls are green?"

"No."

"The energy that bursts from our bodies when the Pearl is broken is the same substance that keeps us alive on our long journey through space. It's filled with nutrients and stabilizers, some of which are even found on Earth. Like Ridium, the chemicals necessary to create Pearls are pulled from Haven itself. The planet's core was a deep green, even with a surface of brown and gold.

"It's this same energy that grants us the ability of flight for several hours after we've landed. It heals our wounds and makes adapting to the environment easier. I still have the smallest trace of it inside my body."

"That's why I survived."

"Excuse me?"

"Oh," I start. "Last spring. I fell off a twelve-story building. And lived. There was Pearl energy around me."

"It only protects those from Haven," he continues. "In its purest form, it would have a destructive effect on your friends here. This protection is the green luminescence you see. The burst, when the Pearl is broken and the Drifter freed, requires extra energy. This is absorbed by your brother and transformed into a common element on Earth."

"Fire," I mutter.

"Crimson would signal a different form of energy. Something I'm not familiar with. Something we may not have any control over."

A chill runs down my neck. "The Authority?"

"Perhaps." He pauses. "We'll keep an eye on it. The Ridium around your wrist seems to respond. Be aware."

I let my arm fall to my side. It's hard not to be aware when the thing pulls my entire body forward.

Ryel glances at the console. "I'm going to speed up. We'll find your brother today. The Resistance wants the two of you together."

I shift in my seat. "They've said this specifically?"

"You heard the message from your mother. You were granted the power. The Key and the Catalyst. One to open the Pearls, and one to channel the energy. Your world is better protected when you're together."

A loud hiss fills the cockpit.

"Crap!" Eva drops the wires she's holding. "They've done it."

Words interrupt the hiss streaming from the circular speaker in the center of the console. *"Academy to shuttle 743. Do you hear me?"* A pause. *"Academy to shuttle 743."*

Even through the static, I know exactly whose voice it is.

"Are you there, shuttle 743?"

Agent Morse sounds muffled, but I can picture his face in the room with me now. His phony encouragement. His condescending smile.

"We don't have to respond." Eva stands back. "He won't hear us if we don't press reply. Not that it does us a lot of good. If I wasn't able to get the communication blocked, the radar's probably a lost cause."

Agent Morse continues. *"We'd appreciate it if you'd let us know whether you're okay or not. I know that's you in there, Jesse. And your friend. We have Skandar back onboard. He won't talk, but we can put two and two together ourselves.*

"Your radar's muddy," he says. *"I'm sure you're aware. But we'll find you. Alkine's determined."*

Eva rubs her eyes. "I did the best I could."

Morse coughs on the other end. *"No reply? I hope you're alright. You better have a damn good reason for all of this, Jesse. You don't know what you're inviting here. Things aren't as black and white as you wish they were. You think you're the hero in this, don't you? You ever consider the contrary? That's what a good strategist does. They weigh all the possibilities before jumping headfirst into battle."*

Ryel stands. "Is this shuttle equipped with weaponry?"

Eva's face tenses. "You mean blasters?"

"That'll do." His eyes settle on an open compartment at the far corner of the cockpit. "Ah, I see. Take the steering, please."

As Eva sits in the pilot's seat, I watch Ryel move to grab a small pistol. He barely examines it before turning back to the console.

"Still no answer?" Morse pauses. *"Okay. Have it your way. But just know that this was a mistake. You're going to regret this, swear to god."*

Before he can finish, Ryel opens fire on the speaker. One shot and the thing explodes in a puff of dark smoke. Ryel quickly puts out the meager flames with the sleeve of his shirt, then sets the pistol beside the wreckage.

"There," he says. "We don't need to listen to that anymore."

20

We cross the rest of the Pacific without any Academy interruptions. Eva disables our radar, though it's probably too late to matter much.

Though Ryel seems constantly alert, Eva and I fall asleep several times throughout the journey. I need it. We've been going nonstop for hours now.

We climb into Skyship Territory to avoid Unified Party checkpoints before crossing into America. Border hopping—exactly what got the Academy in trouble in the first place. Of course, it's easier to sneak by in a shuttle our size. The problem is we're flying blind. Without the radar, everything's more of a guess than a certainty.

It's been four months since I've seen home. Even the Surface looks kind of inviting.

Eva analyzes a map she pulled from an overhead compartment before glancing out the window. "The Fringes are so bright. It's like a different world."

I bite my lip, thinking of Avery. I don't know how she's managed to stay well this whole time, out here in the wasteland.

Ryel turns left, beginning our descent.

"It's close." Eva consults the map again before glancing out the window. "I'll let you know when to straighten us out."

He keeps his gaze forward. "This terrain is not unlike Haven. Warm. Dry."

I cough. My mouth is dry from the temperature-controlled air. "What do you think Morse meant . . . 'you're going to regret this'?"

Eva ignores me, pointing forward. "Now. Bring us level. Syracuse is straight ahead." She folds the map and turns. "He's just being the big, bad agent, Jesse. Trying to intimidate you."

"Yeah, you're probably right," I reply, though part of me doesn't quite believe it. I've had a nasty feeling in my gut ever since the first time I defied the Academy. Even now that we've freed Ryel, it's hard to reconcile the two.

I grip the armrest, trying to steady my nerves. As we lose altitude, New York State's vast, brown desert fills more and more of our windshield. It's a different kind of desolate than Siberia. Even at dawn, the temperature will be hotter than I've felt in months. One hundred and twenty degrees according to the onboard thermometer, and rising. A scorching, suffocating heat that crawls inside your body and kills you from the inside. Everything slows. Mind. Reflexes. We can't be outside for long.

As we approach the dusty collection of buildings that used to be the town of Syracuse, I peer behind us out the side window. I see the silhouette of Rochester—Chosen City #17—glinting far in the distance, a beaming mirage against a blanket of dirt, a soaring metropolis positioned awkwardly at the edge of a desert. The dome of connectors forming the Bio-Net over the city gives it the impression of a protected snow globe. People inside are free from the intensity of the Fringes, their comfort and security paid for by the Government's Environmental Tax. It's the Unified Party's domain, and even though Syracuse could be dangerous, I'd much rather land in the lawlessness of the Fringes than spend even a moment inside a Chosen.

Ryel brings us down in the center of what could be the same street we landed on last spring. They're all the same.

Instantly, flashes of that afternoon come back to me. My first meeting with Cassius, the energy when our powers activated, the fall to the ground.

"I'm shutting off the temp control," Eva warns. "Prepare for the heat." She turns a black knob above her head until it clicks. Earlier this morning, we'd found a pair of Surface outfits in the back hatch of the shuttle—pale, thin uniforms over undershirts. The material's light, designed specifically to refract sunlight. Ryel insists that he doesn't need one. His clothing is white anyway. He should be alright.

As soon as we open the door, the coolness inside our shuttle dilutes, replaced by the brutal heat outside. The air hits my body with physical force, as strong as any missile or explosion. It courses down my throat and into my lungs. There's no comfort here. And this is just the beginning.

We amble down the lifeless street, shells of dirt-caked buildings on either side. A wind kicks up and showers our faces with clouds of dust. It's utterly silent. I hope that means the Fringers are off in another part of town, as far from us as possible.

Eva speeds up until she's in step with me. "I don't see anybody."

"Shh." I push her back. My head darts back and forth, analyzing every closed door as we pass. "Avery's probably waiting inside. Do you remember which way the hotel is?"

Eva points to the left down an alley. I nod and lead the way between the buildings, keeping watch for Fringers. My cheek stings with the memory of being slammed into the hot brick wall last spring. I push the thought away and step into the next street.

Ryel follows, arms crossed, unconcerned with any of the dangers a Fringe Town could surprise us with. Ever since leaving Siberia, he's seemed increasingly impatient. I guess I can't blame him, after all the time we've wasted. Still, he's not exactly the warm and happy type. But maybe he's what I need.

"There." I point to a building half a block away. It's several stories high and dilapidated. If possible, I think it's crumbled even more since the last time I saw it. I stare at the rooftop, at the exact point I'd hung on that morning. I thought I would die there. How wrong I was.

A voice shatters the silence—an indistinguishable, wordless cry from somewhere above us. Deep, but fractured. Eva and I duck instinctively. It doesn't seem to startle Ryel.

Eva covers her head. "What was that?"

"It almost sounded like—"

"Fringers," she interrupts. "They're watching us. We better be quick."

I glance up at the boarded window from where the sound came. Eva's probably right. Fringers. That's the likely explanation. Still, I can't help but wonder.

"That's Avery's hotel," I whisper. "What if they're hurting her?"

Before Eva can answer, the door to the derelict building falls open, its top hinge knocked off. A figure stumbles out, cautious, shielding the harsh sun with her hand.

"Avery!" I forget the others and take off in a sprint. Nothing else matters for a second, not the unbearable heat or the threat of Fringers. I run until I've got my arms around her. I pull her close, unwilling to let her slip away again.

The monster hug doesn't last long. Not as long as I'd like. Our damp skin sticks together as we part. Her hair, grown out some since I last saw her, is pulled back in a ponytail. Her face is dirty and mottled with sweat. Her eyes point down, unwilling to look at me.

I step back. "Is something wrong?"

She shakes her head.

"I can't believe it's you, Avery! All these months, I thought...I wondered if you were alive. I didn't know what they'd do to you."

"Shh." She raises a finger. "There are Fringers nearby." She glances around, lips trembling.

Eva moves beside me, expressionless. "Nice to see you again, Wicksen."

Avery's face hardens. Her breath quickens. It's like she's trying to keep from vomiting.

I lean forward and grab her hand. "Something's wrong. What is it? Are you sick?"

She shakes her head.

"Eva, do we have water?"

"Back in the shuttle." She steps away. "You want me to grab it?"

I nod, then turn back to Avery.

Avery meets Eva's eyes. "Wait. Don't go. Don't leave him alone."

I stare at her face. She still won't look at me—not for more than a glance at a time. "What? Leave who?"

"I missed you, Jesse," she says. "Seeing you here... urgh..." She grabs her forehead. She's sweating even worse now, like the beginning stages of Surface Stroke.

"We'll get you in the shuttle." I move behind her.

"No," she says. "It's all I can do to—" Her teeth clench. "Run away, Jesse. Run."

"I don't understand."

"Run!" She backs into the doorway, bumping against the frame.

My heart sinks. "Avery, you sounded fine on the communicator. I thought you—"

The street erupts.

Footsteps echo in a clamorous beat, kicking up dust and sand in clouds around us. Men in dark battle suits rappel from buildings. The clicks and whizzes of artillery come next, locking on the center of the street where we stand. Avery doesn't move, not even to flinch. She still won't look at me.

I'm too stunned to speak. Everything happens in one moment. Before I know it, someone grabs me by the wrists and throws me to the ground. I eat dirt before struggling to bring my chin up. I can't see anything through the brown cloud that obscures the alleyway.

The air begins to clear. Avery stands beside the hotel door, away from the front steps. She stares at me with wide, pleading eyes.

A second figure approaches from beyond the doorway. I don't recognize the shadow at first, but as soon as her face comes into view she's unmistakable, even with a scar carved into her cheek.

Madame. She's alive. And smiling—the kind of smile that tells me that all she needs to do is raise a finger and I'll be dead.

21

Madame clears two steps down from the doorway, arms crossed. "Pull him to his feet," she orders. "I want to see his face."

The soldier behind me yanks my arms so hard they nearly pop out of their sockets. I wince in pain as I'm brought to a standing position. My face is covered in dirt. I taste it in my mouth, feel the sharp grit between my teeth.

"Ah." Madame smiles. "There he is."

I try to look around for Eva and Ryel, but the soldier's got my face pushed forward. All I see is Madame, and Avery behind her, hunkered against the safety of the building.

I struggle against the man's grip. "What have you done to her?"

"Never you mind." Madame moves closer and grabs my chin, pulling up and forcing me to look at her. I spit. It lands on her cheek, just below the scar. She ignores it. "Look at you. You're not the same boy I met in Seattle."

I kick at her ankles, but she releases my chin and moves away before I can make contact.

She turns to Avery, grabbing her wrist. "He's loyal.

You're a lucky girl. Come, see him. You deserve it after all you've been through."

Avery resists, but Madame pulls her forward until she's within reaching distance. My arms are twisted so tightly behind me that I don't have a chance to move, let alone grab her hand.

"What did she do to you?" I whisper. "Did she hurt you?"

"Jesse," Avery starts. "I don't know what to say."

Madame creeps up behind her. "Say what he wants to hear, darling. You know how to talk to him."

I look past Avery, directly into Madame's eyes. "I'm gonna kill you."

"That'a boy." She glances skyward. "This city is filled with Unified Party Cruisers. You can't see them from where you're standing, but I've got one prepared just for you." She lays her hand on Avery's shoulder. "I'll let the two of you sit together if you'd like. You can catch up."

I notice movement behind her, another shadow in the doorway. With the last bit of leverage available, I shift an inch to the side to see Cassius standing there, expression grim.

My heart jumps at the sight of him. He's thinner than I remember and wears an unadorned white shirt and pants. "Cassius! Thank god. Do something!"

Madame turns to look at him, wiping what's left of the spit on her cheek. "You're supposed to be upstairs."

A boy emerges from the door and speaks before Cassius

has a chance. "He slipped away, Madame." He has the voice of a child, but the swagger of a soldier. "You told me not to hurt him—"

"It's alright, Theo," she says. "We might as well have everyone in the same place."

I wait for Cassius to summon a burst of fire, or at the very least tackle her to the ground. Anything to turn the tide in our favor. But all he does is stand there, looking as helpless as Avery. His eyes meet mine. "Sorry, Fisher. We can't do anything. It took all my strength to get down the stairs."

My mouth falls open. I turn back to Madame. "It's a chip, isn't it? Like last spring…like the one you put in Avery's head."

"Don't worry about it," she replies.

I'm about to respond when Ryel's voice comes from behind me, louder and more forceful than I've ever heard it. "Your attention, please!"

The soldier behind me pivots, dragging my feet across the dirt until I can see Ryel. They've got a half-circle of guns pointed in his direction. Eva's not too far off, threatened by a second firing squad.

Madame marches toward him. "And you would be?"

"My name is Ryel." His voice is remarkably calm. "Let the boy go."

Madame laughs. Then, as she stares at him, the realization dawns on her. "I see. You're one of them, aren't you? An invader."

He swallows. His eyes lock onto hers. "Yes. And I'm asking you to release us before I'm forced to access my special abilities."

Her eyes slit. "What special abilities?"

"I can flatten this entire battalion with a blink of my eye. I can do it standing right here, several yards from you. And you will feel the brunt of it. I can guarantee that."

I stare at him. There's no way he's telling the truth. If he was that powerful, he could have escaped from Alkine's island weeks ago.

Madame clears her throat. "You're lying."

"You know nothing of our people."

"I know more than you think." She smiles. "And you, sir, are lying."

"Is that a chance you want to take?"

She crosses her arms and motions to a soldier beside him. The hilt of a gun slams into the side of Ryel's head. He stays standing, though visibly disoriented.

"Yes." Madame motions to another soldier. "This one will be worth studying. Don't damage him more than you have to." She turns back to me. "We hunt Pearls, Jesse, as always. The Fringes are more chaotic than ever. A war with the Skyships is inevitable. We need power."

"You're not gonna get it," I reply. "I won't let you."

"It will not be your decision to make," she says. "But think of it this way. At least you and Cassius will be together again. No more running. Won't that be nice for a change?"

An explosion rattles the silence. It comes from behind

us with enough force to knock me forward. The soldier releases his grip on my arms. I stumble to my knees. Bits of dirt and wood fly through the air. For a moment it's so chaotic that I can't tell which direction is which. A brown cloud envelops me, thick and hot. It feels like fingernails scratching my body. Just as the echo of the blast begins to fade, a second explosion rips through the street a quarter mile to my right. Then another.

The entire city's coming down.

With each explosion, the air becomes murkier. Soon, it's impossible to see my own hands in front of me. Alarms wail in the distance, sounding from cruisers along neighboring streets. The clicks and hums of readied artillery join the fray, though it's impossible to tell how near or far I am from anything. Madame yells in front of me, but can't get all the words out before succumbing to a succession of coughs.

And then, a battle cry. A hundred voices arrive at once, shouts and yells as dark figures cut through the dust cloud in rapid snapshots. Some carry sticks. Others brandish chains or knives. One trips over my outstretched leg and slams into the dirt. I brush my hand through the air to get a better look. The stranger turns, his face obscured by an oval-shaped, translucent mask. His skin is bronzed, turned dark from Surface Tan.

Fringers.

Another explosion rattles the street. A sulfurous stench clogs the air, along with dark billows of smoke. They're bringing down the city. TNT, or some sort of old bombing device like that.

Unified Party troops rush into action around me and try to ward off the attack. It's still too dark to see, but covered by their masks, the Fringers have the advantage.

A hand reaches out to grab me. I recognize Madame's polished fingernails. I push myself back and kick, connecting with her stomach. She grunts in pain as her arm gets sucked into the cloud again.

I stand and stagger back, off balance. Three steps and I run into someone's shoulders. Before I can fight back, a pair of hands grab me around the biceps and pull me close. The air thins and I see Ryel's face, staring at me through the dust, eyes unblinking. It's as if the cloud doesn't bother him at all.

"The others—" I choke on the dust.

A Fringer bolts past us, nearly knocking Ryel sideways. Shouts and cries fill the street, joined by a few bullets. But in the dust's low visibility, Madame's soldiers can't risk firing. It's hand to hand.

Another body collides with mine. At first I'm convinced it's a soldier, but then I turn and see Eva's panicked face. The three of us stand pressed together, waiting for a fist or leg or blade to emerge from the brownness and attack.

Eva coughs. "We have to get out of here!"

I want to argue, tell her that we've got to grab Avery and Cassius first, but she's right. The longer we stay inside this cloud, the more dirt we breathe in. If it gets much thicker, we're going to suffocate.

Ryel releases his grip on my arms. "I can breathe through this." He points to his left. "Run in that direction until the air is clear. I'll find Cassius and meet you at the edge of the cloud."

"And Avery?"

He bolts away without a word and disappears into the dust. Eva yanks on my wrist, pulling me along as she sprints through the street. We avoid most of the soldiers, now too busy defending themselves against an army of Fringers, and loop around the chaos. Nobody notices us, especially this far from Madame. With every step, the air begins to clear.

Eva stops. I run into her shoulder. "Freeze." She steadies me.

I push on her back, eager to get as far from Madame as possible, but she holds firm.

Seconds later, an empty water tower plunges from the collapsing roof of a Fringe building in front of us, cutting through what's left of the cloud on its way to the ground. The structure collides with the dirt and smashes inward like an aluminum can. I pull Eva to the ground and we huddle as a tsunami of dirt and debris comes at us. Shards scrape against my back, ripping holes in my shirt. My hair whips back behind me, caked with dust.

Once the air settles, we resume our sprint, moving through the tunnels created by the sideways support beams of the tower that stretch in diagonals from the ground.

The air clears considerably past the structure. Soon, we can breathe again.

I cough. "What if Ryel doesn't come back?"

"We have to find our shuttle," she says.

I point back into the expanding cloud. "It's all the way on the other side. There's no way."

"Then a cruiser," she pants. "We'll steal a cruiser."

"I'm more worried about—"

"Jesse!" A voice comes from beyond the water tower. I turn to see Ryel crawling through the wreckage. Two others follow him. I move forward, watching the dust intently, waiting to see who it is.

Avery and Cassius stumble behind him, covered with dirt and sweat. I run forward and grab Avery in my arms. Her hands stay limp at her sides. Cassius pulls me away, breathing heavy. "I saw Madame fall. I can't hear her in my head."

Eva motions us into a nearby alley. "This way!"

We run, all five of us, though each scratchy breath sends bristles of pain through our chests. We arrive on a clear street, free from the carnage of the last one. A building to our right lies wrecked and gutted. Flames lick the air from charred holes. A cloud of smoke rises into the sky, but the wind pushes it back toward the soldiers, away from us.

Cassius stops. "Do you hear that?"

We pause to listen. There are so many noises in Syracuse right now, but I realize almost instantly what he's referring to. He'd know the sound better than me, after all.

A cruiser alarm system.

Eva claps her hands together. "It's coming from over there." She points to a second alleyway, farther from the cloud.

Cassius nods. "If we can get inside, I can get us into the air."

Ryel pushes forward. "Let me."

Cassius flashes him an incredulous look, then meets my eyes. "Who's he?"

"Don't worry," I say. "He's a pilot."

"Alright." He cups his ears. "We've got to hurry. Before Madame gets back inside my head."

We dash into the alley and are immediately greeted by the sight of a government-cruiser loading ramp open against the ground. Cassius crouches to look into the body of the cruiser. After a moment's consideration, he motions us forward. "It's clear."

We rush up the ramp into the cabin. Ryel moves to the cockpit. Avery collapses on the first available seat, breathing hard. The ship rocks with the onset of energy—filtered Pearl energy, most likely. If Ryel knew what was powering this thing, he might not have been so eager to climb into the driver's seat. I wish we had the luxury of worrying about it, but right now we need to get away.

The ramp begins to close behind us. Dust flows into the ship from the faraway cloud. The temperature control kicks in and bathes us in cool air while sucking any foreign particles from the atmosphere.

We're just about to take off when something slams

against the cruiser's backside. I watch as the ramp shudders and a hand grips the top, several feet from where it will close and seal. Moments later, a face pulls itself up to the crack, followed by a thin body. Soon, a boy falls forward, looping around and colliding with the floor. A knife slides to the far corner of the cabin. The kid pulls himself to his knees and grabs for the weapon. The ramp seals behind him.

He turns and stares at us, eyes wild, heart beating so fast I can practically see it. I recognize him instantly.

Avery tenses. "Theo!"

The kid coughs, gripping the knife tightly. "Nice try, guys, but I'm sure you didn't think it was gonna be that easy."

22

Cassius grabbed onto the nearest railing to avoid stumbling. Theo crashed into the secured ramp behind him as they rocketed into the sky, past any remaining fragments of the dust cloud, away from Syracuse.

When the cruiser stabilized, Eva lunged at the kid, trying to force the knife from his hand. Theo ducked and kneed her in the gut, sending her slumping to the corner. He raised the knife.

"Stop!" Fisher yelled.

Theo spun to face Cassius, eyes wide. "Turn this thing around."

Eva remained on all fours, unable to right herself.

"Who's piloting?" Theo pointed the knife at Eva. "Tell them to bring this down or I'll kill her."

Cassius waited a moment, just to make sure he couldn't hear even the slightest echo of Madame's voice in his head. His brows lowered, eyes locked on Theo's. He was free from her. Even if it was only temporary, he had the opportunity he'd been waiting for. His fingers clenched into fists.

Theo's expression wavered as he glanced around the cabin.

"You're outnumbered," Fisher said.

Cassius kept his attention on the boy. "Don't underestimate him."

Theo gave a weak smile. "That's right."

"What was that you said down there?" Cassius took a step forward. "Madame won't let you kill me?"

Theo backed away, still pointing the blade of the knife at Eva. "She didn't say anything about this one. Turn the cruiser around or she gets it."

"Not a good idea."

"You can barely move," Theo scoffed. "She's got you harnessed—"

"I ran," Cassius said. "All the way through the dust cloud, on my own." He advanced another step.

Theo brought the knife in front of him, pointing it at arm's length, shoulders tensed. "She'll find you, no matter where you go. It's only a setback."

Cassius smiled, enjoying the panicked look in the boy's eyes—like a cornered animal. "You know," he started, "when I was your age we had our first parachuting trials. Back at the Lodge, with Lieutenant Henrich. I still remember the control sequence. There's a button to seal the back end of the cruiser. Then you strap yourself in and open the ramp. When you're ready, you let go and release your chute. Did they take you parachuting yet, kid?"

Theo's eyes widened, lip trembling. "What are you getting at?"

"I'm just saying," Cassius continued. "Maybe it's time. Except I don't know if we have any chutes onboard. You might need to go without. We could open the hatch. There's not a lot to grip onto, and we're awfully high."

Theo kept the blade in front of him. "I took down three fully grown men back there. Three times my size. I could do the same here."

"Could you?"

Theo's feet arched. He tensed, then lunged forward.

Cassius darted to the right, but Theo's knife connected with his side, spilling a splotch of blood that stained the far wall. It had been too long—shackled to the wall in the Lodge, no control of his own body. He grimaced as he shifted away from the boy. Theo spun around for another attack. Fisher rushed forward, but the kid swiped at the air with the knife, keeping him at bay.

Theo turned, momentarily distracted. Taking a quick breath, Cassius seized the moment and jumped on him, twisting Theo's right arm behind his back. The boy tried in vain to slash at his stomach. Cassius swung him around and forced him into the wall. Theo kicked at his legs, but before he could do any damage Cassius grabbed him by the hair and slammed his head into metal.

That was it. One move and Theo sunk to the floor, unconscious. His knife clattered to the ground beside him.

Silence.

Cassius gripped his wounded side. "Bandages, Fisher. Please."

Fisher glanced around. "Where?"

"Cabinet to the right," he pointed. "Above Avery's head."

Avery stood and pulled a silver first aid kit from the overhead storage. Cassius lifted his shirt to reveal a dark-red slice mark as long as a finger. Trails of blood ran down his side and stained the waist of his trousers. It wouldn't be the only incision today. The device in his neck needed to come out. So did Avery's.

Fisher pulled a wad of bandages from the kit and started unwrapping them. Eva crouched beside him, still coughing from her injury. Eventually, he let her take over, which was good because she knew what she was doing.

"We'll need a scalpel," Cassius wheezed. "And tweezers."

Fisher winced. "For what?"

He pointed to the back of his neck. "Madame put something inside of me. She was controlling my actions." He motioned to Avery. "Her too."

Fisher turned to look at her. "That's why you were acting so strange?"

"I'm sorry," Avery said. "I couldn't … I couldn't break through. She was using me to get to you."

"And it won't happen again." Cassius leaned against the wall and glanced down at Theo, who lay crumpled on his side. "If I didn't think it'd wake him back up, I'd kick him."

"Who is he?" Fisher crouched low and checked for extra weapons on the boy's belt.

"One of Madame's kids," Cassius replied.

"Another one?"

Cassius nodded.

"What are we gonna do with him?"

"I told you," Cassius said. "Throw him out the back."

Eva stood. "He could be useful. Maybe he knows something we don't."

"He's dangerous. He's not what he looks like."

"Still," she replied. "There have got to be some sort of restraints in here. We'll tie him to one of the seats. Hide the knife."

Cassius sighed. "If that's what you want to do." He winced as pain spread through his side. "Now in that same compartment as the first aid … maybe one down … is a PSK. We'll need that."

Fisher backed up. "PSK?"

"Portable Surgery Kit. I can show you what to do, up to a point." He glanced at Avery. "I hope you're ready for a little discomfort."

She nodded without a word.

After restraining Theo and gathering the kit, Cassius took the lead. He demonstrated the safest technique on Avery's neck while Fisher and Eva watched. It had been a long time since his last emergency medical training module, but he'd always been a quick study. More than that, he'd had personal experience, as the scar on his wrist confirmed.

Fisher flinched as the tweezers went into the small cut Cassius made in Avery's skin. The kit had been well stocked with vials of localized anesthesia, but that didn't mean there'd be no pain at all.

In the end, thankfully, the device had been attached close to the surface. No need to go deep and risk brushing the spinal cord. Within a few minutes, he held the tiny chip between the tongs of the tweezers and began patching her up.

Next, it was his turn. He administered the anesthesia himself.

"It's okay." Eva grabbed a sterile set of tools. "I've got it."

Cassius grit his teeth and closed his eyes, eager to take his mind to another place altogether.

————

An hour later, the cockpit's windshield was a floor-to-ceiling view of unencumbered sky. Cassius stood in the center of the small chamber, hands on hips. The anesthesia was beginning to wear off, but he felt alright. He'd live, and that was the most important consideration.

The door behind him opened, followed by footsteps. Another second and Fisher was standing beside him.

Cassius barely turned. "Aren't you going to talk to your girlfriend?"

"She's resting," Fisher replied.

He nodded. "I can't believe you came to Syracuse."

"What was I supposed to do?"

"Without escorts or a fleet of shuttles or anything."

He stepped toward the pilot's seat. Fisher's new friend was focused on the sky. All Cassius could see was the back of his head. "I can take over. Flying will give me something to do."

The pilot turned around. It wasn't the first time Cassius had seen his face, but free from the adrenaline and horror of the Fringe Town skirmish, it was the first time he'd looked at him properly.

Realization flooded his mind. "I don't believe it. This is the guy from the rooftop. Last spring."

"Ryel," the pilot answered. "And you're Cassius Stevenson. We've got a lot to talk about."

Cassius sighed. "Set a southbound course down the coast."

"Swarms?" Fisher asked.

Everyone knew that the nearer you got to the equator, the more bugs you'd find. There were parts of the Fringes that were uninhabitable down south—too hot and clogged with insects.

"They're less likely to follow us south," he said. "And it will give Ryel here time to tell me everything he knows."

23

The air begins to darken once we cross the border into Georgia. It's got nothing to do with the sun. It's the swarms.

We're high enough to dodge most of them, but they're still visible—dark blotches of prickly movement knocking against the sides of the cruiser like spitballs.

I watch Cassius's face as Ryel recounts everything he's told me.

Haven. Ridium. Matigo.

Despite all the crap we've just been through, his tone is more patient than it was with me and Eva.

Cassius doesn't interrupt once. That's probably the biggest contributor to Ryel's improved mood. He listens with a blank expression, like a soldier waiting to hear his orders.

As I stare at his face—impenetrable, hard—I wish I could be like that. This is big, emotional stuff. But from the outside, at least, Cassius is able to compartmentalize it. Instead of emotional outbursts, he sits calmly in the co-pilot's chair. Even at the mention of our parents, his expression never wavers. He glances out the window at times, closes his eyes here and there, but never speaks until Ryel's finished.

And when he does, it's clear and confident. "So what do we do?"

Ryel turns back to the console. "The only thing we *can* do. Free an army of Drifters and hope that we're not too late."

I stand from my perch on the floor and stretch. "Tell us more about Haven. What was it like?"

Ryel's brows rise. I haven't been able to get much out of him thus far, but now that Cassius is here, he seems more willing to talk.

"I suppose it wasn't completely unlike Earth," he starts. "At least in the beginning. Rural towns and cities, usually separated by vast fields and forests. It wasn't until the first Shifter was born that things really started to change. It's unclear exactly why those on Haven began to evolve with the ability to manipulate Ridium, but the gift was bestowed upon only a few. A recessive gene, I suppose." He glances at Cassius's bracelet. "Before Shifters, Ridium had been a natural part of Haven's crust for hundreds of years. It didn't have much of a purpose ... or so we thought.

"Shifters ushered in a new era. Those who could harness Ridium changed our planet. They were revered. Before long, the element formed the foundation of our buildings ... developed our technology. It was everywhere. Small farm towns transformed into vast metropolises of dark uniformity in a matter of years. In fact, many in the

Resistance would argue that the harvesting of Ridium was what destroyed our planet in the end. Without it, Haven's crust began to decompose. All of our cities were built on a collapsing world. Like laying a rock on top of a tower of paper."

He sighs. "In its dying decades, Haven became a dry, lifeless planet. That's the only way I've ever known it to be."

"Like the Fringes," Cassius says.

"I suppose. In the beginning, the majority of us supported the Shifters and the dynasty they'd built for themselves. It was all we knew. In fact, up until the last few months, I was a pilot in Matigo's army against the Resistance myself. But I defected. Thankfully."

I run my hand across the cold, black bracelet around my wrist. "I can't believe—"

A flash of red overtakes the windshield as something darts in front of us. The bracelet shudders, then shakes uncontrollably. Cassius's too. Our ship lurches.

It's over in a second. The sky clears and the cruiser levels out.

"What was—" I stop myself as I notice Ryel's body, slumped over on the console.

The cruiser dips.

Cassius springs from his seat and places a hand on Ryel's neck. After a moment, he glances at me. "He's unconscious." He reaches to take hold of the steering. "Whatever that was, the sight of it knocked him out."

I move to the front of the cockpit and stare out the

window, searching the blue sky for a hint of crimson. "I know what it is. It's from the red Pearl. He followed us all the way from Siberia."

"Red Pearl?"

I grab my hair. "I don't know ... It wasn't this bright last time."

Another flash, and this one is twice as blinding. The Drifter soars right in front of us, lingering long enough that I see the outline of his body.

Just as he moves out of sight, my bracelet yanks forward and throws me into the windshield.

Cassius manages to hold onto the steering, even as his bracelet pulls to the side. "I'm taking us into the swarm." He struggles. "Nothing would be stupid enough to follow us there."

I don't have time to argue before he begins the descent. The nose of the cruiser dips until what's left of the sky outside is replaced by the dark, moving cloud beneath us.

I swallow, watching the swarm grow closer. Within moments, I can see the individual bugs. Locusts, mostly. Flies. What had started as a blob of movement is now an enormous hive of buzzing wings. Clicking, scratchy legs. And eyes. Thousands of them.

We plunge into the darkness. Torrents of insects slam into the windshield, popping into splotch after splotch of brown, goopy liquid. Cassius pulls up on the steering, trying to level us out so we can land, but we can't see a thing outside. The cockpit lighting works overtime to compensate for the instant shade thrown over the room.

The buzz, even muted by the cruiser, is all-encompassing. A surge of activity bashes the ship from every angle. When we hit dirt and settle down, I hardly notice. The engines die, but it's still noisy. A chaotic pulse. Constant.

The cruiser suddenly seems ten times smaller—a tiny toy, easily broken.

The door behind us opens. I hear Eva's voice before I see her.

"What do you think you're doing?" She notices Ryel's unconscious body and recoils. "Is he okay?"

Cassius rubs his bracelet. "We're being followed."

"So you brought us into a swarm? You think this is a good idea?" She points behind her. "With Unified Party boy tied up back there?"

"We didn't have a lot of options," Cassius responds. "At least we lost him. I think."

My bracelet rattles. Cassius and I exchange glances. Neither of us has to say a word.

The maelstrom of sound outside intensifies. Avery steps into the cockpit, rubbing her arms.

"I hate bugs," she says. "You guys better have a good reason for this."

Eva frowns. "It was a hair-trigger response. How's Theo?"

"Still unconscious."

I hold up a hand. "Wait. Do you hear that? Is it just me, or is the buzzing getting quieter?"

We fall silent, listening to the sounds outside begin to fade. It's still there, but more distant somehow—muffled.

I rush to the console. "How do you clean the windshield?"

Cassius moves to my side and slams the top of a diamond-shaped button. I watch as a mist sprays over the outside of the glass. Four wipers slide across the glass, one from each corner. I peer through as the Fringe heat dries what's left of the cleanser.

Then I see him. The man from the red Pearl, standing mere yards from the front of our cruiser. My bracelet hums, shaking against my thigh.

The others notice him too. Everyone freezes.

The sight steals my breath. The swarm is pushed back in a dome around him as if an invisible force is keeping them at bay. The entire cruiser's surrounded by an air bubble of clear space, half a mile high and equally as wide. The swarm waits, pushed back against the sky like a living, moving Bio-Net.

The Drifter stares at me. Even from his distance, I meet his eyes. Connect.

I know what I've got to do.

24

Cassius pulls on my shoulder. "Back in the cabin. Now."

I allow him to guide me through the door, but I don't take my eyes off the Drifter the entire time. Not until the panels close in front of me and block the view of the cockpit.

He blocks the way, forcing me to meet his eyes. "What do you know about that thing?"

Eva moves past Theo's slumped-over body toward the weapons cabinet. "That's the guy who pushed you out of the Academy, isn't it? What do you think we need...blasters?"

I shake my head.

"We're not going to be able to hide back here forever," Avery says. "What about Ryel?"

She's answered by a loud scrape along the wall, right behind her. She bounds forward, startled at the sudden noise.

Eva freezes. "What was that?"

I rush to the side of the cabin. A second scrape pulls along the hull outside, filling the cabin with an eerie squeal. I lay my shaking palm against the wall and close my eyes to see if I feel anything. My bracelet hums.

Cassius grabs his wrist. "Say something, Fisher."

I turn. "He didn't kill me." I'm greeted by incredulous looks from the others. "When we were falling from the hole in the side of the Academy, he could've killed me, but he didn't. He saved me."

The scraping stops. For a moment, it's completely silent. Even the swarm is a hushed buzz in the background. Then a pair of noisy thumps violently interrupt the stillness. Something slams against the wall. The cruiser shudders, then rocks gently back and forth.

Theo's head bolts up. His eyes widen as he comes back to consciousness. His arms tense, trying to lift through the bonds that keep him restrained to the seat. He takes sharp, short breaths. "Let me go." His voice is a whisper at first, barely audible. Then he repeats himself, louder. "Let me go!" He hears the buzzing. I can tell because his entire expression changes. His mouth drops open as he glances from wall to wall. "Where the hell are we? Where did you take me?"

Another heavy thump sounds on the ceiling. Everyone ducks. Theo's eyes scan the cabin. "What's going on?" He swallows. "What's going on?"

"Shh." I extend a hand to stop him, keeping my attention on the ceiling the entire time. The thumps turn into footsteps. The Drifter's climbed onto the roof. Heavy boots tromp against metal.

Theo glares at Eva. His shrill voice pierces the silence. "You've got my knife. When I get loose, I'm gonna rip your throat out just for that."

Eva grabs the knife and slips it in the side of her boot. "That's not happening."

My shoulders tense. "I wanna go outside."

"What?"

"No. Listen, Eva. He's followed me all the way here from Siberia. The way he looks at me ... I think maybe there's something he's trying to tell me."

Cassius shakes his head. "He knocked Ryel unconscious."

"We don't know that," I reply. "It was the flash ... the red energy or something else."

"So if the energy can do that to Ryel, what'll it do to you?" Cassius glances at the ceiling as another footstep reverberates across the metal.

"Besides," Avery starts, "you can't go into the swarm."

"He pushed it away for me." I look around from cabinet to cabinet. "The bugs, they're not close anymore. I'll be safe. There's gotta be some gear hanging around this place. I'll suit up ... even take a com-pad. I'm not worried about the swarm. I need to go. There's something about him."

Cassius pushes past me and heads to a compartment at the far end of the cabin. "Then I'm going with you." He pulls open the door and frowns. I move to his side and peer in. A dark suit hangs against the wall, sealed into a tight line of plastic. Cassius bangs his fist on the wall. "There's only one."

"It's okay." I pull out the bodysuit and tear at the bag. "I can do this. And if something goes wrong, I've got all of you to help me out."

Before anyone can argue, I pull the suit over my clothes, zipping up the front and fastening the security locks. "Hand me the helmet." I pull the thick gloves over my fingers. Instantly, the suit's temperature regulator kicks in, cooling my body to acceptable levels.

Cassius passes me the dark helmet. "You sure about this?"

I grab it from his hands without a word and secure it over my head. My breath quickens. I can see out the circular window in front, but I still feel constricted. Small spaces have never been my strong suit. I blame it on all that time crammed inside a Pearl, rocketing toward Earth. It's an unconscious thing. I need to control it.

"I'll open the side door." My voice streams from a pair of speakers below my jaw. Everyone looks murkier with the helmet on, slightly darker and farther away. I step past Eva.

"I don't like this, Jesse."

I pause, meeting her eyes. "You never do."

Avery's voice comes from somewhere behind me. "We'll be watching out the windows. If anything goes wrong…"

Cassius grabs the security handle to open the door. "Don't do anything stupid, okay? Take it slow."

I nod. Then, after a moment's pause, he relinquishes his hold on the handle. I grab it immediately and swing open the door. Usually, in a place this close to the equator, we'd be greeted by an endless parade of locusts spilling into the cabin like a tidal wave. Right now, there's nothing. I stop to stare at the swarm pushed back in the distance, a curved wall of buzzing wings stretched into a dome above the ship.

As soon as my feet touch the dirt, I shut the door behind me. No sense risking it.

The ground feels distant under my boots. Inside the suit, I feel contained. Heavier. Taller. I see now why Unified Party soldiers have always been so intimidating. I feel more powerful standing here than I ever did in a Skyship uniform.

Once I'm a few yards from the cruiser, I turn and peer up at the roof. The sound of the swarm drones around me. I try to tune it out.

The red energy streams from the top of the cruiser like a beacon. Its rays pulse in every direction. Beams intersect the swarm wall like lasers pushing them back. I step away until the Drifter comes into view. I focus on the fragment of black hanging on the necklace at his chest and know instantly what it is. Ridium. Not a huge amount, but there's got to be a reason it's there.

I take a deep breath, keeping my eyes on his face. "Hello?" My voice sounds robotic through the speakers in the helmet. Unnatural.

The figure turns immediately. He steps to the edge of the ship, crouches low, and stares down at me. He's got that same vacant look in his eyes. He's reacting, not recognizing. I don't know what's beyond those eyes, if anything.

"Remember? You … we … "

The Drifter takes a high leap into the air and jumps from the edge of the cruiser. For a moment it looks like he's going to fly again, but his feet touch the ground. It all happens in silence, like the pounce of a cat.

He brings himself to full height, arms at his sides. His thick brown hair, obscured by the red glow, blows gently in the breeze. He wears clothing like Ryel's loose-fitting, light-colored garments that suggest Fringe living. Except there's no way this guy's from the Fringes.

The humming of my bracelet intensifies under my glove. It thrashes around, irritating my skin. It doesn't have much space to move, but the way it's shaking I'm afraid it's going to burn right through my suit. I glance over my shoulder at the swarm. The wall of insects stays intact, pushed safely away from us.

I approach the Drifter. Small, careful footsteps. "Who are you? Do you know my parents? Do you know who I am?"

He cocks his head to the side like a dog might. Only it's not cute. Instead, there's a mild threat to it, like he's sizing me up.

"Do you speak?" I remember the girl in Seattle last spring, and hope if I say the right thing his language processing will kick in. "English?"

His lips stay closed, body still.

I take another step forward. "I thought maybe you knew who I was, the way you looked at me. You've been following me. I … something called to me when your Pearl landed. I couldn't touch it, but I knew it was there."

Still no answer. His brows furrow. His head remains still. The swarm drones on.

With a sigh I grab hold of my fingers and pull the glove from my right hand. My bracelet shifts uncontrollably now, spinning around my wrist so fast that it practically burns. I adjust the sleeve on my suit and hold my arm in front of my chest. "My parents gave me this. Ryel said it's made from Ridium. Does that mean anything to you? I don't know what it's for, but it goes crazy every time you're near. That must mean something."

The Drifter's head clicks back into place. He blinks and lowers his chin. The bracelet forces my arm back to my side.

I shake my head. This is going nowhere.

Carefully, I remove the helmet. Maybe if he can hear me without the speakers, he'll understand. I try not to look at the cruiser. I imagine they're panicking right now, watching me slowly dismantle my suit. Cassius is probably about ready to jump out the door.

The moment the helmet's off, the buzzing of the swarm becomes all-consuming. No wonder the Drifter couldn't hear me before.

The heat's more dense and humid than I've ever experienced. It's worse in the southern Fringes. No wonder bugs are the only ones who thrive in it. I hardly want to open my mouth for fear of letting the thick air in.

But if I get answers, it'll be worth it.

"Do you understand?" I shout. "Are you understanding any of this?"

The Drifter's eyes widen slightly. His body shows no reaction.

"Please," I continue. Sweat drips down the back of my neck. "Just tell me who you are."

My bracelet stops. The Drifter raises his right hand and points at me.

I'm thrown off my feet onto my back. My hands fly over my head. The helmet rolls into the distance until it's swallowed by the swarm.

Intense warmth pushes on my chest. I cry out in pain as something burrows under my suit and cuts across my skin. It's like boiling water or the edge of a knife heated by flames. I grab the zipper and try to pull the thing away from me, but I know it won't help. Whatever this is, it's inside. Coming out. There's no stopping it.

The pain continues, blistering and ceaseless. I fear I might pass out. I expect to feel the slick stickiness of blood under my shirt. But liquid would boil. There's nothing.

I writhe in the dirt, kicking up clouds around my feet, unable to stand. I manage to turn on my side and stare at the Drifter from the knee down.

The burning stops.

I grab my chest, heart pounding out of time. It's reassurance that I'm still alive. I yell, but the Fringe air burns my throat too.

I watch the Drifter's legs pull out of sight as he rockets into the sky. Red energy blankets my vision for a moment before it disappears altogether. He's gone.

The buzzing intensifies around me. I roll on my back in time to see walls close in. The swarm descends.

25

They're everywhere.

I can't even move before they're all over me. Legs. Wings. Prickly bodies collide with my suit. Thousands of them. More.

I pull my head inward and close my eyes. My mouth's shut, but I can feel them crawling around my ears, getting stuck in my hair. Too long and I won't be able to breathe properly. It's only a matter of time before a fly tries to work its way into my nostril.

The beat of the wings is deafening, like the thrusters of a Skyship right over my head. It's not a buzz anymore. It's a solid force, an apocalyptic scream.

All the while, my chest stings like someone's tried to cut my heart open. I've never felt pain like this. It nearly drowns out the horror of the swarm. I panic, convinced that the bugs will find a way past my suit, into the wound. Then they'll be inside of me, crawling and biting and multiplying.

I raise my right hand and swat through the air, only to feel a flurry of tics and scratches against my fingers. I kick out, which dislodges a cloud of insects. But they come back. I'm outnumbered, billions to one.

At first I think the pull on my ankles is the swarm somehow organizing itself against me. I'm dragged backward across the ground, too rattled to scream. I fight the grip around my ankle, but nothing comes of it.

My feet slam into the ground and I see a shadow push through the swarm overhead. A figure bends low and grips me by the shoulders. I squirm away, convinced that the Drifter has come back to finish me off. As I push, Cassius's face cuts through the wall of insects.

His eyes are closed. His left hand moves up my shoulder until his fingers hit my neck. With the energy I have left, I grab just below his elbow and help him to pull me to my feet.

He guides me through the pulsing swarm. I stumble behind him, waves of insects pelting me. I've got no idea which direction we're headed. Maybe Cassius doesn't, either. We struggle through a churning sea of black and brown. Pretty soon, it'll be suffocation. Buried alive.

I grip his hand, terrified of slipping away. My nails dig into his skin. It's the least of his worries.

We stop.

I hear a loud thump as his fist pounds against metal. He backs into my foot. I struggle to keep my mouth closed, but all I want to do is scream. My chest burns. I imagine skin melting away, eating into bone.

A rectangle of light cuts through the swarm in front of

us. Cassius yanks me forward. I lose my footing and crash onto metal. Sideways waterfalls of insects spill into the cabin of the cruiser before Eva seals the door shut behind us. They stream to the ceiling and buzz around the light panels in whirling riptides.

Someone rushes to my side. I don't know who. I lie on my stomach and feel the cold metal press against my chest.

"Is he okay?" I hear someone say.

"Jesse?"

"Jesse!"

Then, silence.

———

I wake with a shocked yelp, convulsing from head to toe until my body gets itself under control. I'm on my back now, still in the Unified Party suit. I rip the collar open and yank on the zipper. I pull the rest of the outfit from my body and toss it away. The others stare at me in silence, too concerned and confused to say anything.

Avery kneels at my side. "Jesse, thank god! What happened?"

My chest feels like someone's scraped a hot iron against it.

Without answering, I grab the back of my shirt and pull it over my head.

I hear them gasp.

I look down at my chest, trembling with fear of what I might find.

Even upside down, I can tell it's bad.

Scrawled across my skin are symbols. It's as if someone took a razor and wrote across my body, except there's no blood. Five brown-red burn marks of varying shapes and sizes.

Eva backs away, cupping her hand over her mouth. "Oh, Jesse."

"What did he do to you?" Avery grabs my arm.

Cassius reclines in a seat across from Theo, scuffed up and coughing, but alive.

A diluted stream of bugs circle around the lights overhead. The floor's spotted with dead locust carcasses. I keep an eye on the living as I finally speak.

"It feels like someone lit me on fire." My voice is barely above a whisper. "What's on me? What is that stuff?"

Ryel emerges from somewhere behind my shoulder.

I stare up at him. "You're okay."

He nods before kneeling at my feet. His eyes narrow as he analyzes the symbols on my chest. After a moment of consideration, his eyes meet mine. His expression gives away nothing. "May I?"

I'm not sure what he means, but I nod anyway. Something about his voice calms me.

Ryel scoots forward and extends his arm. As he leans in, his fingers make contact with the largest of the symbols. His face tenses in pain. His eyes close. Suddenly, the burning in my chest starts to numb. It dulls from raw stinging into something more distant. Then, when it's nearly gone, Ryel pulls back.

He lets out a noisy breath, like someone's kicked him in the gut, and rests his clasped hands in his waist. "Can you sit up?"

I push on my elbows and pull my body from its half-lying, half-sitting position.

Ryel rubs his temple. "The last sliver of Pearl energy, from deep inside of me. You'll be more comfortable now." He watches my fingers, as if he expects me to pick at the symbols. "Don't touch them, not until they begin to fade. You'll be thankful that you didn't."

Eva moves in closer. "What are those things?"

"A message."

I shake my head, panicking more as I think about it. "I don't understand. What did he do to me?"

I hear Theo's voice in the distance. "Looks like knife work."

Nobody responds.

Ryel shakes his head. "That wasn't a friend out there. The energy alone was too much for me to bear. I felt it . . . the pain. It's like poison."

Eva kneels beside him. "What do those symbols say?"

"A warning," Ryel replies, and I can tell by his tone that he doesn't want to say any more.

I wince as the burning flares up again.

Eva stares at Ryel, eyes wide. "Well?"

He swallows.

Cassius coughs. "Tell us."

Ryel nods before taking a deep breath. "I am already here." He pauses. "That's what it says. *I am already here.*"

Cassius stands and shakes his head. "I'm getting us out of the swarm, as far away from that thing as possible."

Ryel stays frozen as Cassius darts to the cockpit. Nobody says a word.

The words filter through my ears without sticking. I close my eyes and try to float away, but I can still hear the buzzing outside. There's no escaping this. When I open my eyes, Ryel's staring at me, so pointed and direct that I can barely look back.

"I don't know how he's tracing you," Ryel says. "But it seems clear to me who this message is from."

My lip trembles. I don't want to say it.

"I am already here," he repeats. Lines begin to show on his forehead. "It can't be. There were rumors of Matigo's exile, but no evidence that he'd made it to Earth."

I grab my shirt from the floor and pull it over my head. The cloth scratches the symbols, triggering a short shock of pain. I try to ignore it. I pull my knees close to my chest and rest my head, shaking. I breathe deep and try to think rationally. The discomfort fades, replaced by a cold fear. "It could mean something else."

Ryel frowns. "We must prepare for the worst."

"If Matigo's really on this planet..."

"Then the invasion has begun," he whispers.

26

Sunlight peeks through the upper windows on either side of the cabin as we ascend from the cloud of insects. Cassius brings us into the air without hesitation. I'm not sure where he thinks we're going.

Ryel stands, keeping his eyes on me. "Do you feel strong enough to walk?"

I raise my head to answer, but don't get anything out before the overhead speakers click on. Cassius's voice streams through the cabin. "We've got trouble," he says. "Three ships on the radar. I don't recognize any of them."

Eva straightens to attention. "I'll head to the cockpit and see if I can help him."

Before she can get there, the entire cabin shudders. The gray siding of a ship barrels past our starboard, perilously close. We tilt in its wake before Cassius stabilizes the cruiser. A second ship jostles us again, shooting past the opposite side.

Eva falls to the ground.

Avery grabs hold of her seat. "These are Academy ships." She glances out the window. "I'd recognize them anywhere."

Ryel staggers to the far side of the cabin, hand on his head. Cassius's voice sounds from the speakers again. "They've got us surrounded. Damn, these things are quick."

I swallow. The pain is nothing now compared with what's outside. "Alkine." I grit my teeth. "He's found us."

We rush into the cockpit. Cassius sits at the steering, banging his fist on the wall. Beyond the windshield I see a pair of Academy ships—the two that passed us moments ago. They're flying close enough that I can read the identification numbers on their tail fins.

"There's one behind us too," Cassius says.

Eva rushes to the copilot's seat. Cassius shakes his head. "Should we open fire?"

Avery steadies herself against the rocking cockpit. "We do that, and we might as well declare war on the Academy."

"They know I'm inside," I say. "That must be it. They've probably been tracking us ever since we left Siberia."

Eva drums her fingers on the console. "I did the best I could. The radar—"

"It's too late now." I press my hands against my head, cursing. "Is there any way of hitting them without killing anybody?"

"At this range?" Cassius laughs. "I wouldn't bet on it."

"We can't open fire," Eva says. "Avery's right. It would be seen as an act of—"

"Wait." Cassius motions to the radar. "Do you see that?"

Eva leans in to examine the display. "The one behind us is pulling away."

"Why would it do that?" I scoot between them.

Cassius grips the steering, sweat pooling on his hands. "I don't like this…"

An explosion rumbles behind us. The console lights flash red. Then the alarms confirm it.

"They've clipped our wing!" Cassius releases his grip.

Avery hunkers against the wall. "They're opening fire on us?"

The cruiser takes a violent dip to the left. I try to keep my balance but end up crashing to the floor.

"The stabilizer!"

We begin to pinwheel. The Academy's ships pull away from our nose as we lose altitude.

"Strap yourselves in," Cassius warns.

A second burst comes from below us. By the sound of it, this one's worse. Dark smoke obscures the sky outside. A deafening whistling pierces the air as we plummet.

"Strap in!" Cassius repeats. "Find a seat! I'm gonna have to pull one hell of an emergency landing."

I scoot along the floor, fighting gravity as I reach for the nearest pull-down seat. Once I've got it, I grab onto the belt and force myself sideways up onto the cushion. In moments, I've got the belt secured around my waist. The cruiser rocks in a nauseous seesaw.

I watch as Avery and Ryel struggle to reach the remaining seats at the backside of the cockpit. The nose of the cruiser dive-bombs into the swarm, spearing hundreds of thousands of insects. They splat against the windshield, covering it in thick splotches of oily gunk. It's impossible to see. It might as well be dark out.

Pellets slam against all sides of the cruiser, helpless locusts colliding without a chance. Then, silence.

The skies open up. Insect guts fly from our windshield until there are just enough holes of light to see through. The swarm is behind us.

But the ground...

Cassius does what he can to pull us up. The underbelly of the cruiser slides into the dirt with an awful scrape. Sparks sizzle like fireworks as we speed along the ground. Too many and we'll catch on fire. Too many and we'll explode.

But we begin to slow. The scraping quiets. I don't know where we are, or what's outside, but as soon as the cruiser stops moving, I unclick the seat belt and stand, thankful to be alive.

Cassius bolts from his chair. "We've gotta get out. A couple more seconds and the whole thing could go up in flames."

We rush from the cockpit. Cassius sprints to the back of the cabin and grabs the manual crank.

As the ramp descends and thick Fringe air spills into the ravaged cabin, I notice that Theo's chair is empty. I turn to see his body slumped at the side of the room, face-down along the wall. No movement.

Avery peers around my shoulder. "Is he—"

"I don't know," I mutter, too petrified to go and see.

"Help me with this." Cassius motions Eva to his side. As she takes over the manual crank, he turns and busts open an arms cabinet with his elbow.

Without wasting a moment, he tosses a pistol my way. Avery gets one too. Then Ryel.

When the ramp hits the ground, Cassius gives Eva the last pistol and leads us from the cruiser cabin.

We stumble into the harsh desert landscape. The sun forces my eyes shut. I relax them little by little until it's comfortable to open them all the way. The distant buzzing of the swarm sounds behind us. I don't want to turn and see it.

We stay close, glancing overhead for signs of activity. I don't know where the Academy ships went, but they're not here now.

Cassius curses. "They're leaving us to rot out here. Shoot us down so we'll be easy prey for the vultures."

Eva takes in the horizon. "Alkine would never do something like that."

I glance at Ryel. His eyes narrow. "I hear something."

"The swarm?" I whisper.

"No. It's coming from around … " His words fade as he backs toward the wreckage of the cruiser, treading carefully on the dirt. In moments he's rounded the corner. I tiptoe after, scared to let him out of my sight.

Then I notice them, sitting in the distance. The hazy Fringe atmosphere hides them well. If it wasn't for the reflection of sunlight on metal, I'd think I was imagining things.

Ships, lined in front of our cruiser in wait. From this distance, I can't tell if they're the same ones that shot us down or not. It doesn't matter. They're a problem.

I grab Ryel's shoulder. "Stay close. We don't know who's inside."

Ryel nods. "I don't think we—"

A bullet whizzes through the air, feet from my shoulder. I flatten against the side of the cruiser. The rush of air silences. I look back at Ryel. His mouth hangs open. His pistol falls to the ground.

He doesn't finish his sentence.

Instead, I watch in horror as he topples, face forward, into the dirt.

27

"Ryel!" I fall on my knees beside him and grab onto his shoulder.

His legs tremble before falling still. I watch the clench of his fingers loosen in the dirt.

"Ryel." I shake his shoulder. "Ryel, where did it hit you?"

No answer.

The others join us. I see their shadows before I turn around. They stare down, unable—or unwilling—to speak.

It's not until I hear the tread of boots that I turn back around. And there they are, seven of them. Agents.

In the middle stands Agent Morse, flanked by three on each side. His disappointed expression is framed by a light-weight battle helmet. I scan the length of his arm until I reach his fist. He's armed. They all are.

I stand. My voice comes out a choked whisper. "You shot him."

Morse's brows narrow. "It was self-defense."

"He wasn't gonna hurt you."

Eva pushes forward until she's at my side. "Please tell me that's a stunner."

Morse remains still, his lips a straight, unreadable line.

"He's not moving," I continue. "You *shot* him."

Morse clips his pistol to a holster on his back. "Listen, buddy. You've got no grounds to argue with me right now. Do you know how many regulations you've broken?"

"Oh my god." I stagger back. "You killed him." I glance from agent to agent, shaking my head. "You all killed him."

"Jesse," Morse continues, "you've left us with very few options."

"Did Alkine tell you to do this?"

Morse glances at the nearest agent before answering. "He ordered us to retrieve you. Your transportation has been run to the ground. Mission accomplished."

I look down at Ryel. I can barely stand to meet Morse's eyes. "He was the only one who could tell me anything. He knew about Haven. He knew about the Authority!"

Morse motions for two of the agents to approach us. "Calm down. We'll get you back and make sure—"

Cassius bolts in front of me, hand outstretched before him. I watch as sparks dance between his fingers like a broken transformer ready to burst. "You're not taking him anywhere."

Morse steps back. His face remains firm. "You must be the brother. The Pearlhound."

"Ex," he says. "Take one step closer and I ignite every one of these sparks." He clutches his pistol in the other hand.

"Okay." Morse nods. "We're gonna turn this into a standstill? This is not in your best interest, Fisher."

I move to Cassius's side, pistol raised. Eva and Avery do the same. We're not much against seven armed agents, but it's something. They're not gonna get away with this.

"By any means necessary," Morse continues. "That's what the captain said." He glances over his shoulder at another agent. "Johnson?"

The man jogs backward a few steps before turning and sprinting to the nearest ship.

I squint. His silhouette disappears in the haziness. "What's he doing?"

Morse taps his foot on the dirt. "You wanna play, Fisher? We're gonna play."

"You don't know—"

"No," he interrupts. "*You* don't know. Smuggling some kind of explosive on board the Academy, staging a jailbreak."

I think back to the red Pearl knocking me from the Academy's brig. Falling from the open hole. "It wasn't an explosive."

"Sneaking into a secret bunker," Morse continues. "Hijacking a shuttle and leaving it in the middle of a Fringe town." His eyes widen as he notices my pained expression. "That's right, buddy. We followed you to Syracuse. We followed you all the way to the swarms. The list keeps getting longer, all the things you've done." He pauses. "I don't understand it. The Academy is your home. We've fed you, taken care of you—"

"You haven't done anything," I interrupt.

"Maybe not, but that ship is filled with people that want the best for you. And you're spitting in our faces. Where's the trust, Fisher?"

My hand shakes as I keep the pistol forward. "Locking me up in the brig? Refusing to listen to me? Do you know what it feels like to have an entire chunk of your life tossed out? Maybe it's bad. Maybe I shouldn't even be thinking about it so much, but you haven't even given me the chance to figure any of this out."

Before Morse can respond, an agent to his right pushes forward and removes his helmet. I stare at the guy's youthful face in astonishment. Even when I recognize him, I can't get out his name. Eva has to.

"Bergmann?" she says.

August Bergmann crosses his arms, helmet hanging from the tips of his fingers. "Look, Fisher. Alkine wants you back and he doesn't care how we do it. Cooperate, and I won't have to kick your puny little butt. You know I can do it."

My mouth hangs open. Bergmann's not even out of training yet. He's still probationary. "Does he know you're here?"

Morse steps forward. "Captain Alkine allowed me to make the appropriate arrangements. I thought it would be best to bring men you were familiar with."

Anger seethes inside me. Sure, I'm familiar with Bergmann, but not in a good way.

I watch as Agent Johnson returns from the haze, only he's not alone. A second figure approaches beside him. As they get closer, I realize it's Skandar.

I hear a sharp intake of breath as Eva realizes what she's seeing, but she keeps it at that. Skandar glances over at us. He doesn't smile. His hands are free. I don't see any bruises or marks on his face, but his body language—his posture— seems different than usual.

Morse grabs hold of Skandar's shoulder and pulls him forward. "You've got nowhere to go." His eyes focus on mine, then he nudges Skandar in the side. "Tell him, Harris."

Skandar grits his teeth as he looks up at me. I keep my eyes on Morse for another second before turning. "What is it?"

Skandar shrugs. "Jesse … "

Morse prods him. "Just spit it out, okay?"

Skandar glares at him before continuing. "They brought me back to Alkine's office after those agents captured me. I thought he was gonna be pissed. I thought maybe he'd throw me out of the Academy."

"Go on," Morse coaxes. "He doesn't care what you thought."

He shoves his hands in his pockets, looking like he wants to sink into the dirt and disappear. "Okay." He takes a deep breath. "So instead of throwing me in the brig, he opened a file. It was … it was things they've been saying about you."

My grip loosens on the handle of the pistol. "Who?"

"The Drifters," he mutters. "All sorts of stuff. Good things, bad things. Alkine had organized it all. I don't know… he ran it through programs or whatever it is guys like him do. And he showed me this thing… he called it 'the fork.'"

Eva shakes her head. "What's that supposed to mean?"

Skandar's eyes meet hers, then quickly move away. "It showed these two lines… one pointing up to the right, one to the left. The one on the right had you as some kind of savior. But the one on the left…"

Morse's brows furrow. "Intelligence has led us in two directions, Fisher. Direction One: You use your Pearl powers and save the world from whatever invasion is supposedly at our doorstep. Direction Two: You're the reason for the invasion. You get out—run around here like some kind of fugitive—and something happens. Something triggers. Half of the Drifters we've spoken to warned us to keep you close… said that there are people—*things*—out here that'll find you. It all keeps coming back to one word. Ridium. Whatever the hell that is." He pauses. "I knew you wouldn't hear it from me. That's why I had to bring Harris."

I shake my head. "Ridium." I rub the bracelet against my thigh, then consider the pendant around the red Drifter's neck. That makes me think about the warning scrawled on my chest. I can't feel it anymore in this heat, but I know it's there.

I am already here.

I close my eyes for a second and I can see the symbols—burned flesh.

Morse sighs. "Alkine wanted you safe, yeah, but he also wanted you close until he knew what we were up against. Our intelligence doesn't jibe. It contradicts itself and trails off on tangents. Maybe it's a problem with the translation. But the fork…we've got two overriding roads here, and we can't ignore either one of them."

My grip tightens on the handle of the pistol. "He should've told me. Why didn't he tell me?"

"How are you supposed to explain something like that?" Morse takes a step forward. "How are you supposed to tell a kid that he might be responsible for the invasion of an entire planet?"

Avery moves to my side. "You don't know anything for sure."

"That's right," Morse continues. "And the worst thing you can do is lash out when you don't know the facts. We don't know, Jesse. And until we do, you've gotta stay with us. You might call it a prison, but that's not what it is. The Academy is our base of operations. Gallivanting around in the Fringes? It's getting you nowhere."

"So he lied to me," I say. "Again."

"If Alkine had told you the truth, you'd have gone running off like you always do."

"Yeah?" I glare at him. "Well, I ran off anyway, didn't I?"

Cassius brings down his fist, but keeps the pistol aimed

on Morse. "I don't like this. These guys will say anything to get you back."

I meet Skandar's eyes, analyze his expression. It's not the Skandar I'm used to. He doesn't give me any secret wink or smile to show that he's lying. He barely looks at me at all. He wouldn't play along with this if he didn't believe it was true. Whatever Alkine showed him, it convinced him somehow.

Morse clears his throat. The dryness of the air is getting to him. "Come back with us, Jesse. We're family. We're doing what we can."

I swallow a mouthful of thick atmosphere. "I…"

A voice comes from behind me, breaking my concentration. I glance over my shoulder to see Theo limping toward us, head low and arms at his sides. "What the hell is *this*?" he coughs. It nearly sends him tripping into the dirt, but he catches himself, keeping a slow pace toward the center of our standstill. Sweat drips from his hair. His shirt is torn in at least three places. Even more than usual, he looks like an animal.

I hear the cock of weapons behind me as every Academy pistol locks onto the boy.

Theo continues to approach. His right foot drags along the dirt. He coughs into his arm again, then pulls the sticky hair from his face. "Leave me in there like you thought I was dead," he continues. "Like you *wanted* me to die." He stares at the ground as he mumbles. I can barely see his face.

Avery moves to let him pass. He stops several feet behind me.

Morse motions for the other agents to hold their fire. "It's just a kid."

Theo cackles under his breath, which only elicits more coughing. I picture his body lying against the wall, still.

Morse frowns. "This a Fringer you picked up, Fisher?"

I shake my head.

Theo takes a deep breath. "You're freaking useless. All of you." He coughs again. "Jeez, I feel like I'm about to puke."

He raises his head and stares at us all for the first time. Avery gasps. I take a step back from the shock of it.

Theo's eyes glow a bright red—a glow that matches the energy from the red Drifter. Gone are the pupils and whites. It's pure light, like someone carved out his eyes and replaced them with tiny generators.

Sweat pools on his face. His legs shake beneath him.

The agents raise their weapons again. Morse shouts, "What's wrong with him?"

Cassius puts more distance between himself and the boy. "I don't know."

Theo smiles. "Did you morons do something to me when I wasn't looking?"

Bergmann nudges Morse's shoulder. "Shoot and ask questions later. That's what I say."

Theo stretches his right hand into the air, waving it in slow ripples like he can barely keep it up. "I feel like I swallowed a Pearl."

Morse tightens his finger against the trigger. "You gonna tell me who this kid is, Fisher, or am I gonna have to shoot?"

I grit my teeth.

Theo's lips curl into a wide smile and his hand drops to his side. Despite my better judgment, I lean in closer to get a look at him.

Then come the sounds, like enormous daggers slicing through the air.

Choking. Sick, wet gurgles.

I spin around and lose my footing as I watch the ground rise up to attack the agents.

Sharp knives of black metal slash up from the dirt, protruding with such force and speed that they'd be impossible to dodge. There's one for each agent, the tip of which slams into his body and doesn't stop until it juts back out the top of his head. Armor doesn't stop it. Nothing does.

Ridium. Buried underground. No longer.

There isn't blood at first. It's too quick for that. The noises alone are enough to send me into a dizzying shock. The agents freeze in horrific, unnatural positions before the blades retract into the dirt, leaving massive incisions.

Then comes the crimson. Blood spilling onto the dirt, quickly darkening the brown.

I watch in horror as all seven agents topple to the ground in lifeless heaps. Skandar stands in the middle, looking like he's about to faint.

I can't quite process it. My mind's still stuck several

seconds in the past. Seven agents, dead. Morse. Bergmann. Gone.

Skandar stumbles over to meet us, face drained of color.

Theo closes his fist. He wavers in place before letting out one last chuckle. I turn to see the red fade from his eyes. Before anyone can say a word, he sinks to his knees. His face plants in the dirt. I watch his shoulders rise and fall. He's unconscious, but alive.

Everything's quiet. Nothing but the swarm on the horizon.

We bunch together instinctively, staring at the bodies of the fallen Academy Agents, trying to understand it. Their eyes stretch open, staring at the sun. Soon they'll be barbequed in this heat, cooked meat for whatever predator wants to swoop down and get them. I never liked Bergmann, and what little I knew of Morse I liked even less, but they didn't deserve to die. Not like this.

My bracelet buzzes. So does Cassius's. They tremble like they're applauding the scene around them, like they have minds of their own. Cassius and I look at each other.

Black. The daggers from the ground, the seamless bands wrapped around our wrists. I know he's thinking it too. It's more than just the visual. It's instinctive. It all fits together.

Ridium.

I grab my chest and feel the indentations of the symbols beneath my shirt. *I am already here.*

A blast of triple-digit heat throws my hair to the side. My bracelet settles, but I feel it in my heart now. I don't know if I'm making things better or worse. Have I set something terrible in motion just by coming back to the Fringes? Why didn't Alkine tell me about this "fork" before? If the possible consequences are so horrible, I should have been the first to know.

I repeat Morse's words over and over in my head. The troubled look on Skandar's face lingers with me. And then I remember the red in Theo's eyes, the same red that carved this warning into my skin.

I'm being followed. These aren't just random events. It's because of me.

I don't know what step to take.

Legs shaking, I take a seat on the ground. The heat will consume me if I stay put much longer, but I can't move. Maybe Alkine was right after all. Maybe I'm dangerous. To myself. To everyone.

I close my eyes. It could be better if I sat here and did nothing. Me and the wind. I can't hurt anybody if I'm dead.

28

Cassius leapt into leader mode. It was the only thing he knew to do. He didn't want to consider what had just happened, but they had to move before the heat of the Fringes got to them. The full horror of it all could be analyzed once they were safe.

"Rodriguez." He turned to Eva. "Get us access to one of the Academy ships. Keep the radar operational. If we tamper with it, it'll be a dead giveaway that these agents are gone."

Eva stared at him for a moment, lip shaking. Then, without a word, she grabbed Skandar's arm and pulled him with her toward the line of ships.

"I can help." Avery ran after them, eager to be away from the bodies.

Cassius yanked Fisher from the ground. "Come on."

"That was Ridium," he said. "It was ... it was underground. How's that even possible? Ryel said it only exists on Haven."

"I don't know."

"And Theo ... his eyes. It was like he was possessed."

Cassius frowned. "Madame warned me about him.

Just like she used to tell me I was special. It's the same with Theo. *Special* means dangerous to her."

"He's a Shifter," Fisher continued, "isn't he? Like Ryel was talking about."

"Maybe."

"He...they're all dead. Except Skandar."

"Skandar wasn't armed." He craned his neck to look back at the cruiser. No explosions or fire. Yet. "He wasn't a threat to him."

Without another word, Cassius stepped away, heading toward the cruiser.

Fisher tensed. "Where are you going?"

"Just wait." He moved past Theo's body, then Ryel's, and climbed up the ramp until he was in the cruiser's cabin once again. He bolted toward the weapons cabinet and grabbed the closest stunner. Tucking it in the waist of his trousers, he pulled another and gripped it in his hand.

Then he bounded down the ramp and approached Fisher. Stopping over Theo's unconscious body, he fired two rounds of stun darts straight into the boy's back. They stuck in his skin, steadily releasing tranquilizer.

"What are you doing?"

"We're taking him with us," he said. "Now that Ryel's gone, we need someone on the inside. If Theo really is a Shifter, then that means he's from Haven."

"But Shifters—"

"Are part of the Authority," Cassius interrupted. "I know." He looked down at the kid. "Which makes this a hundred times worse. But if we leave him here, we're not going to get any of the answers we need."

"What if he makes those knives come back?"

Cassius lowered the stunner. "He won't be waking up again for a while, let alone attacking us."

Fisher's hands shook at his sides. "Do you believe what Morse said? Do you think the Drifters are really talking about me like that?"

"Does it matter? What's done is done." He looked at the ground, half expecting more blades of Ridium to pop up and skewer them. "You're not a bad guy, if that's what you're worried about."

Fisher shook his head, then moved to Ryel's body and kneeled at the Drifter's side.

Cassius turned to watch him. "It's no use. That bullet shot right through his heart. Did you see the way he fell?"

"There was so much he could've told us." He turned to meet Cassius's eyes. "We didn't have time."

Cassius tapped his foot. "There's not much we could've done. Considering Madame and everything else."

"He wanted me to build an army. He was so disappointed."

Cassius moved closer. "He's gone. We need to move."

"Just wait a second." Fisher leaned in closer. "I want to check him. There might be something we missed."

He watched Fisher scan the contours of Ryel's legs with his eyes, settling on a single pocket stitched into the siding of his blood-stained clothing. Hand shaking, Fisher reached down and unbuttoned it. As soon as he slipped his fingers into the pocket, he recoiled. "It's like ice. There's something in there, but it's freezing."

"Go on."

Fisher clenched his fist and pulled out a metal box, no bigger than a die.

It was remarkably plain. No symbols or indentations or anything. Its silver exterior gleamed in the sunlight, yet seemed to repel it at the same time.

He looked up at Cassius. "This thing should be scalding out here. What do you think it is?"

Cassius shrugged.

"Feel it." Fisher dropped it into his waiting hand. The moment it touched Cassius's skin, he felt a pleasant jolt of iciness. Even the warmth of his hand didn't seem to heat it. He held it up to the sun to get a better look. "It's from Haven, surely." He tossed it back to Fisher. "Keep an eye on it. Let's get Theo into the ship."

Fisher stood. "You sure this is a good idea?"

Cassius glanced back at the boy's body. "Would you rather leave him to die?"

"Would I be a terrible person if I said yes?"

"No." He sighed. "But I think I can handle him. If he can't tell us anything, we'll chuck him out. Right now, we need every lead we can get."

Fisher nodded. "Okay."

"Alright, then. Help me get him up. Too much longer out here and we'll both get Surface Stroke."

29

Even after all we've been through, it feels safe to be back in an Academy ship. I know I've lost all their trust, and vice versa, but at least it's familiar.

Theo sits in the very back of the cabin, wrists and ankles cuffed to the seat. It's a stronger hold than back in the cruiser, not that he's awake to feel it.

Eva takes the pilot's seat. Everybody else spreads around the cockpit. Cassius stands in the corner, shoulder against the wall. Skandar reclines in the copilot's chair. I sit on the floor next to Avery.

"As far as I see it," Eva starts, "we've got two options. Either we head back to the Academy and beg them to forgive us, or we keep flying around in circles."

"Nope," I say.

She scoffs. "What do you mean, 'nope'?"

"We don't do either. You heard what Ryel said. The invasion's begun. We're gathering an army. That's all we can do."

Skandar raises his head. "But Jesse, you didn't see what Alkine—"

"I don't care what Alkine showed you," I reply. "It's too late."

Cassius taps his foot against the wall. "We can't do anything if we're too weak to fight."

I wince. "I haven't eaten since before Syracuse."

"A few more hours and we'll be exhausted," he continues. "We need to refuel."

Eva frowns. "And where are we supposed to do that? Skyships will have checkpoints. Chosen Cities are impenetrable. Even the Fringes . . . we'd waste all sorts of time trying to find a place with any food."

The cockpit falls silent. Cassius's foot-taps echo along the walls.

Avery stands. "I know the place. It's perfect!" She moves to the console and punches in a set of coordinates.

Eva glances over at the information. "What's Lenbrg?"

"The Fringe Town Avery and I stayed in last spring." I sit up. "Of course!"

Avery turns. "It's peaceful, and it's off the radar. They have food, and it's on the way to Siberia. If Alkine contacts the shuttle, we'll just switch off the volume. Play dumb. It'll look like we're heading back to Skyship. Then, when we land outside Lenbrg, we'll dismantle the radar. Disappear. I can do it. By the time the Academy sends someone looking, we'll be gone."

Eva crosses her arms. "You can disable the radar?"

"I trained at the Lodge," she counters. "I can do a lot of things with a shuttle."

My shoulders slump. "The Fringers won't be happy to see us coming back. Not after all the trouble we caused them."

"We'll have to deal," Avery says. "I'll take a bunch of peaceful Fringers over Madame or the swarm any day."

I glance over to Cassius. "What do you think?"

He's silent for a moment. I notice a twinkle at the end of his finger—a spark ready to ignite. "Go ahead. Wherever we go, we're screwed. Just keep that in mind. We'll recharge, but we won't have long before we have to fight again." He pivots and leaves the cockpit.

I turn back to Eva. With a great sigh she pulls on the steering and changes direction. "Setting a course for Lenbrg," she mutters. "You better be right about this."

———

Every last bit of me wants to give in to sleep, but the fact is, I haven't had a chance to talk properly with Avery since Syracuse. And there are things I need to know before I can let myself drift off peacefully.

We sit in the back of the cockpit. Her head leans on my shoulder, eyes half closed. Eva dimmed the lighting and programmed the console on autopilot. We'll take turns keeping watch.

"How are you feeling?" I reach over and pull the hair from her eyes.

"Don't worry about me."

"What was it like, after Seattle?"

There's a silence before she answers. I can't see her face from this angle, but I'd imagine she's troubled. "I don't remember anything inside the city after Madame showed up. I woke up lying on my back in the cabin of a cruiser."

"If I hadn't passed out, I would've—"

"Shh." She yawns. "They restrained me with some sort of fluid pumping into my arm. I don't know … it made me sleepy, and in a way I was grateful for that because it meant I didn't have to think. My brain was crammed—so many things swirling around at once. I thought about you, and all that happened since we'd left the Academy. I thought for sure Madame captured you. It was only when they brought me back to the Lodge and I realized that she was missing that I could even hope you might have escaped."

I close my eyes. "Do you think she's dead?"

"Now?"

"Yeah," I whisper, "after what happened in Syracuse."

"No. People like Madame don't die."

My heart sinks. She's right. "You were at the Lodge all those months?"

"Mmm hmm." She nods. "After they pulled Madame from the wreckage and nursed her back to health, I still asked about you. I was convinced they were hiding you somewhere. You wouldn't believe how many secret rooms and passageways she's got in that building. Even I don't know them all."

"When did you finally find out?"

"Madame told me when she was well enough to speak.

She told me what Cassius had done and that you and the entire Academy split from the community. I didn't completely believe her. I wanted to, but there was no way to know if she was telling the truth or not." She raises her head and meets my eyes. "You wanna hear the sickest thing?"

"Sure."

Avery smiles. "She kept my room."

"What do you mean?"

"My room ... the one I grew up in. She had it kept just the same as I remembered. I'd have thought that after all those years I'd spent at the Academy, all those months of estrangement, she'd have replaced it with something else. It was so weird going in there and seeing all my old things. I could barely stomach it knowing what I do now. She wanted everything to be like it was back then, like I was her make-believe daughter." She pauses. "I didn't know it then, but she'd been pumping medication into my system on that cruiser ride. And she'd been sneaking it into my food and seeping it through the vents in my room." She runs her hand over her head. "And then one night, they put me under and installed the harnessing device."

"Alkine said coming to look for you would be a mistake."

She falls back to my shoulder. "Of course he did."

"But I don't trust anything he—"

"Listen," she interrupts. "You've got so many more important things to worry about than little old me."

"But—"

"Shh. You know, I can't help but feel responsible."

"For what?"

She sighs. "If I'd never been in your life, you'd never have met Cassius or Theo and none of this would be happening. Pearls would still be Pearls and you'd be a happy Skyship kid getting closer to graduation."

"I was never all that happy." I shrug. "And we both know I was never gonna graduate. Besides, this was going to happen either way. At least with me around, we've got a chance of fighting back."

"You believe that?"

I wince. "I've got to. It's what's keeping me going."

"Good for you." Her eyes close. "I feel stupid for ever thinking you were a wimp."

"You've changed your mind?"

"Of course I have." Her voice trails off. "You're gonna be a hero."

I swallow. Or die trying.

"Now go to sleep, Jesse. We both need it."

I close my eyes. She's right, at least about the sleep thing.

30

Cassius sat at the edge of the cabin. He'd tried to sleep. An hour had passed. Then he took over for Rodriguez at the pilot's seat. Now he was back, and wide awake.

He stared at Theo's slumped-over body from across the room. He was dying to burst forth in flames. He didn't want to attack, necessarily, but he needed to let off steam. Nothing had gone right, and he feared it was only the beginning.

He stood and moved to the boy, stopping inches in front of him. Theo's face was covered in dirt. His ratty hair hung just over his closed eyes.

Cassius clenched his fist to control the fire longing to stream from his fingers. He knew he should leave the kid alone. As long as Theo was unconscious, he wouldn't be a problem. But he wouldn't be an asset, either. And he always had the stunners, if necessary.

Taking a deep breath, he reached out and slapped the boy across the face. The blow knocked Theo's body to the side, but the cuffs kept him in place.

All at once, Theo shook to life. His head slammed back into the wall. His arms and legs tensed as his eyes opened.

Cassius took a step back. "What did you do to those men out there?"

Theo blinked, then closed his eyes like he was about to drift off again. When he finally spoke, his voice came out slurred and quiet. "Where am I?"

Cassius crouched so that he could see the boy's face. "You're chained to a chair, where you belong. What did you do out there?"

"I don't know what you're talking about."

"Shifter. Ridium. These words mean anything to you?"

Theo spit, then coughed. "Is this how you do-gooders get your jollies? Torturing kids?"

Cassius scoffed. "You're about as innocent as a serial killer. Seven men down there, dead."

Theo looked up at him, chin tense, expression grim. "What do you mean?"

Cassius frowned. "The daggers."

"You still got my knife? That's the biggest mistake you've ever made, taking it."

"I'm not scared of you," Cassius said. "So you can cut it with the intimidation."

Theo smiled. "Madame's probably looking for me right now. You've pissed her off."

"Good. Now tell me what you did down there."

Theo shrugged. "I've been tied up like this ever since Syracuse! Of course, it's not gonna last much longer, but you should enjoy the peace while you've got it."

Cassius stood. His mind flashed back to the Fringes—

the energy pouring out of Theo's eyes, the way he stumbled, almost like he was sleepwalking. "You said Madame picked you up wandering the Fringes?"

"That's none of your business."

"You said there was an accident?"

Theo's eyes narrowed. "Maybe I did."

Cassius turned around. "You're a freak, just like the rest of us. You've got no idea what you can do."

Theo stayed silent. After a few seconds, Cassius turned to see if the boy had fallen unconscious again. His eyes were still open. They darted around the cabin, taking in every detail. "This isn't the cruiser. This isn't the same room. What happened?"

"Maybe I don't wanna tell you."

"You trying to scare me?"

"I guess I was wrong bringing you back. You don't know a thing. Too bad. I really didn't want to have to kill you."

He felt a tingle at his wrist. He looked down to see the bracelet vibrating against his skin. It forced itself around in circles like it was about to bore right through him. He glanced over his shoulder. Theo's teeth were grit. A bead of sweat dripped down his forehead.

Cassius reached to grab the bracelet with his opposite hand. Before he could touch it, the Ridium pulled upward. His arm went with it, forced above his head in a sprained position. Theo's concentration remained fixed.

Cassius shook his head. "This is crazy."

Another pull. This time his entire body was yanked

sideways. He stumbled across the length of the cabin, propelled forward by an unbreakable force. The bracelet hit the wall with a heavy clank and stayed there, pinning his wrist to the metal.

He gripped tight, trying to break the pull.

A redness coursed through Theo's pupils. Nothing as dramatic as back on the Surface, but obvious even from a distance. The bracelet started to collapse inward. Cassius yelped as metal mashed his wrist bones. An agonizing pressure constricted his arm. Seconds more and his entire hand would be crushed. "Stop," he yelled through the pain. "Don't you know what you're doing?"

The door to the cockpit swung open.

"What's going on?" Avery's voice sounded behind him, though he couldn't see her. The cabin began to black out around him. His arm pulsed with panicked blood.

"Stunner!" he shouted. "Grab the stunner!"

The bracelet released its hold. His wrist drooped to his side and he collapsed. The Ridium expanded to its usual, seamless state. Color blurred around him once more.

Through the pain, he stared at Theo. The red washed from the boy's eyes like rain-wiped watercolors. Within seconds he was back to normal, except for a smile across his bratty face.

Wasting no time, Cassius lunged for the stunner, wrapped his finger around the trigger, and fired right into Theo's shoulder.

31

The last of the sun sets beneath the mountains in the distance. I hold Ryel's cube in front of me, marveling at the sheer sleekness of it. It's seamless—perfectly uniform. I'm not sure how something so simple can have such a hold on me, but I can't take my eyes off it. I've gotten used to the chill that runs up my arm when I hold it. Now all I want to do is look at the tiny reflection of my face in its gleaming walls.

I've never looked worse. Scratches and bruises cover my face. My hair sticks to my scalp, matted by dirt and sweat. A cut splits my bottom lip. I picture all of the insects from the swarm running around on top of me, fighting to crawl up my nose or under my eyelids. It's a miracle I'm still walking at all.

I reach under my shirt and feel the scars on my chest. They seem to fade with each passing hour. The sting is gone, too, replaced with a dull, sick feeling every time I touch them.

I am already here.

Ryel's words repeat in my head. I wish I knew what they really meant.

The cockpit door opens and a pair of footsteps approach

us. I turn to see Avery supporting Cassius, who grips his wrist.

"He's a Shifter alright." Cassius sits against the wall. "My bracelet … he was able to control it."

I grab my wrist instinctively. "You wanna drop him now?"

"No," he replies. "He's out. I've got plenty of tranquilizers. He doesn't seem to know anything about it. It's like he becomes a different person."

"The red in his eyes," Skandar says. "Like back outside the swarm."

Cassius nods.

Eva glances at the radar. "We've still got approximately two hours until we can think about landing outside Lenbrg."

"The stunner'll keep him down at least that long," he says. "But nobody disturb him. It doesn't end well."

I drop the cube into my pocket. "And then what?"

"And then I hit him with another round from the stunner," Cassius replies. "I can't shake the feeling … If you can free some more Drifters, maybe they can tell us something about him. If he's an enemy, he may be more use to us alive."

Avery frowns. "That's something Madame would say."

"Well," he started, "you don't grow up in the Lodge without learning a thing or two."

———

10:30 PM. Our ship sets down a quarter mile from the north end of Lenbrg. The closer we get, the more I start to recognize the scenery. Last time we were here, we were speeding from a Unified Party battalion on our way to Seattle.

After Avery kills the radar, Eva shuts down the engines and we crowd into the cabin. Theo comes to almost immediately, sitting upright. Groggy, he eyes us one by one. He doesn't smile.

I glance at Cassius. He grips the handle of a stunner and takes a step forward until he's about two yards from Theo's chest.

Theo smiles. "You coward."

Cassius pulls the trigger as his reply. Then twice more.

Three darts of tranquilizer pierce just below Theo's left shoulder. The boy barely reacts, even at the loud thwack, thwack, thwack as the darts stick in his skin. He keeps his eyes locked on Cassius's the entire time. In moments, his head slumps forward. His fingers loosen on the armrests and, eventually, his eyes close.

Cassius lowers the pistol. "We have six hours. Maybe seven, given his size. Keep an eye on the time. We get in, we get food ... rest. Then we're out before dawn."

With that we leave the comfort of the ship for the unbearable warmth outside. We must look like one motley bunch as we approach Lenbrg. We could all use a shower, to say the least.

The moon lights our way, casting a glow on the hilly Fringe landscape. We're heading into the coolest time of the night, not that it means much out here.

Heaps of trash form dark mounds in front of us. They're

the first signs of civilization, George Barkley's collection of junk piled outside the back of his farmhouse on the northern edge of the town. It's where the Unified Party ambushed us before. A shiver runs down my spine. I glance at the stars, half-expecting to see the outlines of cruisers following us.

Up until that point, this had been my one good experience on the Surface. Avery and I had been shocked to find a colony in the Fringes banding together to instill some sense of order. Rather than give in to chaos, they scavenge food and power a generator. There are bound to be other Fringe Towns like Lenbrg, but it's not something you hear about often.

We continue to approach the piles. With every step, the smell worsens. From what I can remember, most of Barkley's collection is nothing more than mass old junk he finds in the ruins of Seattle, but who knows how long it's been since he's seen the bottoms of the heaps. Things could be rotting down there. The oppressive heat definitely isn't helping.

A few more steps and we're bathed in floodlights. Everyone freezes. Sheets of light blare down at us from both sides, so bright at first that I have to shield my eyes. Before I acclimate to the glare, I hear the cock of a gun. Then a voice.

"Oh, hell no." Barkley's gruff, unimpressed drawl comes from somewhere in front of me. I rub my eyes and watch him appear from the light, walking forward with an old-fashioned revolver pointed in front of him. "It can't be," he continues. "Y'all are temptin' fate."

I raise my hands in the air, even as I take a step forward. There's no way Barkley'd recognize Cassius, and probably not Skandar or Eva either, but he obviously hasn't forgotten me. The old man looks more beaten down than the last time I saw him. Tired. He'd helped us get to Seattle and it hadn't turned out well for him.

"Installed these floodlights myself," he continues. "Part of a new precautionary system, thanks to the likes of you. You here with Unified Party cruisers trailin' you again?"

I glance over his shoulder, relieved to see that his farmhouse is still standing. Madame could've easily leveled it last spring.

Avery moves to my side. "How's your son, George?"

The man's eyes narrow. "Alive. You've got a lot of balls coming back here. We pride ourselves on staying out of the eye of the government. You brought 'em straight to us. Still haven't recovered completely." He waves the nozzle of the revolver. "Go back. Wherever you came from, go back. We don't want you."

I slowly lower my hands, sighing. "We need your help."

He chuckles. "Heard that one before."

"It's not like last time. It's ... we just need a place to stay for a few hours. Somewhere safe."

George keeps the gun cocked, not saying a word.

I feel a hand on my shoulder. I turn to see Cassius

standing behind me. "Come on. Let's just take our chances back in the shuttle. This wasn't a good idea."

Barkley shakes his head. "Always knew you'd be back eventually. Didn't think it would be so soon. How'd that army of Unified Party troops work out for you, anyway?"

"We didn't mean any harm," I say.

"Sure you didn't. It was a mistake helping you in the first place. In fact, I ought to—"

A second voice interrupts him from beyond the lights.

"Dude, no way!" Bobby Henderson jumps into sight, a smear of oil on his cheek, black hair grown into a shag since the last time I saw him. Last spring, when Avery and I stumbled into the town, he was the first to find us. Without his help, we'd never have made it to Seattle. Out of everyone we could've found out here, he's the one I was hoping for the most.

Bobby's about the same age as me, yet seems ten times more untroubled. He wears a broad smile on his face as he bounds toward us. Before I can move, he grabs my shoulders and forces me into an awkward hug. When he's done, he moves on to Avery. "Oh, man, you don't know how many nights I thought about you guys. Barkley told me you were ambushed by Unified Party soldiers as soon as you got to Seattle. I hope you didn't worry about us. Those bozos left as soon as they realized they weren't a match for you Shippers."

He steps back and takes us all in. "Most exciting thing that's happened to Lenbrg ever. Of course, my pops doesn't agree, but who cares about him?"

George lowers the gun, shaking his head. "Why the hell are you out here, Henderson?"

Bobby brushes him off. "Don't you worry about it."

"This is my property," he replies. "I'll worry as much as I like. I've told you again and again. Too many times to count…"

"Aw, cool it, old man. These are friends. They don't need you harassing them."

"I ain't harassing them," he says. "You're supposed to be organizing cans in the supply room."

Bobby shrugs. "I got bored. They don't need me, anyway." He glances back at the piles beyond the lights. "Some security system, Barkley. You've got a blind spot there." He points. "And there. And there. I can help you fix it if you want. I'm good at—"

"Shut up, boy." George rubs his eyes before turning to us again. "You better leave. They ain't gonna let you in the city. I can guarantee that."

Bobby smiles. "You let me have 'em, Barkley. You won't even know we're here."

Avery steps forward. "We're really not asking for your help, just some food if you have it … and a place to catch our breath."

"Doesn't seem like too much trouble to me." Bobby beams. "Don't worry, Barkley. I'll take 'em. And you have the added bonus of getting rid of me for a night."

George shakes his head, cursing. "Stay clear of the city walls."

"Yeah, yeah." Bobby grabs my shoulder and leads me to the side. He turns to whisper in my ear. "I've got this awesome place all set up. Wait'll you see it." He pushes me away from Barkley. When we're completely out of sight, the floodlights shut off behind us.

Bobby releases my shoulder and walks in front of me, leading our group around the edge of the town.

Eva moves beside us. "Shouldn't we be heading toward the city?"

Bobby bends over to pick up a rock, then chucks it into the distance. "You heard the man. They don't want people like us hanging out with them."

I glance back at the farmhouse. It's nothing but a dark shadow in the distance. Even the junk heaps are hard to spot. "Where are we going?"

"Just a little more." Bobby points in front of us. "You see that?"

I squint. All I see is another blob of darkness against the sky, like a toe sticking up from the ground.

Bobby doesn't wait for a response. He breaks into a jog, oblivious to the heat. "Sometimes I get sick of being inside the walls. Lenbrg never changes. Plus, ever since you guys dropped by, the city council's been freaking about the chances of another attack. I figure the town needed a lookout. I'm just fidgety enough for the job."

We echo his faster pace. With each step, the details of the dark blob come into view. What looks like a miniature lighthouse stands before us, an awkward structure against the flat horizon. Farther beyond that, I see the outline of a turbine. Blades turn lazily in the breeze.

Bobby bounds to the side of the building and pulls a key from a necklace beneath his shirt. Opening a lock on the door, he ushers us into a tight circular room. It's an uncomfortable fit for all six of us, but Bobby squeezes to the far side anyway. "Shut the door." He grabs a nearby crank and turns.

Skandar pulls the handle, closing us in the hot room. I adjust my collar. "I don't think this place is meant for more than two people."

"Just wait." Bobby continues to turn the crank. Three clicks echo along the walls around us, followed quickly by a half dozen more. Something whirs to life.

Suddenly, a cool breeze fills the chamber. I watch as a dozen fans, positioned at all angles, shoot cold air into the center of the room. Two floors up, directly above my head, is a temperature regulator attached to the ceiling. An old model, and loud, but it does the job. Within seconds the entire structure's temp-controlled, even as Fringe air spills through the open windows.

"Rigged it up myself." Bobby climbs a nearby wooden ladder and sits on the second floor, which is basically a ring of reinforced wood attached to the walls on all sides. "I call it my fortress." He smiles. "Far enough from town to give me space to breathe, but close enough to keep watch for any trouble."

Cassius runs his hand along the wall, careful not to get

too close to the whirring blades of the fans. "You built this whole place by yourself?"

Bobby shrugs. "Nicked a lot of stuff from Barkley's yard. He won't even miss it. I was hoping to snag some new shades for these windows tonight but, you know, you guys are a much better find." He leans back and emerges with an armful of cans. "Catch." He tosses them down to us one by one, followed by an opener. "I forget what I grabbed, but it's all edible. We throw out any bad stuff."

As soon as I've got the opener in my hand, I rip the top off the can and shove my fingers inside, not caring what's in there. I eat so fast that I can't taste anything. We pass the cans around without a word, slurping and chewing and drinking the juice at the bottom.

"Whoa." Bobby laughs. "I guess you really needed that. So Jesse, what've you been up to? Who are your friends?"

It's a long story. Too long to tell him everything, but I give him the shortened version. I leave most of the stuff about Ryel and the Authority and Matigo out, but even without those parts, his eyes widen with every word. It's the kind of eager curiosity I wish I had. I used to be like that, I think. Maybe.

"Well, you're safe here," Bobby says. "I've got scopes looking out every window of the tower. Nobody sneaks up on me here. I see 'em first. In fact, just a few weeks ago I saw a Pearl land outside the east window, about half a mile away. Saw Unified Party Pearlhounds pick it up and everything."

My stomach sinks at the mention of the word. The

thought of the Unified Party hauling Pearls back to the Chosens makes me cringe.

"You can sleep here," Bobby continues. "I'll keep watch. You all look like you're about ready to pass out anyway."

"Thanks," I reply. "And I know it doesn't mean much, but I'm sorry about what happened last time we were here."

"Don't worry about it." He smiles. "Like I said, it was the most exciting thing to happen to Lenbrg in ages."

I nod, but it doesn't mean much. The truth is, I feel like a time bomb. The way things have been going, I'm not sure Bobby knows what he could be getting himself into, even if it is only for a short time in the middle of the night.

"Five hours," Cassius says. "I suggest you all start sleeping now because we'll be back on our feet before you know it."

Skandar yawns.

"I'll settle for three," Eva says.

As for me, I'll take anything I can get. Anything without a surprise or an attack or some terrible combination of the two. It's not much to ask, but it would mean everything in the world right now.

32

I manage a fitful hour of sleep. An hour and a half, maybe. And then I feel it.

At first I think I'm still dreaming, that this is one of those blissful, sail-away-on-an-island-of-peace dreams that you never want to wake up from. But as the feeling coalesces, as the hairs on the back of my neck stand up, I know that this is no make-believe.

I sit up. Most everyone else is passed out. Bobby's crouched on the second level, leaning on the base of one of his lookout windows. I can't tell, but I think he's asleep too.

A Pearl. I've felt this too many times not to know what's happening.

Careful not to disturb any of the others, I tiptoe to the door and ease it open. Without a sound, I step into the night air.

I see it instantly, hurtling down like a meteor. It leaves a line of green in the sky as it approaches. I pray it didn't pass a Chosen City on its way down. If their scanners had enough time to pick it up, we'll have Pearlhounds all over us. But if I break it and let the freed Drifter sail back into the air, they won't know where to look. If they come looking at all.

I stretch out my arms like I'm about to catch a baseball. The Pearl keeps its trajectory, right toward me. I imagine alarm systems going off, like they used to at the Academy when a Pearl was this close. I picture crowds of people running from the deadly force. And here I am, waiting for it.

The Pearl begins to slow, controlled by my fingertips. I pull it closer, every inch causing more somersaults in my heart. No one else can feel this. Nobody else ever will.

Before I know it, I'm holding the green orb in my hands. I stare into the deep waves of energy. It's been a while since I've been able to luxuriate with a Pearl like this. My heart swells with the healing warmth of it. This is better than sleep.

I survey the horizon, half expecting Alkine or Madame to jump out and steal the Pearl. Instead, Bobby's voice cuts the silence of the night.

"I didn't want to mention it," he whispers, "but I knew I saw you catch one last spring."

I turn, still holding the glowing orb.

His mouth hangs open in astonishment. "I've never seen one so close."

"Duck," I say, and toss the Pearl into the air. It casts a wide arc behind me. Bobby hits the ground. I close my eyes and feel the path of the Pearl through the sky. When it's high enough, I break it.

"Christ almighty." Bobby stands and shields his eyes as a firework of energy blazes through the darkness. It's brightest at the center and dissipates as it streams toward us. By the time it reaches my skin, it's only a tingle. Like feathers brushing against me.

I grit my teeth and whisper to myself, "Please come back, please come back."

I spin and watch the Drifter shoot into the air, away from us. "Damn it." I kick the dirt. "They never come back. Never when you need them." I turn to Bobby. "I think it must be instinctual or something, like caged animals. They just wanna get as far away as possible."

His eyes are wider than ever now. He carefully brings himself to his feet, shaking his head in disbelief. "You—" He chokes on his words. "What—" I've never seen him tongue-tied.

"There's a lot you don't know," I say. "A lot nobody does. Pearls aren't what they seem."

He looks toward the sky. "I guess not."

My shoulders slump. "We've got a fight on our hands, from all angles. I don't even know if I'm helping or hurting." I lift up my shirt.

Bobby gasps as he stares at the markings scrawled across my chest. "Who did that?"

I point to the sky. "One of those. But not a good one. At least, I don't think so."

"You're freaking me out, man."

"I know." My gaze falls to the ground. "Be thankful, Bobby. Stay here. Stay where it's simple."

"I don't know what you mean."

I turn and trudge back to the lookout tower, still abuzz

with the energy. "You will," I whisper. "If we can't stop this, everyone will."

———

Another hour and my eyes fly open.

The door to the room hangs ajar. A thin figure stands just outside, staring in.

I bolt up, slamming my head against an overhanging piece of wood. The others wake around me, in varying levels of disarray. The fan blades continue to whir, giving the tight space a loud hum.

I keep my eyes locked on the boy.

The eyes.

Two pools of crimson pin me to the ground. Theo stretches an arm to lean against the doorframe. Moonlight illuminates his face as he moves closer. His expression is vacant, but his eyes are unblinking. They're all I can focus on.

His head tilts slightly to the side.

Bobby jumps down from the second level. "Who the heck—"

Theo opens his mouth as if to speak, but says nothing. It stops Bobby cold.

Arm back at his side, Theo lurches away, moving into the open like a zombie.

Eva sits up. "What's wrong with him?"

"There was enough tranquilizer in those darts to keep him down." Cassius stands. "I don't understand." He moves toward the door, watching Theo continue his steady pace away from the lookout tower. It's like he's taunting us. Daring us to follow him.

Cassius steps forward. I stand and grab his shoulder. "Don't go out there. You saw what he did to Morse and the others."

"I'm not gonna let him." He yanks from my grip and steps outside.

"Cassius!"

He ignores me. I glance back at the others before deciding to follow him into the darkness.

Theo's eyes continue to pierce the moonlit Fringe landscape—pinpricks of red. He moves backward faster now, but never once looks away.

Cassius kicks up dirt in his relentless pace toward the boy. I stay a few steps behind.

Cassius's left arm flies into the air. At first I think he's giving me some sort of signal. I open my mouth to call out, but before I can say a word, something lifts his entire body from the ground and flings him to the side like a piece of trash.

He hits the dirt several yards away. I back up as Theo's eyes lock onto mine. My bracelet trembles. I reach over and pull it down to my side, right next to the cube of metal in my pocket.

Theo freezes. His arms lie limp at his sides. He takes short, repeated breaths. "I am already here," he says. His eyes pulse against a backdrop of stars. "You ... your brother, your friends. Everyone. They're too late."

I pull my bracelet behind my back. "Who are you?"

His lip trembles. "That Ridium around your arm. Your parents thought they were saving you. They were only buying you time."

I lean in, trying to get a better look at his expression. "Are you … are you Matigo?"

"No."

"Then what—"

He closes his eyes. When they open again, the red flashes away. His mouth falls open. "Help me."

I stare at him, fighting to understand what it is that I'm seeing. It's like a switch flipped and he's a different person again. He's a twelve-year-old. A kid.

I take a step forward. "What do you mean?"

Before he can respond, Cassius pulls himself to his feet. Theo turns and notices him. His eyes widen. He pushes the hair from his face and balls his fists. Cassius does the same, coupled with torrents of fire that burst from his hands in bright explosions before the Fringe air swallows them up.

Theo nearly loses his footing at the sight of it. He looks up to the stars, then back at Cassius. "How did you—" Rather than finish his question, he turns and sprints away.

I move forward but Cassius darts in front of me, blocking my way. "He's mine," he whispers. "Wait here. I'll be back."

"But—"

He takes off without another word. In seconds, he's almost out of sight.

To hell with waiting. I take a deep breath and head after him.

33

Cassius watched Theo disappear into the darkness. The kid ran with incredible speed and endurance for someone who, moments before, had been staggering around.

He didn't look back to see if Fisher had followed. He couldn't lose Theo. If the stunners weren't having an effect any longer, Cassius needed to end this. Nobody could run for long in the Fringes without passing out, even at night. The kid would eventually run out of steam. He had to.

The ground sloped until it became a gentle hill of dry vegetation and boulders—hundreds of hiding places for nasty critters. Cassius remembered struggling through this same landscape in search of Fisher. Only back then, he'd been on his last legs. It was amazing what an old can of fruit could do.

He whipped through a row of prickly bushes, scraping his ankle but refusing to let it slow him down. All the time, he kept his eye on the small figure below him. Then he had an idea.

He spotted a rock, about the size of his fist, and scooped it into his hand as he continued down the hill. His line of vision was perfect. Theo wasn't thinking strategy.

He coughed. His lungs were already parched, and filling with dust every time he took a breath. But he had a clear shot. He concentrated.

Winding up, he chucked the rock forward and watched as it connected with Theo's shoulder. The force sent the kid crashing to the ground. Cassius knew it wouldn't be enough to stop him cold, but it'd slow him down. He bounded to a sprint, almost tripping several times down the hill.

Theo rolled to the side and pushed up with his legs to flip to a standing position. His dirt-stained face tensed as he watched Cassius approach. He raised his fists.

Cassius tackled him. The two toppled to the ground, bashing against the warm dirt. Cassius went for Theo's neck. Before he could reach it, the boy bit down on the side of his hand, hard enough to rip flesh. Cassius kneed him in the gut and rolled away, grabbing his bleeding hand. He staggered to a standing position, breathing heavy.

Theo lay still for a moment before recovering and pushing to his feet. "I'll kill you, Stevenson."

Cassius believed him. There was something insane—feral—hidden behind those eyes. It'd been there the entire time, forcing its way out in glimpses.

Theo tossed a fistful of dirt in Cassius's eyes and lunged forward, punching the side of his face while he was blinded. Cassius slumped sideways before bending forward to catch himself.

Theo didn't give him time. The moment Cassius was

most vulnerable, he balled his fists together and brought them down on Cassius's spine.

Cassius fell, face forward, to the earth. He could hear Theo's breathing above him. Then he felt the boy's boot connect with his side, clobbering his already injured torso. Again. Again.

"You're an idiot!" Theo cried. "You're stupid. Worthless. You're a joke compared to me."

He'd kick until he couldn't move his leg anymore. Cassius knew it without even looking at the boy. He'd attack until the wound from earlier reopened and Cassius bled to death. He was Madame's boy. He was a killer.

Cassius hadn't been all that different himself, before Seattle.

So he knew what he was fighting against. His instincts were right. Nothing but death would stop this kid.

He closed his eyes and focused. Each blow weakened him further. Hand-to-hand was pointless in the heat. Cassius only had one trick that Theo didn't.

He clenched his fingers at his side. He tried to ignore the kicking, forget the physical pain, and focus on what was happening internally. He summoned anger. Anger had worked in the past. And with everything that had happened, it wasn't difficult to find inspiration.

After several false starts, he felt the warmth rise inside of him. It wasn't like the heat of the Fringes. Instead of slowing him down, it gave him energy.

The flood built up—reserves strengthened by hours

without a decent episode. He felt it come to the surface, ignite the veins down his arms, and teeter at the tips of his fingers.

He rolled to the side, exposing his stomach, and extended his fingers before Theo could kick again. A burst of fire streamed from his arms, so thick that it formed a wall between them. Cassius grit his teeth, expecting to hear howls of pain as the flames consumed the boy. His Unified Party training kicked in. He knew what he had to do. For himself, and for his friends.

Theo backed off. Fire engulfed him. Cassius watched the boy's hands flail, but he didn't scream.

Cassius pulled up to a crouching position, his entire body bruised and throbbing. Billows of smoke engulfed the air above Theo's head. The fire dissipated. Theo swatted at his face as if there were a hive of bees buzzing around him. He dropped to the ground and rolled in the dirt, smothering his flame-eaten clothes until the fire was put out. All the while, he stayed silent. Not even a little shriek.

Cassius stood and gripped his midsection, breathing hard. He watched Theo brush the dust from his clothes and jump to a standing position. He was unburned.

His eyes fell on Cassius. They were red.

Cassius stared at him. He waited for something to happen, some kind of reaction. "Why aren't you—" He stopped himself. There was no use asking questions.

Theo took a step back. His eyes pulsed. "Madame said

you were a pyro. She never said the fire came from your *hands*."

Cassius frowned. "You should be burning. You should be—"

Theo shrugged. "Guess your flames are kind of wimpy, Great Cassius Stevenson."

Cassius shook his head. He knew it had nothing to do with the fire. He'd seen what it could do too often. He'd watched the Lodge burn last spring. He'd felt the Chute explode. His fire hurt everyone—killed some. The only thing that it hadn't burned was his own skin.

His mind flashed back to something Madame had said in Syracuse. *You and Theo have a lot in common.*

Did that mean he was immune to Cassius's fire?

The glow in Theo's eyes intensified. "You wanna fight? Come on."

Cassius backed away. "You don't know what you are."

"This world . . . " Theo paused and brushed dirt from his elbow. "You don't belong in it. This is Matigo's world now."

Cassius coughed. When he covered his mouth, he noticed spots of blood on his hand. "Do you understand what you're saying? That name—"

Theo's brows rose. He wiggled his fingers as if he was just getting used to them. "I've . . . I've never felt like this before. Back in the swarm. The heat—"

"Cassius!" Fisher's voice called from the distance. Cassius

turned to see his brother come stumbling down the hill, breathing hard.

Theo backed away, grabbing his midsection as if he was trying to protect something.

Fisher jogged to Cassius's side. "What's happening?"

"My fire didn't hurt him," he responded.

Theo looked up at the stars, then brought his arms out to his sides, rippling his fingers over the air like he was about to conduct an orchestra. "It's beneath me," he said. "It's everywhere."

Cassius felt his bracelet begin to hum. Fisher's too. He took a step back, his shoulder colliding with his brother's.

"Do you know about the Authority?" Fisher asked.

Theo closed his eyes, blotting the red energy. "Now I see it. It's all around us. I am already here. I have always been here."

Cassius gripped Fisher's shoulder. "We should run."

"My bracelet's going crazy."

Before they could move, dark wraiths punctured the ground. Coils of blackness reached into the sky like hundreds of ghost hands joining together. Cassius spun in a circle to watch the darkness form. It spread in shadowy sheets, curving up over their heads and blocking every possible exit.

It had no depth. It was like he was slowly going blind. More and more of the world fell away. The horizon began to disappear around them as the Ridium climbed into the air. It looped and split, like vines of ivy spreading along a wall. Gaps were filled. Stars were swallowed.

A spherical room had been built around them.

Theo raised his fists in the air. Ridium blotted out the last of the sky. Only the maniacal red glow of his eyes gave a sense of perspective.

The oily mess seeped into the dirt and rocketed forward under their feet. Cassius lifted his boot before the stuff could ensnare him in its grip.

His mind began to play tricks on him. Directions skewed. If he were to walk forward, he wasn't sure the darkness would support him.

Black. Everywhere.

Cassius closed his eyes, then opened them again. There were no holes or chasms for the moon to poke through. This was all-encompassing. It was as if his senses had shut down.

The outside breeze was little more than a memory. Walls blended with the slick, Ridium-covered floor. The blackness had become so complete that it seemed to stretch on forever. Had Cassius not seen the chamber created right in front of him, he might have believed it was endless. The hairs on his arms stood on end. His bracelet settled.

Fisher pivoted, searching for an exit. His breathing quickened. Cassius grabbed his arm to steady him. It would be too easy to have a panic attack in here.

Light spilled into the chamber as spiraled holes began to carve themselves into the walls. Cassius could see Theo's silhouette now, cast by the meager moonlight that streamed into the room.

"What have you done?" he shouted. His voice echoed along the blackness.

Theo massaged his fists, smiling. It was that same cocky smile he'd worn back at the Lodge. "You don't belong here." He chuckled. "You really don't."

Cassius gritted his teeth. "What's that supposed to mean?"

"King Matigo can't have what he wants if the two of you are here too."

Fisher stepped forward. "How do you know all this?"

Theo dropped his hands to his side. "Because I'm not supposed to be here, either. I'm going to take us all away."

The ground rumbled, throwing Cassius and Fisher to the floor. The entire chamber pushed up on them, like an elevator moving ten times too fast. Cassius glanced out the nearest spiral opening to see a patchwork of stars falling.

Only they weren't falling. The chamber, somehow, was *rising*. They were moving away from Earth.

A curl of blackness danced from the floor in front of Theo like a serpent. He reached out his arm and allowed it to wind around his wrist. Cassius watched, then looked down at his own hands. The bracelet. The daggers outside the swarm. All Ridium.

The black coil shot from Theo's arm, cast a wide arc, and landed with a ripple on the ground where it fused instantly with the rest of the darkness. "Wow." Theo laughed. "What a ride."

Cassius stood. He had to keep his arms spread to stay

balanced. The chamber's ascent was silent, but not without the constant rumble underfoot. "Where are we going?"

"Up." Theo smiled. "Up and up and up. Past Skyships, past the stars. Away from it all."

Cassius shook his head. "You don't even know what you're talking about." He barreled forward, hoping to catch the boy off-guard. He pounced on Theo, grabbing him by the collar and pinning him to the ground. "Stop this. Stop whatever it is you're doing."

Theo's eyes pulsed. "But I can't." His voice came out innocent. "I don't know how."

Cassius punched him in the side of the face. "You can't do anything if you're unconscious."

"Cassius!" Fisher's voice came from behind him. "I just saw a Skyship. We're moving fast."

A drop of Ridium fell from the ceiling and spilled on Cassius's back, extending into a clawlike shape until it pulled him up and flung him to the far side of the chamber.

Theo grinned as he sat up. "I'd lay off if I were you."

Fisher ran to Cassius's side, eyes wide and panicked. "He's controlling the entire room. If we don't stop this thing we'll be in space."

Cassius glared at him. "Don't you think I know that?"

Theo jumped to his feet and strode forward. "Try and throw me out the back of a cruiser," he chuckled. "Tie me to a chair. *Shoot* me."

"You're sick," Cassius said. "You're gonna kill us all!"

"No," he replied. "Not sick. What's sick is that I've been

slumming it down there for so many years. I don't belong with those people on the Surface. I'm a Shifter. Like my father." He paused a moment to marvel at the chamber around him. "It all makes sense now. It's coming back, like a piece of my brain's been triggered." He chuckled. "All those years waiting. For the two of you to find each other … for our targets to reveal themselves. He's been hiding in the Fringes the entire time. He's already here."

Fisher clenched his fists. "Matigo."

Theo sighed. "He'd like nothing better than for me to do it … get rid of you right now." He continued to approach. "Ridium. That's the key to this invasion. Not Pearls. Pearls are for foot soldiers, for the common Drifter. Ridium is for kings."

With a flip of Theo's hand, Cassius's bracelet lurched to the ground, dragging the rest of his body with it. Fisher's too. He watched, helpless, as the floor devoured his fingers. It pulled them in like quicksand. There was nothing to hold onto.

The Ridium transformed into a chute of darkness. Everything went cold as the surface sucked him in. He took a deep breath just before the Ridium covered his face. His arms flailed, legs kicking at the blotchy mess, but it was pointless.

Seconds later the Ridium parted with his body, oozing upward in a stringy mess. The blackness settled back into a ceiling above his head, but there was no ground left underneath. Only sky, and hundreds of miles to the Surface.

34

I scream. Or at least I make the motion. Whatever sound comes out doesn't reach my ears before the wind pulls it away. Gusts of air tear me in every direction as I tumble in messy circles. It's all a blur, an endless abyss of navy blue.

Second free-fall in as many days. Only there's no Drifter to save me this time.

Cassius plummets behind me, a dark lump against the stars. I can't tell where his face is. I can't see anything. Every passing second the atmosphere pulls me in a different direction until I'm not even sure I'm falling anymore.

I'm flipped over and the world is upside down—long stretches of gray, an endless wasteland. My ears pop. It feels like they'll burst and bleed all over the place. I tuck in my arms, but nothing stops the pain. The sky does its best to rip me apart. It doesn't matter if I'm the Pearlbreaker, not if there aren't any Pearls to break.

The wind twirls me back around so that I'm staring at the vessel of Ridium. It looks like a black bubble from here—a perfect oval of darkness. Theo's up there, or whoever he is now.

I feel a weight dislodge at my hip and watch as Ryel's cube of metal shoots into the sky above me. I reach out and try to grab it before it's snatched away.

Too late. It disappears into the sky, sucked right up to the vessel.

I close my eyes, praying for a Pearl. A shuttle. Anything.

Then, light.

A floodlight above us, stronger even than George Barkley's outside of Lenbrg. It forces my eyes open, though I can barely look at it.

The wind steadies until it's replaced by a soft hum. My body warms. My limbs stop flailing. I lose track of everything around me. Theo's vessel disappears. The stars fade into nothing. The ground becomes an afterthought.

I'm frozen, lying on a bed of stabilized air in the middle of the sky, bathed in light.

And then I'm somewhere else entirely.

An entire world flows beneath my feet. I'm flipped around so that I can stare down at it like a bird. Gold meadows give way to a vast, sandy desert, then to chasms so dark and deep that I'm sure they must be carved from Ridium.

Seconds later, the landscape turns a charcoal gray.

Lights. Rows and rows of them, so tightly packed that the entire world illuminates in a blinding grid.

It all comes unbelievably fast—more and more of it. I can barely process each new sight. Towers. A crater. A black city wide enough to devour an entire planet.

I blink.

A hallway.

Cassius stands beside me. I turn to him. I feel like everything inside of me is all messed up, but I think this goes beyond physical. I'm disoriented in so many different ways. I expect the floor beneath me to open into sky.

"Did we hit the ground?" I cup my hand over my mouth when I hear my voice. "Are we dead?"

Cassius glances around the hallway. He clenches his fingers and taps his foot, as if trying to get used to his body. "Did you see all of that?"

"The cities?" I ask. "The desert?"

"Everything," he whispers. "It was all too much. I couldn't even concentrate. Were we flying?"

I hold my hand in front of my face and bend each finger. "I don't know. I don't know what's happening."

I wouldn't be surprised if Cassius told me that we were in the Lodge. Everything around us has an air of expense to it. From the deep red carpet running down the marble floor to the gold-framed art and photography hanging around us, the corridor reeks of excess. A glass ceiling hangs overhead, constructed in an ornate tiered formation. Beyond it lie the stars. It's night.

Recessed lighting bathes everything in a peaceful glow. The temperature is perfect, without that dry, reprocessed feel that you get in shuttles and Skyships. There's energy underfoot too. I'm not sure what it is.

I grab my hair. "This is freaking me out. First Theo, then we're falling... now this? I think we're dead, Cassius.

Like, seriously. Maybe we died back in the swarm and this is all just a dream."

He swallows. "Feel your chest."

I wince, knowing that the burn marks will make it real. Hand shaking, I reach under my shirt and run my fingers over the familiar symbols, still etched into my skin. I step back without saying a word.

Cassius glances up to examine the glass ceilings. "That light…"

"Ryel's cube," I say. "It slipped from my pocket when I was falling, just before the light came down from the sky."

"You think it had something to do with this?"

I think back to the unnatural coldness that seemed to emanate from the cube. "We don't know what it is. It's from Haven. It's gotta be."

"We could still be falling," he replies.

"Dead," I whisper.

"Would you stop it with that word?"

Something sounds in the distance.

Cassius freezes. "Did you hear that?"

I listen as footsteps round a corner somewhere. "Someone's coming."

Cassius moves to the wall, looking for an exit. "Quick. There's gotta be a way out."

We're too late. A motion at the end of the corridor catches my eye. I turn to see a man approach us, head high, expression serious. His lean body is covered in a head-to-toe suit of black. It has a faint gleam, like Ridium. I flatten against the wall, even though it's obvious he's going to see us.

But somehow, he doesn't. He approaches at a constant pace, shoulders up, lips tugged at a slight frown. His eyes are red, like Theo's were when we left him.

He walks directly past us, moving down the hall with all the emotion of a robot.

Cassius takes a cautious step from the wall. I reach over to stop him, but he's too far away. The man in black continues his march down the hallway. Cassius takes another step.

Then, when I'm sure they're about to collide, something amazing happens.

The man in black—or his shoulder, at least—moves right through Cassius. It's like a cloud, dissipating into swirls of gas until he's on the other side.

Cassius's eyes widen. "Did you see that?"

I freeze, hoping that the man didn't hear him. But he continues onward, giving no indication that he's seen or heard us at all.

Cassius takes another look. "Let's follow him."

I peer down the corridor and watch the guy move farther away. "I don't know … "

"We're here," Cassius says. "I don't know how we got here, but it doesn't matter. We might as well make the most of it."

He starts off after the man. Cursing under my breath, I follow.

We trace the guy's footsteps past several intersections of hallways before we make a turn and head up an impressively tall staircase. I'm not sure how big this place is, but apart from the glass ceilings, I haven't seen a trace of the outside world this entire time—only the same, ornate corridors.

The stairs lead us to a separate room that branches from the roof in a sphere of glass. It reminds me of an enormous Pearl. All it's missing is a green glow.

We stand at a narrow landing, squeezed up against the man in black. I take the chance to peer around the side of his face and search for features that might give me an indication of who—or what—this guy is.

He looks a little like Ryel, and it fools me at first. I even whisper his name, not that he's able to hear me. The differences make themselves known in time. Longer nose, a scar just in front of his left ear, and most worryingly, the glint of red in his eyes.

I don't have time to linger, as the doorway to the room opens before us. The man strides in without hesitation. Cassius and I tiptoe behind. We arrive on a vast expanse of carpet, exquisitely detailed in pattern and shape. The designs meld and flow into place, cycling around each other in a slow, hypnotic pace. The longer I look at it, the less convinced I am that it's carpet at all. Nothing here is completely as it seems at first glance.

The glass walls of the spherical chamber are entirely translucent. I glance behind me and marvel at the endless fortress below us. I can't tell where it ends. Maybe it never does. I peer through the glass ceilings. Pathways of silver-white light form an impressive maze of corridors and rooms. I'm reminded of the images I saw after Ryel's cube activated. Lights. Everywhere.

And it's true. Everything is like this. All around the structure, 360 degrees.

I notice more bubbles like ours, rising into the air above the paths of light in the distance. But beyond that, everything's more or less at the same level. It's like the carpet under our feet—an unending patchwork. A grid stretching into the horizon.

There's smoke too. Or clouds of some sort. It's difficult to see them in the night, under the stars. The lights of the complexes show me the difference. Some are brighter. Others shine from beneath a layer of thick atmosphere.

The man kneels in front of us, knees on the ever-changing carpet, head bowed. "King Matigo." His voice is barely above a whisper, as if he's afraid to speak at all.

I break from the cityscape outside to focus on the inside of the room.

Cassius nudges my side. "Hey, do you see anybody?"

"What?"

"Look." He points past the man in black to an enormous, rounded desk. It's not made of wood, or metal, but some stonelike substance that reminds me of granite. "It's just red, right? You see it too?"

I blink. Then it snaps into focus, out of nowhere. A figure sits behind the structure, glowing such an intense red that I can barely look at him. I can't discern any features, only the faintest idea of a shape. And even that's blurry. It's like a black hole of red Pearl energy. And to my astonishment it moves. And talks.

"Lieutenant Thamus," the voice starts. It's halfway between a boom and a whisper. An impossible voice. "Number 976. Do I have that correct?"

"Of course, sir."

The red energy flickers. "I was gazing at the stars, wondering."

There's a pause, but Cassius breaks the silence. "It's Matigo," he whispers. "Are we on Haven?"

I push his shoulder. "Shh."

He takes a cautious step forward. "I don't think they can hear me."

The red energy pulses. "Aren't you going to ask me for clarification?" Matigo's voice changes again. It's more thunderous now. Muffled, even, like it's coming from a broken speaker.

Lieutenant Thamus stands, hands clasped behind his back. "Of course, sir."

Something pounds the top of the desk. It could have been Matigo's fist, but there's no way to be sure through the glare of the energy. "I was wondering why we've yet to quantify the number of stars in the universe. I'm compelled to conduct an inventory."

The lieutenant nods. "Perhaps after our mission is complete, sir."

"Perhaps." He pauses. The energy dulls for a moment. "I was also wondering about tomorrow. I am concerned."

Thamus bows again. "I understand completely."

"Our foremost experts have assured me that the process will run smoothly. These past three months have been hard on him. The initiation ... it is not always pleasant, especially for such a young body. But he has his father's talents." He pauses. "And I don't intend to back down. I am not a coward, and neither is my son. If it is good enough for the Resistance, it is good enough for me."

Thamus takes a deep breath. "Everything has been orchestrated with great precision. Every variable has been considered. We have eliminated the possibility of surprise."

The energy pulses. "You've come to collect him, then?"

"If King Matigo wishes it."

Cassius tiptoes forward, past the lieutenant and closer to the desk.

Matigo speaks. "I don't fear for his life. Death is insignificant in the grand scheme of things. I would sacrifice a child ten times over to see this through."

"I understand."

"Good." The energy flickers. "The Resistance has already sent their champions, and with them, an attempt at blocking our systems. Ridium is the key to our success. If the Resistance hadn't coerced a Shifter, we would not be having this discussion now."

"Yes," Thamus says. "We are still investigating the possibility of a defector."

The energy quivers, as if sighing. "It doesn't matter who did it. All remaining Ridium is under the Authority's control once again. There's precious little left after our initial assault on Earth. Haven's southernmost pits are more heavily guarded than ever before. They may have halted our efforts momentarily, but the dam will puncture. It is inevitable."

I look at Cassius. "The Scarlet Bombings. Do you think that's how they got the Ridium under the surface of Earth?"

He shrugs.

Thamus swallows. "May I ask you a question, sir?"

It's silent for a moment. The energy softens. "You may."

"Why him? Why your son?"

Matigo takes his time before responding. For a second I think he's going to ignore the question altogether, but then the energy moves again. "You might ask the Resistance the same thing. I have become a target in this war. Those close to me have become targets. There are other Shifters on this planet, but they will have their own ambitions. There is a legacy to uphold. I cannot make this journey, not yet. Not until I know that it is safe. And if I cannot do it, someone of royal blood must be allowed the honor." He pauses. "You will take him to the pits at dawn and he will be submerged in Ridium. I have a team of Shifters ready to construct his craft and get him safely to Earth. Then, when the time is right, I will send a Herald after him and our invasion will begin."

Lieutenant Thamus nods. "What if he will not go willingly?"

"He is my son." Matigo laughs. "He is honored by the opportunity. He is *excited*."

Cassius creeps around the side of the desk, trying to

get closer to the energy. When he's near enough to reach out a hand and touch it, something pushes him back. He glances at me, eyes wide with surprise. "It's like there's a wall here," he whispers. "It's not even warm or anything. It's just ... nothing."

I shake my head, unable to give any explanation.

Just then, something catches my eye, off to the side of the room. A boy appears from nowhere, sitting on a stool next to the wall, twirling a dagger in his hand. He wasn't there before, I'm sure of it. Thamus ignores him completely. There's no indication that Matigo's seen him either.

I crouch low to look at the boy's face. He can't be any older than five. His brown hair covers the tops of his eyes so that it's hard to get a decent look at them. The blade of the dagger reflects light from the city beyond as it shifts effortlessly through his fingers. "Cassius." I keep my voice low. "Come over here."

Cassius moves past Thamus and crouches beside me to look at the boy. "It's him," he whispers. "Of course it's him."

I bring my head down and meet the kid's eyes. And I see it. Instantly. There's a familiar expression in them—a warped curiosity. A slightly rattled look.

I turn back, heart in my throat. "Theo."

The boy stands. I back away, scared that he heard me. I push Cassius to the doorway and we watch as Theo approaches Thamus. The red energy pulses behind the desk.

The dagger falls still in Theo's hands. He sheathes it at his side and crosses his arms. He's just a kid, but the way he stands—the look in his eyes—there's nothing innocent about it.

"My son," Matigo's voice booms. "Soon you will undergo a journey. A test run. You may be lonely for some time, but I will not be far behind. They are using an energy transport system against us. We will use Ridium against them. It has already been set in motion on Earth. There's only one thing standing in our way, and it belongs in the hands of the Resistance." He pauses. "Sons. Children, like you. And once they are disposed of, there will be no stopping us."

The words blast through me like an explosion. They echo, as thunderous as Matigo's voice. *Disposed of.*

I stare at the five-year-old Theo's face, committing everything I've heard to memory. Ridium. Shifter. Herald. Submerged.

Disposed of.

Suddenly, everything collapses around us. The walls fragment and fold into each other. Theo's body disintegrates right in front of me. The hypnotic carpet swirls so quickly that it becomes a starburst. We dive into the endless sea of lights. They begin to change, multiply, and spread apart until they're stars.

It's cold. Then windy.

I'm in the middle of the sky again. Free-fall.

Only I'm not falling anymore. Ryel's cube tumbles from the air and lands in my hand. Something carries me.

Someone.

It takes me a moment to see him. My mind is so muddled. But then I notice the glow. Green, all around me. A cocoon of Pearl energy protects my body. If deflects the wind until I can't feel anything.

A pair of arms support me, stronger than they look. The Drifter's face comes into view as he gently holds me in the air. I meet his eyes, though I can't speak. I let my body droop against his hold, confident that he won't drop me. I've got no reason to be, but the Pearl energy makes everything feel better.

The Drifter speaks. "You saved me. Now, I shall save you."

My shoulder jerks back as I hear his voice. "English?"

He nods. "English."

"Wait." I analyze his face, looking for markings, hair color, anything to identify him. "Are you—"

"You freed me," he interrupts. "From a dark machine. There was a tunnel. Darkness, all around."

"You're the guy from the generator back at the Academy," I say. "From three nights ago. I didn't know if you'd lived." A smile breaks out on my face. I don't mean it to. It fades as soon as I remember the events of the night. "Hey ... what about Cassius?"

"He is with my friend," the Drifter replies, his voice calm and low. "You are both safe. It's lucky you found a senso-cube. It bought you some time."

"That's what that thing is? A senso-cube?"

He nods. "You and your brother were suspended in the air for nearly thirty minutes. Frozen, like statues."

The thought makes me cringe, not only for the sheer weirdness of it, but for the thought of what Theo could have done to us in that time.

I glance toward the stars. The vessel of Ridium is gone. Theo's disappeared.

The Drifter's grip loosens around my midsection. "We are nearly on the Surface now. My transport energy is beginning to fade. I won't have many more flights left in me."

The sun begins to rise over the mountains. Not enough to kill the darkness, but the sight captivates me. It's been so long since I've been this high in the air. I used to witness sunrises like this every morning out my dorm window. I've been on the Surface too long.

Before I know it, the Drifter's feet touch ground and he places me in the dirt. I lie there, trying to get my bearings. Only when I'm sure the earth won't collapse underneath me do I stand.

Cassius is beside a second Drifter. I shift to scan the stark landscape. We're back outside Lenbrg, right where Theo conjured that vessel of Ridium. I crane my neck and search the stars, past Skyships to the darkest part of the sky. He's up there. He wanted to kill us.

Matigo's son.

We have to stop him.

35

It isn't long before I see the others come over the hill toward us. They must have seen the glow from the Drifters. Avery takes off at a sprint toward me, then wraps my torso in a tight embrace.

The second Drifter helps Cassius to his feet. We stand in a bubble of dim green, which is already starting to fade.

The Drifters tell us their names are Talan and Sem. Sem's the one who plucked me from the sky, and he speaks better English than Talan. The language processors in their Pearls vary in structure, he says. Some are damaged during transport, and others move more slowly to cater to individual brain functioning.

"Where have you been?" Avery clutches my arm. "By the time we headed outside, you guys were gone."

"Theo's escaped." Cassius steps past her. "He's Matigo's son. He wants to kill us."

Eva follows him. "Matigo has a son?"

Sem looks down at his fingers, watching the last of the Pearl energy drain from his body. "The boy's shifting powers have been unlocked. He's in control of Ridium now, just like his father. But he's young. Inexperienced. We may be able to strike before he has a chance to do any major damage."

I turn to face him. "How are we supposed to do that?"

Sem stares directly into my eyes. He looks strikingly like Ryel. "Pearl energy is the most powerful force we have. If we can knock him off balance, we'll attack when he's most vulnerable." He sighs. "Talan and I are nearly dissolved of our energy. We won't be much help in this regard."

"But you're talking to the Pearlbreaker." Skandar moves beside me. "Jesse can get more Drifters."

Sem extends his fingers. "Let me see your arm."

I hold up my right hand. He grabs hold and pulls me closer. "Ridium, I see. Your father gave this to you?"

Cassius kicks the dirt before turning to face us again. "It was in the form of a box, at first. It melted and … and now we can't get them off."

"These are a problem in the hands of a Shifter like Theo." Sem glances at Talan. "Though they might be something more."

I swallow. "Ryel said that it could be programmed."

"A Shifter can do many things with Ridium," Sem says. "Not the least of which is programming. It's possible that your parents coerced a Shifter to imbue these bracelets with a purpose." He drops my hand.

I stare down at the blackness. "Like what?"

"That isn't clear, but once a chunk of Ridium is given a purpose, it will follow its programming until another

Shifter tells it otherwise. This could be a problem, or a blessing. Only time will tell."

Cassius rubs his wrist. "I don't like the sound of that."

I let my hand fall to my side, forgetting about the bracelet for a moment. "Drifters. We need Drifters."

Sem nods. "We must attack the boy, and soon. But we need all of the artillery we can get."

"Okay." I turn and face the distant mountains. I close my eyes so that nothing can distract me and work through the events of the past few days, considering my options. Allies and enemies, and everything in between. When I open them again, a single vision fills my mind. "Okay. I think I know what to do." I turn back. "What's the nearest Skyship?"

Eva shrugs. "There are a couple storage ships just south of the Canadian border."

"No." I ball my fist. "It needs to be one of the larger ones, but nothing with a heavy Tribunal presence."

"Then Altair," she replies. "Skyship Altair. Southeast of here."

"What are you thinking, Jesse?" Avery's eyes narrow.

Cassius smiles. "He's thinking we need to steal some Pearls."

"We've got two options," I say. "Break into a Chosen or find a storage facility on one of the Skyships. We can't just stand here waiting for Pearls to come to us. We need a lot of them, and quick."

Eva frowns. "And what about Theo?"

Cassius curses under his breath. He clutches his bracelet and meets my eyes. "I'll handle Theo. At least until you can break the Pearls."

Sem moves to Talan's side. "And we will do what we can to help. Unfortunately, I don't think I will be able to enjoy the benefits of flight for much longer. We'll require use of your shuttle. But we can help organize any freed Drifters. We can make sure your efforts aren't in vain."

I nod. "Then let's get this over with."

Eva points back to the hill we'd come over. "Shuttle's just past that point."

Sem meets my eyes. "Lead the way, Pearlbreaker."

———

Two hours after dawn.

Skyship Altair hovers over the Idaho/Montana border. It's too far from either coast to be much of a government stronghold. Eva says she's heard it's mainly a recreation and business center. Not a lot of money stored onboard, but given its size, it must need a plentiful amount of Pearls to keep it airborne. This will be our target.

The sun beams into every window of our shuttle. The Fringes are bound to be baking, even this early in the morning.

Cassius sits in the pilot's seat. "So that room we saw, with Matigo and his lieutenant. That was a memory?"

Sem nods. "A reconstruction. Important events are stored in senso-cubes on Haven. The Authority controls all of the planet's history. I suspect that particular cube was stolen."

"I found it in Ryel's pocket," I say.

Sem's brows rise. "If he was indeed a pilot with the Authority, I suppose he would have had the opportunity to grab a cube before joining the Resistance. Usually they're simple to trigger, but Matigo likely had security in place on that cube. You were lucky it managed to activate in the air. Perhaps due to the vast amount of Ridium above it."

Cassius brings us back level. "Any tips on Theo?"

The Drifter frowns. "Don't underestimate him."

"Yeah," Cassius says. "I think I've got that." He turns to me. "As soon as the officials on Altair see this Academy shuttle land in the docking bay, they'll likely send people after you."

I grit my teeth. He's right. Unless Alkine's pulled off some sort of diplomatic miracle while I've been gone, all those onboard the Academy are still fugitives from the Sky-ship Community.

"I won't stay long," Cassius continues. "Just a quick drop-off. Use the others to create a distraction."

"Yeah," I say. "We'll do what we can."

Sem nods. "We need to be on the offensive. We can't drag this out."

"Good thing," Cassius responds. "Because we're almost there."

My knees shake with nervous energy. I think about last spring, when I was a simple Skyship trainee floundering in a program that, at the time, seemed too big and too difficult to bear. Now, only four months later, I'm planning an assault against a Skyship.

I think back to what Morse said in the Fringes before Theo killed him. I could be the trigger for this invasion. Has it already happened? If I had stayed back at the Academy like Captain Alkine wanted, would we have had more time to prepare?

There's no chance to second-guess myself now.

We stand in the docking bay of Altair, watching the ship pull away. I don't know what Cassius thinks he's doing, going after Theo on his own. I've learned not to question him, but it doesn't sit easy with me.

Before leaving the ship, I grabbed a pistol and tucked it in the waist of my pants. The cold metal is a constant reminder of the risk I'm about to take. It should raise my confidence. Maybe I'd feel better if I was a good aim.

"Find the main security center and keep watch." I turn to the others. "If something happens, I'm counting on you guys to throw them off track. Create a diversion ... or something."

Eva crosses her arms. "That's very vague, Jesse."

"I know," I reply. "But if the Pearls are stored on the lower levels, I won't be able to see what's happening in the city. If they've got a security patrol after me, I'm blind against them."

Avery shakes her head. "You're not doing this alone, Jesse."

"The fewer of us that go, the less obvious it will be."

"You need a backup," she says.

Sem nods. "The girl is right. Talan and I will scout. If necessary, we may be able to provide the distraction you need."

I meet Avery's eyes. I try not to let my heart make a stupid decision, but even weighing the pros and cons leads me to the same response. "Okay, Avery. You're coming with me."

Eva glances at a shuttle full of commuters in the distance. "Don't feel too secure, people. Once Jesse starts breaking Pearls, it's going to be like the Academy times a hundred. People will feel it. The entire ship will."

I take a deep breath, turning to Avery and grabbing her hand. "You really wanna do this?"

"Do *you?*" She squeezes my fingers.

I don't answer. Instead, I clutch the pistol under my shirt, say a few prayers, and hope for the best.

36

After ascending twelve levels, Avery and I arrive in a broad, low-ceilinged plaza just below the domed city at the very top of Skyship Altair. It's an underground shopping center, reeking of perfume samples. The light overhead is impossibly bright, the faux-marble tiles polished and gleaming below our feet. Slow, hypnotic music plays softly in the background. It calms my rollicking heartbeat, if only for a moment.

I watch shoppers as they pass by. Even this early in the day, the wide plaza is crammed with activity. "The more people, the better chance we have of blending in." I step forward. "We need to find a ship directory."

We push through the crowd, past holographic advertisements and decorative fixtures. Fountains, indoor gardens, the latest gaming pavilions.

And then he catches my eye. He emerges from around the corner of an electronics store, still covered in his dark bodysuit. The red energy has completely faded, but I recognize his face immediately. It's the face that I hoped was my father's. The face in the swarm.

I grab Avery's arm and pull her close. We flatten against the wall. "It's the Drifter, from the red Pearl."

She cranes her neck, but the Drifter's quickly swallowed by the crowd. "Where?"

"Not far." My bracelet buzzes. He's getting closer. "This isn't good."

I scan the shopping center, searching for escape routes. I can't see the Drifter anymore, but I'm sure it was him. The trembling of the Ridium confirms it.

"There!" Avery points to an exit on the other side of the plaza, in between a pair of clothing stores. We'll have to cut through the crowd to reach it, and risk running right into the Drifter, but there aren't any other options.

I stand on my toes and try to gauge the Drifter's whereabouts. "Do you see him?"

"No, but it's so crowded."

"We're gonna have to chance it. Follow me."

We take off at a sprint across the plaza. The Drifter spots us immediately.

I watch his arm stretch out. People fall like dominoes around us, yanked sideways through the air before they land in a heap along the wall. Broken dolls. That's what they look like after he's done. They don't even have time to scream.

Avery slams into my shoulder as I freeze, in awe of the Drifter's power. She pushes me. "Come on!"

"How's he—"

Floor tiles pull from the ground and explode in splinters

around me. The Drifter's hand glows red as he steps forward, eyes pinned onto mine.

I glance around the plaza, looking for something that I can use against him. Lights flicker overhead. The calm music continues to pour from speakers around us. Gaming pavilions function in the distance.

And then it occurs to me. It's all electricity, everything around us. Energy. Pearl energy.

It's a long shot, but I have to try.

I close my eyes and reach into the air with both hands. I was able to summon energy from the Drifter back on the island in Siberia. If I can do that, maybe I can rip it from the transformers and wiring inside this ship.

The mall continues to deconstruct around me, ripping violently apart at the red Drifter's whim. Screams echo along the walls as the remaining crowd scatters in all directions. Benches fly into walls. Plants tear from their pots and shred into pieces. I don't know how he's doing this, but his shots have missed me so far. Other than a few small nicks, I'm fine.

My skin tingles. I pull down through the air and ball my fingers into fists at my side. I open my eyes.

The lights shut off. The music dies and the pavilions fade to a stop. Thin streams of green energy fall from the ceiling like a fine rain. Inch-long slivers. Fragments.

I push out and direct them toward the Drifter. They cut through the air like a thousand porcupine quills, puncturing his coat and lodging themselves in his skin. He stumbles back. This is hurting him. Good.

The red in his hand fades. Alarms start to blare in the distance. Bodies litter the ground. Those that weren't hurt have escaped into the shops. They cower, watching us.

I grab Avery's hand. "So much for keeping things calm."

We dash through the darkness, past the exit, and arrive in an unadorned, concrete hallway—a claustrophobic underbelly to the mall's hyper-lit, kinetic energy. These types of places are usually pretty empty. The alarms will draw any guards toward the shopping center, but we've got a few moments before they arrive.

Podlights flicker at equal intervals on either side of us. We rush around the nearest corner without a word.

"Did you kill him?" Avery huffs as we power down the second corridor.

"I don't think so," I say. "All I did was slow him down."

As if in response to my words, the exit door breaks from its hinges behind us. I hear footsteps. Turns out I didn't slow him down as much as I thought.

Avery grabs my wrist and steers me toward an emergency door to our left. My breath catches in my lungs as we barrel down another corridor. I can't take much more of this before I collapse altogether. I'm not a marathon runner.

The Drifter's feet pound behind us, an ever-accelerating drum pattern. He's faster than I expected. Maybe it's the red energy, or maybe I made him angry.

We plunge past another door and head deeper into the Skyship. Then another. I grab the pistol from my waist. With every turn we make, I expect to cross paths with a security force. But we're good for now. This is maintenance territory—the inner workings. Unless there's a problem with the ship itself, we should go unnoticed.

I feel the Ridium hum against my skin and wonder if Theo can feel it too. The way he controlled the substance, I wouldn't be surprised if he knew where I was right this moment.

I wipe the thought from my mind. I don't need to be worrying about Theo. Not yet. Something catches my eye. A symbol on a door at the end of our corridor. I pull Avery to a stop.

"Jesse!" She struggles against me. "We've gotta keep moving."

"No. Don't you recognize it?" I point to the symbol, a bolt of lightning surrounded by an intricately bordered circle.

"Power station," she whispers.

I nod and race to the door. Large ships like Altair have no less than four stations like this spread around the vessel. They're what pump the Pearl energy around. The ship's hearts.

"It's a dead end," Avery warns.

"I know." I grab the handle. "But I have an idea."

"You're gonna get us killed."

"No," I say. "If there's a Pearl inside, I can use it."

"What if it's empty?"

I lay my hand on the door and close my eyes. I can feel it inside, a warm presence calling to me. "It's not."

I wrap my hands around the trigger of the pistol and fire into the door, just below the handle. The lock blasts away. We slip inside.

The light from the hallway outside is eaten by darkness. The floor to the station is illuminated by thin, orange diamonds running along the sides, a sign that we're close to the reactor. A metal door lies closed at the far end of the corridor. It's likely more than a foot thick—too much for my dinky little blaster.

I rush forward, jogging down the hall until I feel the buzzing energy of the door under my fingers.

Avery moves behind me. "I don't like this, Jesse. He's coming."

"I can do it," I whisper. "There's Pearl energy on the other side, funneling in the reactor." The hair on the back of my hand stands on end. "The Drifter's gone. It's halfway drained already, but I can use what's left."

She turns, surveying the dark. Her gaze shifts toward the ceiling. "This place is like a tomb. If you're wrong…" She can't finish the sentence.

I run my hand along the surface of the door, feeling for cracks or holes. Anything. Already, my body feels stronger. I lay my cheek against metal, pulling.

My heart swells. I feel a waft of air brush against the back of my neck. I'm surrounded by energy. I could bathe in it if I wanted. I take a step away, furrow my brows, and grasp on with everything I've got.

"Jesse." Avery turns. "Did you hear me?"

I don't need to respond. Strands of green light coil from within the doorway, escaping through microscopic holes and cracks in the metal. They flower around me, winding above our heads. Trails of light swirl in the darkness. Some wind underfoot, curling beside my feet until they find refuge with a neighboring strand. The door rattles and hums, on the verge of pulverizing into dust. The hallway flashes a brilliant green. I close my eyes and become one with the energy, letting it wash over me like a wave of soothing bathwater. It encircles my body, cleansing cuts and bruises from the day. My lungs expand with the freshest, most revitalizing air imaginable. I feel whole.

A door slams off its hinges. The sound pulls my eyes open once more. I spin around to see the silhouette of the Drifter at the opposite end of the hallway, still and menacing. Both fists glow with a vibrant red—violent Pearl energy ready to kill me if I don't act soon.

Avery backs into my shoulder. The Drifter holds out a hand. The corridor rattles. The scars on my chest burn, though it's quickly countered by the bolstering cocoon around me.

Before he can make a move, I let it all go. I thrust my hands forward and feel everything leave me. The green wave shoots through the hallway in a turbine, twisting and swirling so fast that the strands blend together, one undecipherable from the next.

I watch the energy slam into the Drifter. It knocks him back in a violent pulse. He flies across the connecting corridor and slams through the neighboring wall, pushed faster and farther by the oncoming energy.

The ground drops beneath us as the Skyship lurches downward. The thick metal of the door cracks behind me. Avery slips. She holds her head in her hands, protecting herself from oncoming rubble. The rows of orange lights blink frantically before settling. The ground stabilizes as the ship corrects itself. One power station deactivated. If I hit all of them, we're going down.

I watch the last of the Pearl energy dissipate through the distant hole in the wall. The Drifter's gone, knocked way off course. I pushed him away, maybe even killed him.

I help Avery to her feet. "Are you okay?"

She nods, visibly shaken. "I thought what you did last spring was something. That ... that was amazing, Jesse."

"Yeah?" I take a deep breath. "There's more where that came from." I glance behind me. I can see the empty generator through the cracks in the thick door. Scraps lie at my feet. "Come on," I say. "Let's go break some Pearls."

37

Cassius gunned the accelerator, arcing the Academy ship high into the stratosphere, far enough from Skyship Altair that it seemed a distant dot below him. He'd never driven an agent's ship before. The controls were remarkably similar to those of a cruiser, but the speed was amplified. He could work wonders with this. He'd need to.

Last time he'd engaged Theo, the boy had the upper hand. He had control of the environment, even in his unstable mental state. The trick this time was to hit him first, draw blood before he could react. He knew precious little about Ridium, but it was certainly dangerous, especially under Theo's control.

Cassius took stock of the weapons available to him. Cannons, mounted on the front underbelly. Tractor beams—useful only if he had the chance to pull Theo into the ship with him. A pair of missiles, though he doubted that human weaponry would be of much use against an alien substance like Ridium. If the black vessel was anything as strong as the bracelet around Cassius's arm, he'd be fighting against the indestructible.

As he piloted the ship, his mind kept coming back to one thing. Pearls.

Matigo obviously feared them, or feared how they could be used. Otherwise, he wouldn't have gone to the trouble to send his own son to Earth as some sort of sting agent. He wouldn't be after Fisher, either. If Fisher succeeded in finding more Drifters, Cassius hoped they knew what to do.

He took a deep breath and began to bring the ship down. Theo's vessel appeared on the radar as a dark blotch, like a storm cloud ready to belch thunder and lightning. Cassius was directly on top of it now.

First, he'd unleash a volley of cannon blasts. If that didn't work, he'd have to get closer. One way or another, he needed to engage Theo directly. If he couldn't kill him, he'd hurt him. Weaken him until the Drifters could finish him off.

The ship gained speed as it cut through the air, descending like a dagger piercing the sky. The black, spherical vessel neared. Cassius waited until he could see it clearly before letting loose.

He fired a round right into the surface, spinning sideways to avoid crashing into the vessel. Explosions lit up the atmosphere around the sphere of darkness but left no mark. As soon as the smoke faded, Theo's vessel remained untouched, floating silently in the sky.

He rounded in a wide loop, ready to test the missiles.

He doubted they would be any more effective, but he had to try everything before risking a closer encounter.

As he turned to approach the vessel, he noticed a quiver of movement from the darkness. He pulled a pair of specs from the cabinet overhead and slipped them onto his eyes, magnifying his vision twofold.

The blackness stirred in front of him like a monster ready to attack. He slowed his approach.

Out of nowhere, the vessel developed a long, snakelike arm. It flew from the darkness, extending a winding tendril through the sky, directly toward his ship.

Cassius cursed. In one motion, he released the missiles and pulled up, cutting a vertical climb back into safe territory as the black extension wound after him.

The missiles detonated along the shell of Theo's vessel with little effect. Cassius brought the Academy ship upside down, spinning so that he could make a quick escape.

Too late.

The black tendril grabbed onto his stern with an awful clamp. Metal squealed behind him. He laid on the accelerator. It was no use. Within seconds, the entire ship yanked backward.

He slammed into the console, then forced a glance over his shoulder. He was expecting to see the entire ship tear away from him. Instead, a violent thud on the windshield sent him flying with enough force to snap his seat belt. He hit the ground sideways and rolled to catch a glimpse of the windshield. A black film of Ridium blotted out the sky.

All at once, the backward pull intensified. He tried to grab onto something, but it was too quick. He flew forward through the air and collided with the console again. The speed of the movement forced him into the windshield, dangerously close to the Ridium outside.

His bracelet clamped onto the wall of black, craving to rejoin the element. He stared at the doorway to the cabin, wishing he could escape. Theo had hold of the entire ship now. He could do anything he wanted. He could smash him like a piece of tin.

Cassius closed his eyes and succumbed to panic. He was miles above the Earth, closer and closer to a lunatic who could control everything around him. And all Cassius had was fire. Fire wouldn't do anything up here, not against Matigo's son.

A deep rumbling sounded underneath him, then a violent tearing as the Ridium ripped the Academy ship to pieces. The cabin door splayed open, eaten by an enormous black mouth of jagged teeth—a razorblade funnel that sucked Cassius in and spit him back out.

He landed hard on dark flooring. The familiar sheen gave the entire room a pristine feel. His bracelet sunk to the ground, forcing his arm with it.

Then, Theo's voice. Nowhere, and everywhere all at once.

"So you lived," he said.

Cassius flipped over so that he could stare at the ceiling.

It was the same color as the floor, of course. Everything was. Smooth. Black. Alien.

His eyes darted around, searching for Theo. His right wrist kept him pinned to the ground, but he kicked his legs anyway, struggling to get up. "Where are you?" His voice sounded smaller than usual. He didn't want to sound like this, not in front of Theo.

"You shouldn't have been so nasty to me." The boy's voice rang out from somewhere behind him. "I remember everything. It doesn't change what's going to happen, but I could have made it easier for you if we'd been friends."

Cassius squirmed on the ground, trying to pull his hand free. "I know who you are. You're not some poor junkie's kid from the Fringes."

"Surprise."

Cassius heard footsteps. Then, out of nowhere, Theo appeared beside his left leg, arms crossed. Cassius tried to kick him, but Theo quickly fashioned a coil of Ridium from the ground, keeping his ankle in place.

Cassius glared at the kid. "Did you know the whole time?"

"Not before the swarm," Theo responded. "Not before the crimson."

"The red Drifter?"

"Matigo's herald." He nodded. "Sent to Earth to kick things off when my father was ready."

"Where is he?" Cassius strained to look up at Theo. "Where's Matigo?"

Theo crouched, one leg on either side of Cassius's. His smile widened—that same sick expression he'd worn when they'd first met at the Lodge. "Anywhere. And everywhere."

"What's that supposed to mean?"

"A broken world like this one is so much easier to conquer." He paused. "My father knows this. You're all at war with each other, and you don't even know what's coming."

"I saw you," Cassius spit. "On Haven. I saw what he was going to do to you. Bring you down to the pits. Submerge you … or something."

Theo nodded. "We're Shifters, me and my father. There aren't many of us on Haven, and even less who can manipulate Ridium as well as we can." A spout of blackness emerged from between Cassius's feet, like the eruption of a volcano. Theo grabbed hold of the top and formed it into a perfect sphere. It hovered over his hand, spinning like the model of a planet. "It won't mean a thing once it's all gone, but for now it's going to help us take over this planet."

Theo shot the black sphere into the air, where it exploded in a hundred sideways raindrops that diffused into the walls around them. "A skilled Shifter," he continued, "can program a task—or several—in specific order, and the hunk of Ridium will carry that information until it's completed its mission." He stepped to Cassius's side and sat, staring down at his bracelet. "I can feel it now. That chunk around your wrist was given a set of three tasks by a traitor to the Authority." He ran his hand over the surface of the bracelet. "Task one: Transform from the shape of a cube to a pair of bracelets, one for the Pearlbreaker, one for his brother."

Cassius remembered when Madame had first presented him with the mysterious black box. It had taken Fisher's key to activate it. His wrist hadn't been bare since.

"Task two," Theo continued. "Relay your mother's recording from Haven. Reveal all of the amazing things you can do to save your world." He laughed for a second. Then his smiled faded. "Task three won't matter much longer."

"Tell me." Cassius squirmed.

Theo nodded. "Your parents thought they were smart. The bracelets, even back when they were some boring box, have been programmed by a Shifter to transmit a constant signal to the stars."

"So what?"

"So ... " He smiled. "They're a filter. They let in the good Pearls and keep out the bad."

"How?"

He shrugged. "Green, red ... it's different energy. It's a frequency game, Stevenson. Like a radio blocking a certain station." He lifted his finger. Cassius's bracelet lifted into the air, stopping half a foot from the ground. Frozen. "Like I said, Ridium's a powerful substance. I don't know how the Resistance found a Shifter willing to undercut the Authority, but this little thing, along with Fisher's, was their last great hope."

He let the bracelet fall to the floor again. It landed against the Ridium without a sound. "There are thousands of them, Cassius, right at the edge of space, circling your planet. Red Pearls, everywhere. More than I can even imagine. This far up, you might even feel them if you close your eyes and concentrate real hard." He smiled. "And all I have to do is get rid of you and your brother."

Cassius winced as the coil tightened around his leg. "What about the red Drifter? He was in a Pearl. He came through okay."

Theo nodded. "He wore a tiny piece of Ridium around his neck—the last remaining treasure in my father's collection. It was a gamble, but Ridium attracts Ridium. The natural bond between the objects was enough to break through the transmission." His brows rose. "That's how I came to Earth, after all."

Cassius craned his neck to see around the room. "You came here in *this*?"

Theo laughed. "Are you kidding me? All I had was enough Ridium to get me safely through space."

"Submerged," Cassius said. "You were submerged in it."

"Exactly," he replied. "And I shifted it into a kind of ship. A barrier between me and the stars. Like a Pearl, but better." He paused. "It was supposed to be untraceable, but Madame's radars must have picked me up when I landed. I don't know … I guess she had reason to search the skies after you and Fisher showed up."

A ripple coursed through the ground as he continued. "I had no memory when I got here, wandering through Fringe Town after Fringe Town until she picked me up.

An accident, she'd said. I'd had an accident. That's all." He turned away, eyes focused on the distant wall. "But Ridium's everywhere. It came down with the Scarlet Bombings that destroyed your cities. It's been seeping underground ever since, waiting for Matigo to use it. Every last bit of the stuff that was on Haven is now on Earth. The entire planet's a weapon for those who can use it."

Cassius felt a pain in his chest, like the wind had been kicked out of him. "I thought the Scarlet Bombings—"

"Were a pre-strike," Theo interrupted. "Yeah, they were. They set everything in motion. The warming of the environment, the fighting. Skyships. Chosen Cities. And Ridium. Everything's been counting down to this moment."

Cassius winced. "So what are you going to do?"

Theo grinned. "First, I'm going to let the rest of the Authority in. Then, oh great Cassius Stevenson, I'm going to kill you."

38

Altair's in full freak-out mode. I'm sure of it, even though I can't hear the sirens anymore. If the destruction in the shopping center wasn't enough, the lurch from the disrupted generator would have set everyone on edge. We've stabilized now, but sudden drops in altitude don't make for a very subtle sneak attack.

Avery and I stumble back to the main corridor of the Skyship, stopping at a maintenance directory on our way. The nearest storage center is one level below us, not far. It's a matter of blending until we get there. We can't allow a security team to get the jump on us, not when we're so close.

My mind flashes to Cassius. It's not a productive thing to worry about, but I can't help but wonder if he's alright. Theo was a deadly opponent even before Lenbrg. I know Cassius is strong—he could take us all down if he wanted to—but is it enough?

I brush the thought aside and try to envision the mission before me. I see us breaking into the storage room. I imagine the explosions. Pearls, everywhere. Light, everywhere. So bright I have to shield my eyes. I feel the buzzing—how great it is to break one, how dangerously empowering. I try to imagine this as an assignment. Schoolwork that needs to be turned in. Goal. Objective. I bet this is how Cassius sees things all the time. If I can tap into his wavelength, I can be like him. A soldier. But it fits worse than that too-tight suit I had to wear during Visitation Day last spring. I'm not the guy that gets things done. My life's been a series of starts, not finishes.

Avery and I crouch against the wall outside the storage center. "They're gonna be on edge," I say. "After what happened in the reactor, they'll be sending teams down."

She nods. "We'll have to be quick. They don't know what you can do."

A tremor runs down my spine. "I can feel it, even through the wall. There are dozens of them, just sitting there."

Avery grabs the pistol from my side. "Here, let me handle this."

"You're gonna shoot them?"

She blinks. "If there are guards."

"It's on stun, right?"

"Don't worry about it," she says. "I'll do what's required to protect you. I used to be a decent shot in my day."

"But—" I stop myself. She doesn't want to hear it. She doesn't care how much I hate hurting people, how selfish I feel when these kinds of things happen because of me. She's right. This became a war weeks ago. There are casualties in war, some of them innocent. There will be a whole lot more if we let the Authority invade.

The energy hums around me like a swarm of insects, tugging at my skin, trying to work its way inside. I swallow and block it out for now. It's too scattershot, anyway—too far away to be of any use.

I take a deep breath. "Let's go."

We sidestep to a pair of wide doors. Avery keeps the pistol close. The foyer of the storage center will be open to the public. It's part of the Tribunal's effort to increase Pearl education, or at least that's what they say. They even grant field trips to kids so they can spend a day learning how the energy is processed. God, I hope there are no kids here today.

I hear whispers immediately. They're calling me, like old friends. A trail of invisible energy pulls me forward. I'm a fish on a hook. My fingers tense at my side, then ball into a fist. I don't even realize I'm doing it.

An oval door spreads apart in front of us and reveals a wide, empty foyer. Avery grabs my wrist, pulling me back to her side. She knows the energy is strong. It'll yank me forward too fast if I let it. "Easy," she whispers.

I shake my hand and try to wash the bristling prickles from my skin.

A crescent-shaped stone desk sits at the far end of the entry room, manned by a single receptionist behind an extended computer pad. A pair of armed guards flank her on either side some distance down the wall. They stand beside thick columns that support an arched glass ceiling. Fancy.

My feet tingle. A wave of Pearl energy pushes my legs forward in awkward steps toward the desk. Fast, until I'm almost running. Avery struggles to keep up. I push back on my heel, but instead of stopping, it catches on the ground and I'm pulled to the side. My hand moves up from my pocket to my hip, forcing out my left elbow. It's hardly subtle.

The receptionist notices. She shifts uneasily in her seat before standing. We're not even halfway across the room before she motions for the guards to intervene.

Avery raises her pistol. "Stop."

Instantly, I realize how pathetic this is. The weapon might scare the receptionist, but it sure as hell isn't going to intimidate the guards. They're outfitted with all the latest defenses. One wrong move and they'll blow us to bits. I've gotta do something.

My eyes close. When they open again, it's like I can see right through the wall behind the receptionist. I mentally catalog my way through the Pearls in the store rooms beyond. My heart beats fast. They call to me, each one. Whisper and hum, a collection of eggs ready to hatch. It's almost too much. I push my hands over my ears. Avery glances nervously at me.

The receptionist throws her hands in the air, head darting between the guards, expression frantic. The soldiers pull weapons from their belts, each about three times the size of Avery's pistol. So much for taking them by force.

"There are too many," I respond through gritted teeth. My chest tightens. I land on my knees, hands pressed against the floor.

The guards step forward. "Drop the weapon," the nearest one says. "We'll shoot. Count of three."

I close my eyes again. I try to push aside the noise and focus on individual Pearls. I leave my body for a second, visualizing myself grabbing hold of one in particular. I note its location and move on to another. Two at once, one in each hand. I tilt my head back and imagine them floating toward me. All the while I fight to maintain control and not get lost in the maelstrom of energy around me.

Everything snaps away. I've got it.

We're connected, me and these Pearls. It's as if the voices have suddenly gone mute. I see the Pearls rip from their bindings and float through the storage room, breaking glass and plastic and whatever else they've got to travel through before reaching me.

They're coming.

"Jesse." Avery taps her foot nervously. She can't feel them like I do. It sucks for her, not being able to feel them. Not knowing what's coming.

I struggle to my feet. I curl my forearm like I'm lifting an invisible switch and take a step back as the force barrels toward me.

The receptionist backs into the wall, mouth open. "Shoot!" she begs of the guards. "Can't you shoot?"

A powerful green glow emerges from each side of us, growing brighter and bigger as the Pearls soar through the open corridors.

The Pearls gain speed and zip right at me, stopping

inches from my chest. Avery presses against my back, prepared to use my body as a shield when they break.

I hold my hand flat in front of me and push on the air. The Pearls loop around and head toward the desk. They slow, like they're rolling through syrup, before stopping completely.

I thought I'd have sympathy for the guards, but it's instinctual. The whispers return, calling to me in their unpronounceable language. Gone are the doubts about what to do. About hurting people, even killing them. The Pearls hang in front of me, begging to be broken. Taunting me. The green glow from inside is as hypnotic as ever—a swirling chaos, destroying and rebuilding itself with every passing moment. The receptionist ducks behind the desk.

I close my fist without hesitation. The Pearls explode. Waves of energy force through the room. The desk crashes against the wall, leaving a cracked dent. The guards topple over like figurines, their weapons tumbling from their hands. Their armor's blown from their bodies, cracked into pieces.

The force hits the glass ceiling above us. A cascade of splinters rains through the lobby, striking the ground in a series of jagged clinks. Green light pours through the holes in the room and courses through the circuitry of the ship.

A pair of Drifters emerges before us, all twisted and disjointed before they unfold and soar to the ceiling. They loop around transparent girders and paneling revealed by the broken glass before curving down and making a clumsy, rolling landing. Unlike the other Drifters I've freed, they've got nowhere to go.

Pearl energy hums inside my body like a city-size generator. My head spins. Avery catches my shoulder just before I'm about to black out.

"You're okay," she says.

I pull away from her and stumble toward the mangled desk. "There are more. I've gotta get them all."

She grabs my shoulder to steady me. "Are you strong enough?"

I nod. "I can feel it. The energy helps. If I absorb it, it makes me stronger." The blackness fades from my vision and my head stops thumping. I'm not going to faint.

The Drifters settle in heaps on the floor near the entrance to the room. Both wear simple white clothing like Ryel and the others, though it's hard to see anything beyond the bubble of green energy coating their bodies. One's an older woman. She could be someone's grandma. Her graying hair lies in tangled curls, framing a haggard, worn face. Her eyes are wild with fear. The other is a young man, maybe two or three years older than Cassius and me. He corrects his balance after landing hard on the floor. The two stare at each other for a moment before backing into the wall like scared animals.

I hold out a hand, afraid that they'll run away. "Wait! Stop."

They don't understand me. In moments, they see the doorway and bolt for it, slipping past the opening into the corridor beyond. They leave a trail of green behind them, a sign that they're not of this world and, worse yet, a moving target for Altair's security.

Avery watches them slip away before turning back to me. "You go break the rest. I'll run after them, see if I can get them calmed down before something happens."

I nod. I don't want her to leave, but it's important that we don't lose the same allies we're trying to free. "Try to get their language processor to kick in. If they can understand you, they'll trust you."

"Right," she says. "Be careful."

"Of course."

And then it hits me. I notice the bodies of the security guards for the first time. The receptionist. I turn to Avery, but she's already gone.

My hands shake. I stare down at them.

Weapons, that's what they are. Weapons that can kill.

I want to head over and check if the three Skyshippers are alive, but I'm scared of what I might find. So instead, I take a shallow breath and try to put them out of my mind.

What have I done? What am I doing?

No, I tell myself. Be like Cassius. Do what Alkine always told you. Don't let emotion get in the way of it.

I'm bad, but maybe it's for a good reason.

I focus on a point on the wall and forget them. The Pearls are calling. I have work to do.

39

The ground transformed beneath Cassius. It opened and spread under his back, propping him into an awkward vertical position—half standing, half hanging. It reminded him of being chained up inside the Lodge. Theo paced before him, his expression more rattled by the moment. He turned and waved his hand in front of his chest. Cassius felt his bracelet melt to liquid around his wrist and jump from his skin, right into Theo's hand. Theo manipulated the Ridium into a ball and lobbed it across the room, where it stuck to the far wall and flattened. "It's done," he said. "Melded with the rest of it, free from its programming. Once I get Fisher's, my father's Pearls will blanket the planet." He flashed a wide smile. "And you without an army. Things didn't really go the way your parents planned, did they?"

Cassius swallowed. Ridium crept over his ankles.

Theo approached. "Matigo wants you dead, but I haven't decided how I'm going to do it yet." He dislodged a chunk of Ridium from the ceiling. Cassius watched it land in the boy's hands and transform into the shape of a knife, just like the one Theo had held on the Surface. "There'd be a certain symbolism in a blade through your heart. After all, you and your friends took my favorite knife from me." The black point dissolved. Theo shrugged. "I'll think about it some more. Fisher's nearby. We're on a course for Skyship Altair now."

"What?"

"Ridium seeks Ridium," Theo said. "Remember? It's giving me signals. I feel Fisher, running like a rat through the bowels of the ship. We're nearly there."

Cassius squirmed. "You're just a kid."

A strand of Ridium crawled behind him and yanked his hair back, forcing him to meet Theo's eyes.

"I'm royal blood," he responded. "I'm not *just* anything."

"Yeah?" Cassius replied. "Well, without my father, there'd have never been Pearls in the first place. Green. Red. It doesn't matter."

Theo smiled. "But it does. Red Pearls are self-extracting. They don't need a Breaker. And once we kill Fisher, the Resistance has nothing. You should have started earlier." He laughed. "How many do you have? Ten? Twenty? Of all the thousands of Pearls that have fallen since the Scarlet Bombings, you don't—"

"Shut up."

"Hit a nerve? I'm sorry." He turned and walked away. Cassius watched him extend his hands and spread them apart through the air like he was opening a set of invisible curtains. The entire front side of the vessel blossomed open to reveal an enormous hole through which Cassius could see Skyship Altair. The ship looked like a toy in the distance, hovering unprotected in the open sky.

"See that?" Theo stared out the opening. "The entire ship's coming down, I'll guarantee it. We don't care about Skylines and Surface law. We see what we want and we take it. I'm going to send a message. An opening salvo. If Madame taught me anything, it was a sense for drama."

Cassius took a deep breath. He pictured Fisher down there, unaware of what was approaching. He hoped that his brother had managed to do something—*anything*—that would help defend against Theo. If not, this would be an extermination.

He stared at Theo from behind, marveling at his slight frame, his lopsided shoulders, and stringy hair.

Skyship Altair pulled closer until the gray of the top level filled the entire opening. Buildings. Transport. People. Shippers, yes, but people nonetheless. The line between Surface and Skyship had utterly broken. They had no idea what they were up against.

Altair's control deck was no doubt trying to radio the strange black vessel by now, but they'd have no luck. There'd be no precedent for this, and nothing to do but attack.

It came surprisingly fast.

A barrage of missiles fired from the ship's defense cannons. Cassius watched as they approached with blistering speed, spiraling up toward the hole.

Theo wiped his hands in front of him, closing the window as Cassius flinched from the oncoming fire. Explosions sounded outside, muffled by the wall of Ridium. The vessel stayed remarkably stable. After three more volleys, the ground shuddered beneath Cassius. The entire room began to melt.

He watched the walls drip around him. The ceiling caved in, raining down on both boys. The wet floor climbed up Theo's body, looping around his legs up to his hips. It covered his lower half in seconds, forming what looked like a shiny metallic bodysuit. It rose to his chest, then spread down his arms and covered his hair until he all but disappeared against a backdrop of Ridium.

He turned to look at Cassius. A round hole revealed his face, but everything else was covered in black. Hair, ears, shoulders. Theo laughed, brows raised. "Cool, huh?"

The restraints melted around Cassius. His wrist felt cold and naked without his bracelet.

The vessel continued to collapse. Soon, the city of Altair revealed itself around them. They'd broken through the dome overhead, triggering a deep, constant siren. They'd landed.

Ridium poured through the streets of the Skyship like floodwater, decimating everything in its path until the ground was covered with a thin layer of black. Buildings shuddered as the substance pounded into walls. Benches and tables were pushed along the stream—trees uprooted. Anyone unlucky enough to be walking on the top level found their feet stuck in the blackness. Some fell. Some were covered.

Cassius collapsed to his hands and knees. The hole in the overhead dome continued to widen. By the time the security mechanisms rattled into place to repair it, it could be too late.

Theo moved forward, hands at his side, in his suit of Ridium. There was no sign of Fisher, Drifters, Pearls, or anything that could put up a fight. Cassius knew that he had to find a way to stop him, but the boy was protected head to toe. Fire hadn't hurt him back on the Surface. He was the Authority's champion for a reason. He was indestructible.

Then, an explosion.

The ground rumbled. The blast had come from somewhere on the lower levels. Cassius didn't know what had caused it, but its effects made themselves known immediately.

The ground lurched under his feet. The ship sunk. No emergency thrusters. Something had happened.

The Ridium fused into the ground around him, soaking into the bowels of the Skyship like water into soil. The blackness on the streets faded as it spread through the inner workings of the ship. Cassius cursed. This kid was apocalyptic.

He was doing it, just like he said he would. Theo was bringing down the entire Skyship.

40

The corridor rocks violently around me. Alarms blare, so loud that I have to cup my hands over my ears. It threatens to kill my concentration, but I fight past it and recover my balance.

The ship lurches under my feet, then back up again.

I take a deep breath, soaking in what's left of the energy from the freed Drifters. I let it refresh my body, boost my energy. Then I close my eyes and focus.

I reach into the air and pull down, feeling for Pearl energy. They're close. My fists bunch at my side. My eyes flip open as several Pearls come at me, ripped from separate rooms. Wood smashes in the distance. Metal dents. They're like wild spirits escaping. A stampede.

The ground slants. I lose my footing momentarily but keep my attention on the pathway of the Pearls.

The entire corridor glows green as five of them hover through the hallway. I open my fist and press my palm into the air, beckoning them forward.

A thought stops me.

Just two Pearls had all but decimated the lobby. If I

break five at a time, right in the middle of the ship, I could bring everything down.

I let the Pearls settle in the air. They float in a circle around my head, bobbing impatiently. There are more in this storage center. I need them all.

Before calling them forward, I visualize the layout of the ship. Avery and I had studied the directory for only a few minutes, but I'd made sure to note the location of the closest exit to the top level.

My chest buzzes with excitement as the warmth from the Pearls envelops me. I use the added strength to hone in on the remaining Pearls and pull them from storage until I have seventeen in total. They fill the corridor with a blinding glow. I can barely keep my eyes open. The whispers are back, loud and from every direction. The Drifters want out.

They'll have to wait a few moments more.

I bolt back to the lobby with a string of Pearls following in my wake. It's easy to control them now, this close. It's like they're helping me, like they know they need to follow.

I clear the half-open door and take off into the bowels of the ship. The ground rocks underfoot, throwing me to the wall. The Pearls follow suit. They echo my movement like they're attached by invisible strings—a bundle of glowing balloons behind me.

As soon as I turn the first corner, I'm ambushed by a trio of soldiers. I skid to a stop. The Pearls bunch around the top of my head, bouncing against the ceiling, denting metal. I notice the soldiers' eyes widen, even past their visors.

Before they have a chance to compose themselves, I pull a Pearl from above me and clench my fists. It breaks directly in front of my chest and sends a shockwave through the corridor. The security squad topples as soon as the force hits them. I watch the energy hit the walls, fluttering metal like paper.

A Drifter emerges at the end of the corridor and shoots around the corner. I only see it for a split second, and don't have time to chase it around the ship. I can't spare too many of these Pearls.

Luckily, the stairwell is close.

It's also clogged. As soon as I make the turn back into pedestrian territory, I'm met with crowds of people, all bustling around on fast forward, panicked. When they spot me, their panic turns to awe.

They flatten against walls, scared to get too close. I sprint through the crowd and make a beeline for the stairwell. The Pearls sink below my shoulders when the space restricts.

I push past Shippers on the stairs, elbowing my way up two flights. Some people duck out of the way. Others slip and fall. I don't stop to look at any of them. I climb, face forward as the energy blocks any distractions. I can't keep the Drifters bound inside for much longer. I'm scared that if I don't get to the surface quick enough, they'll break and set off an explosion in the middle of the stairwell—the worst possible place.

With each step, it gets harder to control. I bite my lip

and keep my fingers straight. People scream around me, but all I can think about is the release—when I get to the top of the ship and let the Pearls explode.

The thud of my feet on the steps disappears. Everything does, as the energy envelops me. It pulls at my hair, tears at my clothing. I feel sick. These things are forcing me. I've never had so many so close.

One level more. One flight. Five steps.

I arrive at the top level and sprint to the center of a stone plaza, careful to move away from buildings. I don't even notice how thin the air is until I stop. I take two choked breaths before finding my voice and shouting.

"Move out of the way!"

My panicked cry gets the attention of every single person in the plaza. They turn and stare. I hear shouts, but they're buffered by the whispers of the Pearls around me.

I sink to my knees and bunch my fists, letting go.

Sixteen explosions pinwheel around my body.

A whirlpool of energy swallows the plaza, spreading through the top level like a black hole. I don't know how many people duck. I don't know how many buildings are damaged by the force. I don't see anything beyond the wall of green, but I know, from the indescribable maelstrom consuming the plaza, that this was a bad idea.

41

Cassius watched as a security battalion emerged around the corner, sprinting across the Ridium-soaked streets toward Theo. But before the soldiers could come close to reaching the boy, daggerlike cones of blackness cut up through the ground, spearing their bodies like meat on toothpicks. Soldier after soldier succumbed to his power. It was a massacre.

Cassius stepped forward, careful to keep his eye on the ground in case something came at him too. The Ridium continued to fade around his feet, working its way into the circuitry of the ship.

The wind intensified as more and more atmosphere was sucked out of the hole at the top of the dome. The ship continued to sink. Without a clear view of the space beyond the city, he couldn't tell how close they were to hitting the ground. When they did, the resulting explosion would be enough to tear the Skyship apart.

Someone grabbed his shoulder. He pulled away and staggered forward, in fear for his life.

"Cassius!" A familiar voice called him back. He turned to see Fisher's friends, Eva and Skandar, standing before him. Their eyes focused on the distance, past his shoulders to Theo.

Cassius coughed. "Where's Fisher?"

"We don't know," Skandar said. "He went with Avery."

Eva's mouth fell open as she watched Theo continue to fight back the ship's forces.

"He's covered in Ridium," Cassius explained. "There's no way to stop him. He's going to bring the ship down."

Eva was about to respond when a loud explosion rocked the opposite side of the ship. Cassius turned to see an expanding flare of green energy blossom from the far side of the city. It coursed above the tops of buildings, spreading upward and outward like a tidal wave.

He shielded his eyes from the brightness, but forced himself to keep looking. The longer he stared, the more details he could make out. There were bodies, glowing brighter and stronger than the rest of the green. Drifters swirled amongst the chaos. They circled in loops through the sky, riding the wave of energy.

"Fisher," Cassius whispered.

Eva moved to his side. "I've never seen so much Pearl energy in one place."

"It's coming at us." Cassius took a step back. "It won't dissolve in time."

She glanced down at his wrist. "Your bracelet!"

He felt the breeze tickle his bare skin. A shiver went down his spine. "We can't let Theo get the other one. Fisher has to stay as far away as—"

The Pearl energy crackled above them like sheet lightning, splintering the rest of the dome. A few more direct hits and it would burst altogether.

Cassius bolted toward Theo. The boy continued to fend off security forces in front of him, but it stole all of his attention. If Cassius could take him by surprise, he'd have a chance of buying Fisher and the Drifters some time.

It was reckless, he knew. If anything, he should be running the opposite direction, but he couldn't let Theo get that bracelet.

A few hundred yards and the boy was in reaching distance. Before Theo could react, Cassius bounded toward him, grabbed his shoulders, and pushed him to the ground. He grunted in pain as he collided with the Ridium. It was like tackling a cold statue.

The air around them heated as the Pearl energy pulsed closer. Theo pushed up and sent Cassius flying from his back onto the ground. The sky darkened. Seconds later, the green tidal wave ripped through the air. Cassius held his hands over his face, expecting to be hit full-on. Instead, the energy funneled into what looked like a sideways tornado and barreled straight at Theo.

Knocked off balance, the boy tried to shield himself, but the Pearl energy came at him with too much power. Cassius watched as the Ridium tore from his small frame and fell to the ground in splotches of black.

Now that Theo was unprotected by his suit, the energy blasted him to the ground. Cassius staggered to his feet and watched as the force from the Pearls threw the kid across the top of the ship, kicking him around in painful somersaults like a human tumbleweed. He prayed that it would be strong enough to drag him away entirely.

Before Theo reached the outer edge of the ship, the boy managed to conjure a thin shield of black, deflecting a wall of green back into the air and slowing himself to an uneasy stop.

Cassius took shallow breaths, watching the kid's still body. Tendrils of smoke curled from Theo's back. His face was buried in the ground. He wasn't moving.

Pearl energy. It was the key. It hurt him.

He turned back to the city with only one question on his mind.

Where was Fisher?

42

I regain my senses as the energy dissipates around me. As soon as I feel capable of standing, I peer at the dome, half a mile above my head. There are visible cracks, even from this distance. I shouldn't have broken the Pearls all at once. I should've known there would be consequences.

But that's just it. I didn't feel like I was in control. It's like they were breaking me.

Without looking at any of the fallen Shippers that litter the plaza, I take off at a sprint, following the flow of energy down the city.

I soak it in and let it push my feet forward. I run faster than ever before. It's half me, half the Pearls. That's okay. If I'm going to round up the Drifters, I'm going to need as much strength as I can muster.

The streets of Altair are empty. Pedestrians have filtered to the lower levels, forced downward by the unstable air pressure. It's all deserted. The Pearl blast took care of anybody who was left.

As I continue forward, the ground darkens underfoot. My right wrist feels heavy. At first I'm convinced it's exhaustion and nothing more, but then something forces my arm down. It's desperate to join the black pavement below me.

Ridium, and it's everywhere.

I hear footsteps behind me and speed up. Then a voice. "Jesse!"

I glance over my shoulder and watch Avery come after me. I slow for a moment and let her catch up.

I pant. "Where did you come from?"

"I lost the Drifters, Jesse." She struggles to match my pace. "They flew up the stairs. They're here, somewhere, on the upper level. I'm sorry."

"Don't worry about it," I say. "I think Theo's here."

She glances at the ground and her eyes widen. By now, we all recognize Ridium. Nothing on Earth is that black— that pure.

We take the next few streets in silence. At this speed we'll clear the top level in under five minutes.

But it's not to be.

At the next intersection, we begin to slow. Half a mile later, we keel over. I lean my hands on my knees and cough. It's the air pressure. The dome's coming down. The wind now pushes on us with powerful force, swirling trash around the intersection like a cyclone. And there's smoke.

I don't notice it at first because it's so transparent, but the atmosphere's definitely heavier. Multiple explosions throughout the ship have freed gases that we shouldn't be breathing. I glance at the sky and notice ships and shuttles all around us—dots in the darkening blue. Passengers are evacuating in all directions, heading toward safer ships. We're standing in the middle of approaching disaster.

"We're sinking," Avery says. "Can you feel it? What's happened to the emergency thrusters?"

I turn and stare at her in silence. Part of me knew this from the moment the ground rocked back in the storage center, but there were too many other things to worry about. And now, the Ridium. Not even someone like Cassius could deal with all of these factors at once. Not even someone like Alkine.

I think about the people unable to evacuate. The docking bays will be the first to hit the ground, and the worst damaged when they do. There'll be nothing left. No survivors. This has been the Skyship Community's biggest fear since the fleet first launched into the stratosphere. A ship can't be allowed to crash. And if it hits anywhere but the Fringes, the casualties could be in the thousands. More, even.

I cough. It's a struggle to keep standing, let alone move forward. If Theo's here, as powerful as he was back inside the vessel, there's no way I'll have enough energy to fight him.

Just then, I notice a flash of green out of the corner of my eye. I peer at the sky, searching for its origin. Before I can spot it again, the entire street's lit up.

I watch as a crowd of Drifters joins us in the middle of the intersection. They descend from the sky like angels, landing gracefully on the pavement. I see Sem and Talan among them, carried to safety. Instantly, I feel stronger. I arch my shoulders and take a deep breath, spinning in a slow circle to take them all in.

They're as unique as human beings in shape and size. The elderly stand next to children, next to adults and teenagers. They are my people—more than I've ever seen in a single spot. And without saying anything, I know they're here to help.

They step forward until they're close enough to touch. None of us speak. We don't have to. We know what we need to do.

I take a deep breath.

With a renewed sense of purpose, I lead them out of the intersection toward the rapidly disintegrating blanket of green beyond. We may not be much of an army, but the knowledge that they're behind me gives me the confidence I need to keep going forward.

Several intersections later, I see Cassius.

My first instinct is to run and check if he's alright. Then I notice Eva and Skandar standing several yards behind him. Alive.

Their expressions transform when they see me. I know how we must look—Avery and I the focal point of an army in green.

I stop and study the scene. Cassius jogs up to me.

"Thank god," he says. "Theo's down, but I don't think it's permanent. You've gotta move." He glances at my wrist. "On second thought, you've gotta get out of here."

I squint to see past the wreckage. At first I don't notice Theo against the expanse of blue. Then my eyes settle on a body. Small, right at the edge of the ship. One strong gust and he'll be pulled past the dome, shattering the glass and falling to his death.

"The Pearl energy," Cassius continues. "The blast was strong enough to knock him down. But he wants your—"

My bracelet flies from my wrist and transforms into a black ball. It sails across the length of the ship to Theo's outstretched hand. He stands, legs limp and crumbled, shaking with exertion. But he wears a wide smile as he knocks the ball of Ridium high into the air. In seconds it hits the dome. Unstable cracks shatter. I feel the breeze, unnatural against my bare wrist.

"No!" Cassius turns, and I see that his bracelet is gone too.

I meet his eyes. "What happened?"

"He's got them both." Cassius curses. "They've been programmed to block the Authority's signal. They were keeping the red Pearls at bay!"

I look down at my bare skin, then back at the Drifters. The ground pushes up on us as the Skyship continues to sink.

I watch Theo sink to the ground in the distance. He's on his knees now, smirking.

A shadow falls over him. I crane my neck to see a dark ship approaching. A round of detonations rings against what's left of the dome, breaking the remaining glass. A Unified Party Cruiser flies into the city, so low that we're forced to duck as it comes barreling overhead.

It loops around, just above the buildings of the city, and opens fire.

The Drifters shoot up from the ground one after another behind us, darts of green piercing the sky with staggering speed. In seconds, they're out of sight, taking Sem and Talan with them. I wish I had time to tell them to stay, but they're frightened. It's instinctual.

We're alone.

I pull energy from all around me—what's left in the air, what's left in the ship itself—and prepare for an attack. But the cruiser doesn't fire on us. Instead, it lets loose a barrage of ammunition at the edge of the sinking ship, carving enormous craters in the pavement. Theo disappears in a cloud of smoke.

The cruiser makes a diagonal descent, aimed at the widest portion of open space available. Just when I think it's going to set down, it makes a sharp turn and crawls toward us, inches from the ground.

I see the outline of Madame's figure behind the glass of the cockpit. I watch her grab a device on the wall beside her and hold it to her lips. The front of the cruiser hisses as the outside speakers switch on.

"I'm opening the side hatch." Her voice is amplified as it streams from the cruiser. "I strongly suggest you come inside. Altair is poised to hit the Surface in less than a minute. I'm afraid there's no time for dawdling."

I glance at Cassius. We stand together. Us. Avery. Skandar. Eva.

The dome collapses completely. Shards of fiberglass rain on the decimated city, joining the rubble from the explosions. Theo's body is somewhere behind the cruiser, though it may have fallen into the ship when Madame's firepower crumbled the ledge.

"We have to go," Cassius whispers. "We have to."

I nod, then meet the eyes of the others to let them know it's okay.

It's really not, especially with Madame in the pilot's seat, but it's our only choice. Escape with her or die in Altair's imminent explosion.

I lead the charge toward the cruiser, hands over my head to shield myself from falling rubble. Madame is dangerous. We shouldn't be allying ourselves with her like this, but there isn't time. This is survival.

The inside of the cruiser feels clean. We pile in, all five of us, before the hatch shuts. Immediately the ship gains altitude. We're thrown to the back as Madame climbs into the air.

When I'm able to stand, I rush to the nearest window and peer outside, trying to spot Skyship Altair.

I catch sight of it just as the lower levels plunge into the ground. An intense, miles-long fireball ripples from the underbelly and spreads up, demolishing every piece of the structure. Buildings collapse on the top level, pulled toward the surface, folding in on themselves. There were evacuees—I saw them. But there's no way that every single resident found their way off the ship in time. There wasn't enough warning. Nobody knew what was going to happen.

If Theo hadn't perished before, he's surely dead now.

That's a small consolation, considering the rest of the casualties. But it's not enough.

Avery comes to my side and throws her arm around my shoulders. She pulls me close. We collapse on the floor, together. I'm done. I can't do anything. I can barely move.

This is it. This confirms it.

I'm no hero.

43

Cassius forced himself into the cockpit, breathing hard.

Madame glanced up briefly to acknowledge him. "Have a seat."

He strode to the copilot's station and collapsed in the chair. He wanted to put up a fight, to curse her out or hijack the ship, but he didn't have the energy. He was afraid that he'd never be able to get up from this position again.

"They grow up so fast, don't they?"

He turned his body so that he could stare at her without moving his head back and forth. "Theo."

She turned the cruiser southward, which was fine because Cassius didn't want to look at the smoldering blaze that used to be Skyship Altair. The farther they went, the more relaxed he'd be.

"I always knew he was dangerous," she continued. "Rough and unbalanced, but I sensed something in him. Something similar to what I sensed in you at that age. And when I found him, I knew I needed to keep an eye on him. Anything that connects back to you, Cassius, is important to me."

"I'm nothing like him," he countered.

"Apparently not."

He met her eyes, only for a moment. It was hard to summon up any fear—or even much loathing—for her after what had just happened. Somehow Madame paled in comparison to the Authority.

She stared forward, focused on the skies. "You know what they say about keeping your enemies close. I track all of my children, but Theo was different. He needed constant monitoring. He didn't arrive with a message like you had. I didn't know where he was from, but I always knew where he was going."

"You tracked him?"

"Of course." She smiled. "You didn't think I'd let him roam free, did you?"

"Then why didn't you do something sooner?"

"That Fringe ambush in Syracuse stole the wind from my sails. I was without an army, but they could never take my wits. I escaped, at the expense of my battalion." She glanced sideways at him. "But as you know, there are always more soldiers. They're expendable. You and Fisher? You're keepers."

"Stop gloating." He felt his fist begin to burn, eager to release a torrent of flame. He could do it if he wanted. He could drag her to the floor, knock her unconscious, and be done with it.

She pursed her lips. "You know I don't approve of such things. The fact is, we've entered a new stage now."

He scoffed. "You don't know the half of it."

"I'm sure you'll tell me in good time. You never were one

to hide things." She paused. "For now, what has come between us in the past must be regarded as history. I'm willing to—"

"I don't want to hear it."

Her brows rose. "Would you rather I'd left you there to die? Do you think this is easy for me, Cassius?"

"You always meddle. Some things are bigger than you."

"You've been through quite an ordeal," she said. "I understand."

"Stop it. Stop talking like that."

"Like what?"

He gritted his teeth. "Like you're being filmed or something. Like you're playing a different person. I don't want you here. I hate you."

She remained silent for a moment, eyes on the sky. "You have nowhere else to go. Word of this will spread, and spread quickly. The Tribunal will blame an event like this on the Unified Party—"

He grabbed his hair, face shielded from her. "I don't care."

"True or not," she continued, "that's what they'll do. This may trigger the war we've always feared. It will be traced back to you and Fisher. Maybe not immediately, but it will happen. You are not safe anywhere."

He looked up at her, eyes watering. "And I'm safe with you?"

She sighed. "You are familiar with me. That will have to do."

"I could kill you right now." He shook his head. "All it takes is a thought."

"You could." Madame smiled, then let out a soft chuckle. "But you won't. We both know that."

Cassius turned away. He couldn't look at her anymore. He couldn't watch her smile as everything sunk around them. He glanced out his windshield.

A flash of red.

"What was that?" He pivoted to get a better look.

Madame's face bristled. She moved her attention back to the skies in time to see a second orb of red energy shoot past them like a comet plunging to Earth.

She laid off the accelerator, visibly shaken. The red energy came and went in less than a second and the air was clear again. Her mouth opened. "I've never seen—"

"A red Pearl." Cassius leaned forward.

She turned to him. "What?"

He felt the emptiness on his wrist. Theo may have perished, but Matigo's son had accomplished his goal. The bracelets were gone, and with them the scrambling power of the Ridium. "You don't know as much as you think you do. You don't know anything."

She swallowed. "None of the scanners detected—"

A second Pearl interrupted her, carving a turbulent path about a hundred yards to her left. She gawked out the window and watched it fall before turning back to the controls.

"History," Cassius said. "You wanna forget the history between us? We're gonna be lucky if we have any history left."

44

They start falling soon after the wreckage of Skyship Altair disappears from our view. Eva's the first to see one, but soon all four of us are plastered against the windows, staring out at the Surface below.

They drop like regular Pearls, but far more frequently. It's like Cassius said. Without the opposing force of our bracelets, the floodgates have opened. There are dozens of them at any given moment. Even without seeing it directly, I know they're everywhere.

Some might be striking Skyships or Chosen Cities. Many will hit the Fringes. There will be Pearls in Siberia, dangerously close to the Academy. They'll land in Africa. The Commonwealth. The ocean, maybe. They're blanketing the Earth. And here we are—six of us in a tiny cruiser. Insignificant.

Avery's shoulder touches mine. I can feel her trembling. "They're not stopping," she whispers. "They just keep falling, like a hailstorm."

I shake my head. "They're coming too soon. There are too many."

We did everything we could, I tell myself. We followed the breadcrumbs. We were careful. Would things have been any different if I'd listened to Alkine and stayed at the Academy, confined?

I'm a disaster. One after another, my allies have been ripped away. Killed.

Mr. Wilson. Ryel. Morse. Bergmann. I didn't listen, and now they're dead. And I'm sure it won't be long before the rest of us follow suit.

I turn around and lean my back against the window. I can't look outside anymore. I can't watch them land.

I can almost hear Theo's laugh echoing in the sky. He'd love this. He'd consider it the greatest honor—the son paving the way for his father.

I kick at the floor and let out a deep sigh before burying my head in my hands. Then, allowing tears to spill over my fingers, I wipe my face and stand. "I should go see Cassius."

But before I can take a single step, the door to the cockpit opens and Cassius walks out. He takes a breath as he scans the cabin. Then, voice trembling, he speaks. "We're going underground."

We turn to look at him. Eva crosses her arms. "Where?"

"There are Unified Party bunkers spread all around the Fringes. The closest is in Nevada. Madame has access. We'll be safe until we can figure out what to do." His eyes meet mine, pleading with me not to argue. I sense that he's already had a difficult enough time talking with Madame up front.

"We can't stay on the Surface," he continues. "And we're not in a position to..." He stops himself. "We're going underground. That's all."

I expect someone to challenge him, but nobody responds—not even Eva. There's little choice, really. We don't have the energy to fight. We wouldn't know where to start if we did.

All of a sudden, green light filters through the windows, bathing the inside of the cabin in a soft, calming glow. I turn back to the window and see them instantly.

The Drifters fly on either side of our cruiser, encircling us in a protective formation. I can see their faces from this distance, and make out their plain white clothing. They're here, Sem and Talan and every one I freed on Altair.

I spin around. My heart beats faster, or maybe it's the energy outside. "Look." I point. "In the sky. It wasn't all for nothing. They're here. They're following us."

"It doesn't matter," Cassius says. "We're going underground either way. We can't do anything like this. We'll die, and then we won't be of use to anyone."

I nod, even though I hate the thought of it.

I am already here.

Now Matigo has his army.

The cruiser lurches beneath us. Skandar rushes to the window. "We're heading down."

Avery crosses her arms. "That was quick."

"The ground's opening," Skandar continues. "I see it."

Cassius sighs. "Say goodbye to all of this, at least for a little while."

I take a last glance into the sky and watch the storm of red Pearls. Is it defeat? Are we running away? What would my parents want us to do?

I shut off the questions. They'll drive me crazy if I let them control me. Cassius is right. We can't do anything in this condition. The world will have to defend itself for now.

The windows darken.

The ground swallows us whole and everything's silent.

45

Thirty-eight hours later:

The silence is what kills me.

I don't know what's happening above us, on the Surface. Every minute that passes could mean another life extinguished, another city decimated. On the other hand, maybe none of the Authority's Pearls have broken yet. The Unified Party communication feed cut out shortly after we landed. Last we heard, the Chosen Cities considered the red Pearls an attack by the Skyship Community. A new form of technology. Then they started to hatch. That's when the feed broke. We're cut off.

We're clueless. Clueless and isolated.

But we're not going to get anywhere on guesswork. This is a war, and you don't enter a war blindly. It took some convincing, but everyone understands now. We're safe, and safety is a luxury we need to harness while it lasts.

Our bunker lies in the middle of a Fringe desert, far from the nearest Chosen and invisible to the unknowing eye. It will be our home for as long as necessary. Without the bracelet, Matigo has no way of tracking us. He wants to kill me, I know that. After all, I'm the Pearlbreaker. That's never been as important as it is now.

But I don't know where he is. Or who he is. If he's been here for a while, he could have blended in years ago. He could be anyone. A Fringe leader, a government official. Maybe even a member of the Academy.

Sem and Talan took care of triggering the remaining Drifters' language processors. Twelve out of nineteen are now speaking fractured English. They seem to become more fluent with every hour that goes by. We'll be ready soon. They can give us information.

I spent the first ten hours sleeping. I didn't want to. The thought of what might be happening over my head made me feel too guilty to sleep. I couldn't abandon the fight just as it was starting. It was a coward's move.

But it's the right one. Confinement. Not the way Alkine was keeping me a prisoner back home, but a different type.

Cassius and I are the Resistance's champions, and champions don't go and get themselves killed at the first sign of danger. They learn and they discuss, and when they have a plan, they execute it to the best of their ability. I guess in a way, Alkine was right.

This war was always coming. One way or another, Matigo would have found a means to invade. In the long run, there was nothing either Cassius or I could do to stop it. At least that's what I repeat in my head to make myself feel better.

The Unified Party bunker is remarkably spacious, much more so than the Academy's holding pen back in Siberia. The eerie stillness makes it difficult to imagine that the events of the past few days actually happened. After a night of drug-induced sleep, it feels like I might have dreamed the entire thing. Even the scars on my chest are beginning to fade.

But it wasn't a dream. The destruction of Skyship Altair was only the first strike.

The door to my room opens and Avery enters. I feel stupid, sitting on the corner of my bed like a little kid when I should be out acting like the hero I'm supposed to be, but she caught me at a bad time.

She joins me on the bed. "The Drifters are all awake. We're calling a meeting in thirty minutes."

I sigh. "I wish I knew what was happening up there."

She bumps my shoulder. "The Chosen Cities have been fending off Fringers for years. The Skyship Community has their defenses. You can't worry about what you can't control. You need to get your strength up." She pauses. "Look at you, you're malnourished."

I shrug. "I've always been skinny."

"Madame sent Talan and Sem up to the Surface to report. They haven't come back with anything major. No Theo, either."

"He's dead," I mutter. "I'm sure of it."

"Maybe." She sighs. "The world will do without us for a little while longer."

"I don't like this place."

"Neither do I. It reminds me of the medical labs under the Lodge." She shivers. "Bad memories."

"Madame's still okay?"

"She hasn't tried anything yet. Cassius is keeping an eye on her."

I grip the edge of the bed. "Of course he is."

"I think she's just as shell-shocked as we are, Jesse. This is new territory, even for her."

I glance up at her. "I still don't like being this close to her."

"You think I do? I was under her control for weeks. She's done horrible things to me, and I feel like punching her in the face every time I see her. But she knows how this place works. And more importantly, she's got contacts and access to the Unified Party. I think we're going to need everything we've got at our disposal."

"Yeah," I reply. "I understand it. That doesn't mean that I have to like it."

She lays her hand on my knee. "Are you okay, Jesse?"

"It's all real," I say. "Ever since Syracuse. There's no putting this off or forgetting about it. It's real. I mean, I always used to procrastinate at the Academy. I wasn't anybody's idea of anything. Not a good student, not a good agent. Not even a very good friend."

"Stop." She squeezes my leg. "Jesse, don't say things like that."

"I'm not even a good Pearlbreaker," I continue. "Think about it. There's only one of me in the universe—only one

person who can do what I can—and I screwed it all up."
I lie back on the bed, staring at the ceiling. "There was supposed to be an army waiting for them, and what have we got instead? A bunch of Drifters, two of them kids. And... and our greatest enemy down here looking after us. It's ridiculous."

Avery leans back with me. Her hair falls against my shoulder. She whispers, "Theo was more powerful than anybody could imagine, maybe even more powerful than you and Cassius combined. And you beat him. You lived."

"Yeah, but we—"

"Never mind the buts," she continues. "You beat him, and that's what we're going to do to the Authority. This is our planet, Jesse. We have the upper hand. It may seem dark now, but when we climb up to the Surface, we're going to be ready. You and Cassius? You're the champions. You don't get to be called that without a reason."

I close my eyes and let her words filter into my brain. Part of me doesn't want to hear it, but the other part pulls it in like a drug. I need to hear it, even if I don't want to.

"Avery?"

She smiles. "Yeah?"

"I love you."

Her smile turns into a laugh. "Shut up, Fisher. Don't you go getting all mushy on me. That's one thing champions don't do."

I give a hollow chuckle. It falls silent for a moment.

Then, just as I'm about to fall asleep again, I yawn. "I guess I'd better get up."

"I guess you should. You don't win wars sitting in bed."

I nod.

She smiles. "You know, we're not letting them take our planet."

"No," I whisper. "We're not."

I repeat this mantra in my head, and wonder if my parents had to repeat something similar back on Haven. They were able to lead a Resistance against Matigo before I even knew what a Pearl was. I'm not them, but if they could do it, I must have that same strength of will in me. Somewhere, buried like the Ridium under the Surface.

I stand and stretch. One step at a time. Breakfast.

It's easier to focus on small things. If I linger on the bigger picture for too long, I start to freak out. I have to sit down and close my eyes and remember that I'm still alive.

I'm Matigo's biggest enemy. Without me, Pearls are just useless balls of energy. Ryel wanted me to build an army. I wasn't fast enough. There are twenty-eight of us down here, waiting. We're small, but it only takes one to make a wave. Altair was just the beginning. We'll do what we have to. For Ryel, and Morse. And Mr. Wilson and all of those people brought down by Theo. We owe it to them.

We may not like it, but we are the Resistance now.

© Emma James

About the Author

When he was a young boy, Nick James's collection of battle-scarred action figures became the characters in epic storylines with cliffhangers, double crosses, and an unending supply of imaginary explosions. Not much has changed. The toys are gone (most of them), but the love of fast-paced storytelling remains. Working in schools from Washington State to England, Nick has met thousands of diverse students since graduating from Western Washington University and braving the most dangerous job in the world: substitute teaching. Luckily, being dubbed the "rock star teacher" has granted him some immunity. He currently lives and teaches in Bellingham, Washington.